A GREATER DISGRACE

a Nosemitt & Sniffle mystery

Marilyn D. Brown

For Nosemitt,
whose real name is quite normal:
with great affection
and with the reminder that this is not a portrait,
let alone a biography.

Printed in the U.S.A. by Independent Publishing Corp.
St. Louis, Missouri

They drove in silence through the snowy town, the cab driver sensitive to the young lady's occasional tears and respectful of the old man's air of collected command. When he had picked them up at the old Tapton estate, two miles west of Sunford's city limits and "newly" converted a decade ago to an elegant small hotel, the driver couldn't help noticing right away how pretty she was in spite of her odd outfit and her red eyes or how the old man, his left hand enfolding the young lady's right hand, could not have seemed more pleased to have her by his side, despite the marks of grief in both faces.

She wore an ancient black coat considerably too large for her and, if the mothball scent meant anything, rarely worn by anyone for years. Perhaps it was reserved for mourning, the driver thought. On her head was a hat that could only have belonged to some long-dead ancestor, a hat trimmed with a similarly extinct unrecognizable fur, balding in dime-sized spots. Possibly it had been chosen for its black lace veil effect, which did nothing to enhance the hat, let alone the wearer. Her gloves, also black, did not precisely match, though the driver had noticed that only because she kept trying to cover them with her purse. She must have realized too late, he thought.

Her companion wore a long heavy gray overcoat of obvious quality and carried a black umbrella and an old but not shabby briefcase. His glasses misted over from time to time, and yet he had difficulty keeping a little smile in check every time he looked at the young woman by his side. He leaned forward now to ask the driver about the history of the area they were just entering, a little section of Sunford that had locked itself off from the present. Its streets were still of cobblestone; its lamps appeared to be real gaslight. The buildings retained a look of age, although here and there a vacant lot awaited transformation.

"We call it The Pot," the cab driver said with a grin, pleased to be free to speak at last. It had not been a long ride; it only seemed so.

"A suburb of Sunford?" the old man asked. He wondered if the driver's grin were one of affection or derision– it did not occur to him that the driver might simply be glad to end the silence. "It says 'Fondue' on my map. Is that correct?"

"Fondue, yes, but not a suburb– the original town of Sunford and officially its north quarter, although it's a complicated story about the name and there are half a dozen versions about how 'Fondue' came to be selected," the driver said. He seemed to enjoy being able to answer these questions. He liked the tour guide role, though he only rarely got a chance to play it.

"And is there a favorite legend? Have you an opinion as to the real source of the name?" the old man asked, interested in many and varied subjects, not least of all the driver himself, who couldn't be more than a few years in the trade. He had the fresh-faced look of a college student of the fifties and definitely did not seem typical of his contemporaries. The cabbie's appearance was deceiving, for he was in fact a youthful forty-two. He had left Sunford after high school but returned to help his family.

"Yes, sir," the driver said enthusiastically. "My grandparents helped settle this town. They were in on the feud that gave it its name. There was so much fighting over everything all the time that folks said people here wouldn't be happy unless the pot was always bubbling. So, for a while they called the town Stewpot, but then of course someone took offense because Stewpot sounds a lot like Stupid. They argued over a name for years until someone who had traveled through Switzerland on a church mission spoke up and suggested Fondue Pot. They argued over that and finally compromised: Fondue for the town and The Pot as a kind of local nickname. When the town expanded and became the little city of Sunford, this section kept both its old names. Every now and then it threatens to secede from Sunford."

"Quite entertaining," the old man said, busily looking at the mostly brick properties on both sides of the street. "I see they kept the flavor in some of the street names. Here we are on Cheesebubble Lane, and I am particularly fond of the name of our destination: Stirconstantly Street. I gather business still prospers here; I see signs of rehabilitation and renewal all around."

"It's strictly small business here, sir— nothing that pollutes the air is allowed. No factories. Like this address you gave me, number eleven Stirconstantly Street— that's not a brand-new business here in Fondue, but it might be the smallest. The two ladies you are calling on have lived here for half a dozen years— but I guess you know that."

"Yes," said the old man, "but go on; I know only a very little more about them and would be delighted to learn anything."

"Maybe you know they moved here when one of them lost her husband? The other one's an artist, divorced. Made a studio out of one of the back rooms. Theirs is the only duplex in Fondue, but maybe we'll have to call it a triplex now that they're remodeling and making an office in the front. It was a regular house when they bought it; then they hired a pair of carpenters to make it into two separate apartments for themselves. Anyway, they both live there. Fondue has a lot of restrictions on what goes into the environment but it has no commercial zoning and very few regulations about how you change the inside of a building. As long as it still looks like the original structure on the outside, and the plumbing and wiring are up to code inside, nobody says anything. You can work out of your house, as long as you don't manufacture anything dangerous. It has always been an independent, contradictory little community. People here like it that way."

The old man, deciding that the driver liked it that way too, pulled the business card from a small case in his breast pocket and studied it for not the first time. He had acquired it from Gnatalia Ballwin, one of nearby Polk University's now former benefactresses, who had sent it to him over a year ago; and he had kept it because it intrigued him, as human nature invariably did. He had wondered when he first saw it how it could possibly succeed in a goal of bringing business to its entrepreneurs; he had thought it could not engender anything more than curiosity and amusement. Yet now here he was, calling on the pair in question, having been drawn to learn more about them and see if they could help him in this time of need for a kind of background anonymity. They seemed to epitomize the quality. He had observed with a deep but simple pleasure that the card was pale ivory; the ink was dark gray, not quite black. He very much approved.

---

* * v p i * *

NOSEMITT & SNIFFLE
you will find us
a pair of ones, Stirconstantly Street
Fondue

the pot thickens

"You seem to know them fairly well," he said to the driver as he put the card back in his card case.

"Spottily. In Fondue everybody knows each other by name at least, but my mother has served on several boards with Ms Nosemitt.

You know a lot more about them than I do if you know what the 'vpi' stands for."

"I assumed from my informant that it was some kind of private investigators. I do not know what that V stands for– 'very' perhaps." "My mother says never assume anything about anyone, especially about Ms Nosemitt or Ms Sniffle. She says they'll defy assumptions." It had not been until the first mention of the driver's mother that the young lady in the back seat had looked at him. He was a youngish man, she realized. He had a mother. With this second thought one tear began again, and her uncle reached over to take again her gloved hand in his. The driver, seeing the woman's face through the rearview mirror, stopped talking and just drove. In a few minutes they reached Stirconstantly Street and turned left. They stopped in front of number eleven, and the driver hurried around to help both passengers out. The old man smiled and gave the young man directions to come back for them in thirty minutes. "Then perhaps I shall be able to tell you the significance of 'vpi'," he said. The driver smiled but there was no doubt that he was hoping for a more substantial tip than that.

For a moment old man and young woman stood in front of the house/studio/office of the pair of ladies known to them at present only as Nosemitt and Sniffle. The man, who prided himself on his ability to ferret out all manner of information, had been stopped cold in his efforts to learn anything about their identity other than that these were their pseudonyms of choice, the names they went by in many but not all circumstances. He had learned many other things– for example, that Ms Sniffle painted under yet another name not her own, Nigel. He knew that she also wrote under that name; but no one with whom he'd made contact had the slightest memory of her real name. Ms Nosemitt had sat on boards not only in Fondue and greater Sunford but in the community where she had been born. He knew where that was and he knew on what boards; he knew her political leanings and her charitable preferences; he was aware of her widowhood but not of her husband's name; and her own name for all practical purposes might as well have been Nosemitt. So far, anyone living who knew more was not telling.

It was this fact which added to his interest in them, intrigued him as did their card. Sniffle had first come to his attention for her accidental solving of a baffling mystery at Polk University ten years earlier. Ms Ballwin had been impressed less with her professional method than with her oddly accurate intuitive inclinations. She seemed to have the right instincts, whether facts supported them or not. Facts often came around and cooperated later. He had always found that trait a valuable one, especially as he himself lacked it. It came out in his communications with this benefactress that Sniffle had never claimed sole credit for her fortunate discoveries. She had made it quite clear in a letter to Ms Ballwin that a frequent correspondent of hers– Nosemitt as it turned out– had been crucial in formulating many of the questions she had pursued.

At that time Nosemitt was not widowed; the two women were good friends and confidantes. A year later, following the death of her husband, one or the other of them asked the other to consider sharing living quarters. They found that neither was willing to give up her own home and move in with the other, nor were they willing to merge their decor styles. In fact, neither wished to give up her privacy completely; and yet for financial reasons as well as for companionship and security reasons, they went ahead despite the obstacles they themselves posed. They resolved the problems by seeking a new location where they could share a home, each with her separate quarters. The early Polk experience had made them feel that they could work together on small investigative projects where nothing major was at stake. Minor, even petty, mysteries; bloodless crimes; vague puzzles were within their scope. On a casual basis they had succeeded in finding a number of lost items for friends, although each was fairly absentminded about where she had placed objects of her own. They regarded themselves as very persnickety individuals, very particular investigators. They thought their card made that clear, though few others thought so.

Walter Wrothwell had filed their card in his card case and their odd names in his memory, having no need for their services at the time; but now he thought that he did. He needed not professional detectives but intuitive and discreet and unobtrusive agents on his own behalf. If they were quietly eccentric, so much the better. No one would take them seriously, and they would likely learn that much more. They struck him as the ideal agents to find out who had murdered Harriet, and yet he had never met them. He found himself eager now to do so, and yet their insistence on a kind of anonymity must have been contagious. "Shall we say you are my niece, Vanessa?" he asked with a gleam in his eye.

"I *am* your niece, Uncle Walter," Vanessa said impatiently. Her uncle had been behaving oddly ever since they began this ridiculous journey from St. Edwards. She had not wanted to come here; she did not wish to learn more details. Let the police do their work and leave her alone. Why had she needed to come along to interview two distant private investigators? Amateurs by the sound of it. No, by more than the sound of it– amateurs at best. Her uncle's informant had *not* said "less impressed with Ms Sniffle's professionalism." Vanessa knew for a fact that she had said, "totally oblivious of professional skills but surprisingly on target." Vanessa had hoped the police back home would say she could not leave and was unhappy that they had agreed with her uncle that a brief change of scenery would be good for her. The train trip to Sunford had been exhausting, though not to her companion. The rooms at the Tapton were tolerable but she preferred home. Nevertheless, here they were, standing in front of a door with an absurd sign on it, freshly repainted by the look of it and, by a closer look, frequently repainted too:

NOSEMITT & SNIFFLE

in dark, plain lettering on the frosted glass, followed beneath in smaller and smaller lettering like an eye chart,

V P I
No case too large nor client small
though we may choose
to refuse them all.
Nevertheless, welcome!

"Do you really think this is quite the place for us?" the exhausted young lady asked the energetic old man.

"Certainly," he replied, more delighted than ever. "It is practically unknown, which suits our purpose exactly; it is out of the way, entirely unassuming. I find it quite charming." He shaded his eyes and peered through a defect in the frosting to see if he could detect anything but could not. "It seems to me the only question is whether we will be quite the clients for them. I do think we will find them extremely discreet."

"Discreet beyond a doubt," Vanessa agreed irritably. "But what about competent? What about competent?" She began to get shrill, and the tears started again. "I'm sorry, Uncle Walter, but really, we have no idea if they are competent at all. And I don't know why you keep saying 'our' purpose when I have no purpose for being here and want none."

"Now, Vanessa, you have been through quite an ordeal. As to their competence, that's what we are here to learn," he said; and he reached for the door handle, which fell to the ground. The door opened anyway and they entered– she angrily, wearily, suspiciously, but he with faith and eager anticipation.

They found themselves in a small unlit waiting room, temporarily furnished with two decrepit chairs that some sharp-clawed cat had once frisked and scratched upon, a low table similarly attacked, and an old wrought iron bulbless lamp for reading nothing by. Three walls were in conflicting states of disrepair– wallpaper strips and tiny paint squares pinned or glued in odd places– but the fourth wall had been beautifully covered in an incredibly soft and soothing off-white fabric which set to great advantage a large and strikingly, not to say unexpectedly, fine painting. Vanessa dismissed it at first as a hazy attempt at a landscape not unpleasing, but Uncle Walter saw a great deal more in it and he found it hard to look at anything else. He knew they were in a good place; and though he did not have intuitive leaps before the fact, he trusted his instincts always when in any really difficult circumstance. He believed with a sedate pride that they had never failed him.

Vanessa did look at everything else and was not encouraged. The two abused chairs were littered with upholstery samples, making sitting in them awkward at best. The table held two small partially used cans of paint stripper, a scraper, and a battered roll of paper towels. A gallon of paint thinner perched at a precarious angle against the lamp, which leaned more dangerously yet against the wall. Vanessa straightened both. "Thank you, my dear," Uncle Walter murmured; "quite a little minefield, I think, but presumably a work in progress."

"It is not safe to wait here," she said emphatically, looking stiffly overhead at the exposed wires leading questioningly to a phantom ceiling fixture. In fact, it was on the floor in the corner. A cluster of extension cords dangled from an antique hat rack. She removed her paperback novel from her purse and tried to concentrate on reading, but her eyes kept returning to all the hazards.

"Perhaps we should ring," he suggested, spying at last a tiny wall button under a sample of fabric. He had no idea if it was connected; but as soon as he pushed it, a slow scraping sound from within started up and increased and quickly seemed to be gathering strength to burst through the door. Then it shut abruptly off. From a remote part of the house a voice called out, "What do you mean there's someone here? I didn't hear anything."

"How could you hear anything with that screeching in your studio? Are you back to experimenting with audio art?" This second voice seemed mildly exasperated.

"It's not screeching," said a defensive voice; "it's– oh, it's the new bell. Sorry!"

"What new bell? When did we acquire a bell?"

"I'm sure I told you that I bought a bell."

"I hope with that sound it makes, you were given a bell."

"Do you think it will occur to either of them to come open the door?" Vanessa asked. She wanted only to leave.

"I'm rather enjoying this," Uncle Walter said, cupping his ear and straining toward the door in hopes of catching the sound of approaching footsteps. There was no such sound. Vanessa listened intently, sighed, and returned to page one of her novel. Without warning, the door opened. Vanessa was so startled that she dropped her book; her uncle stood up immediately, reached out to shake hands with either or both of the inquisitive pair who stared at him from the door, and introduced himself. "Walter Wrothwell and my, um, great-niece, Vanessa Kettle, here to inquire about the investigative services of Nosemitt and Sniffle. May I assume you are they?"

"I'll be damned," the taller one said. "Business."

"How did you even get in?" the shorter one asked, taking several steps forward and brushing past Uncle Walter, whose hand was still outstretched. She removed a broom from its position propping a navy pillowcase whose function appeared to be to act as a window shade. Immediately the winter light flooded in, and Vanessa had to shade her eyes against the unwelcome glare. "Much better," the proprietress said and carried the broom and pillowcase off to some remote part of the house.

"It is not better at all," the other one announced and grabbed up the cans of paint thinner and two of the five extension cords. "Excuse me one moment, please," she said and disappeared. Walter looked at Vanessa and smiled. She sat down, shaking her head. He remained standing, trying to hear what was going on. He could make out only fragments: "I told you I could not tolerate having anyone see this place looking this way... not ready." That was the taller person's voice. He could not hear the reply. Then, "No, coffee will not make everything all right. If you don't care how it looks, you come out of your studio and help deal with this." Aha, he thought; the short one is Sniffle, and it is not the artist who wants things in order. "Vanessa, my dear, it may comfort you to know that this interview may be as difficult for Ms Nosemitt as it is for you." Vanessa was indifferent.

Five minutes later, the two women returned to invite uncle and niece in. Ms Sniffle had changed from a paint-streaked sweatshirt to a clean shirt with only one ink stain on the sleeve. Ms Nosemitt had put shoes on. The aroma of coffee wafted out from the kitchen, and a path down a narrow hallway had been cleared to a rather surprisingly calm and comfortably decorated room. An arched doorway with the door itself open led to what must be the second apartment, but they appeared to be standing now in Ms Sniffle's part of the duplex. All the paintings on the walls enchanted the old man. He felt a strong and solid affection for both of the women, a respect based in part on his attraction to their style, so different from his own, but based even more on their desire for privacy. He was a man who understood the need and the desire for secrets in life and valued complexity in people. Now he gently guided Vanessa to the most comfortable chair in the room, while he chose a seat nearer to Nosemitt and Sniffle. He was about to introduce the sad matter at hand when Sniffle walked out of the room.

"I guess I will wait," he said to Nosemitt.

"Please don't," she insisted. "Sniffle cannot tolerate hearing any details about murder. She will be back and will be quite fine once you have outlined the facts to me– perhaps sooner; one never knows."

"How do you know it is a murder ?" he asked.

"Oh, it is quite painfully apparent. Your mother, I assume?" she asked, turning to Vanessa. "We are so very sorry, genuinely sorry. Mothers and daughters… it is difficult." Vanessa reddened and looked helplessly at her uncle. He simply smiled gently and acknowledged the accuracy of the assumption.

"My niece, Harriette Kettle– perhaps you have heard of her?" he began.

Nosemitt shook her head apologetically; and from the other room where she was not, in fact, studying another painting to try out in the waiting area Sniffle called out, "The etiquette columnist?"

"Indeed, yes," Uncle Walter called out, quite pleased.

"How did you know that?" Nosemitt called back. No answer.

Sniffle returned via the kitchen, bringing four teaspoons and four mismatched cups with her, plus a notepad and pencil for Nosemitt, who already had both, and a box of tissues under one arm. She left again and returned with a tray carrying the coffeepot and milk and sugar. Vanessa watched in dismay as Nosemitt emptied pencil shavings out of one cup and wiped all cups with a tissue; "None for me, thank you," she said very softly when Nosemitt started to pour.

"Now then," Sniffle said, returning, "I think I can deal with this."

"I'm pouring already," Nosemitt said; "there's no need for you to handle anything."

"I meant Mr. Wrothwell's narrative. I feel more ready."

"My niece, Harriette," Uncle Walter began again, "was found ten days ago in the most upsetting circumstances."

"Dead, I suppose," Sniffle mumbled, making notes on the extra pad. Vanessa was offended and looked away. Sniffle apologized while Nosemitt immediately explained that this was her only way of adjusting to hearing the details. She had to start from a distance and move in quickly.

"Well, yes," Uncle Walter continued, "although I was referring to something a bit more specific. The circumstances were rather tawdry, especially when you consider Harriette's occupation– or, if not tawdry, then bizarre at best. At least one of the local newscasters has made a mockery of the incident, which is one of the reasons I felt Vanessa should get away. I am grateful that the police concurred."

"Please just tell it and get it over with," Vanessa urged him. Her voice was strained and her hands kept fidgeting with her gloves, which she kept putting into her purse and then removing. Both women noticed that they did not match and were enchanted. They had not yet made up their minds about the hat; but, loving the absurd and eccentric, they were charmed by the young woman's taste.

"How could anyone make a mockery of an event of this kind?" Nosemitt asked.

"It is the irony of having been an etiquette columnist of course. She was found lying in a– well, this is painfully blunt– in a gutter in an out-of-the way little section of town with crumbs strewn all over her." He put his hand gently on Vanessa's arm.

"Was she there on purpose? Was she visiting someone? Had she just been eating?" Sniffle asked. Nosemitt frowned at her; good Uncle Walter looked puzzled; Vanessa was disgusted.

"It was in the middle of the night," she said tautly and angrily; "my mother did not make a habit of visiting gutters, to eat or otherwise. Not during the daytime either. I do not understand your questions at all!"

"There, there, my dear," her uncle murmured. "I am sure there is a good reason."

"I did not word that well," Sniffle said. "I meant to ask whether Ms Kettle was in that area of town for some known reason or had she been abducted and taken there? Was her car nearby? And the crumbs seem so odd that I just wondered if someone actually threw them on her as a peculiar insult, or is there a rational explanation for them? Please excuse me; questions don't always pop into my head in the clearest form. And then I am so bad about just blurting them out."

"I understand," Walter said. His niece merely looked at her own lap and pulled at the seam of one of the gloves, creating a new hole. "Perhaps if I continued?" The two women nodded. "Yes, well, then, Harriette's car was parked in her own garage ten miles away, but she herself was found early in the morning by a resident who went out to sweep the small amount of snow that had fallen during the night. The snow is quite important, not least of course because Harriette would not have been found so early had there been none. However, it was a fluke snow. You see, all day the temperature had been unusually mild for December; but at one in the morning there was a sudden dramatic dip; the thermometer had been registering fifty degrees throughout the day and then it was down below twenty. Harriette was wearing a lightweight coat, actually a man's gray windbreaker, and so the police have chosen to reason that she was murdered before one."

"Likely," Nosemitt agreed, "though not conclusive. Surely they have more they are going on besides the jacket? And why does the snow matter? Knowing when the temperature dropped would seem enough."

"Quite true, when that you put it that way," he said in a way that left Nosemitt wondering if he were testing them. "It is important to us, of course, as it is the reason my niece was found more quickly. As to the police having other evidence, I believe they do. Our objective in calling on you, however, is not to reproduce their findings. They may or may not discover the truth, but it is my conviction that they are on the wrong track entirely; and from the haste with which they agreed to let us leave St. Edwards, I venture to say they don't want any more of my suggestions."

"Are there many specific suspects?" Nosemitt asked. "Did your niece– your mother, Vanessa– have enemies?" She felt a strong need to include the young lady.

"Not really, not personally," Vanessa said firmly. "The police are wanting to think there might have been some connection with her daily column. She constantly received letters from so many strange people that they think it is possible one of her replies might have set off a very disturbed person. Or perhaps my mother was a victim simply because some crazy person thought it would be a twisted thrill to go after her.

They think it possible that the crumbs really were an intentional insult, as Ms Sniffle suggested. I can't believe it."

"May I ask the cause of death?" Nosemitt said quietly.

"The preliminary report indicated poisoning. And, yes, Mother had been eating, to go back to another of the questions you asked. But I know that she was not poisoned by the person with whom she had dinner. That is absolutely out of the realm of possibility."

"But of course her dinner companion would have to be one of the suspects," Nosemitt said.

"Impossible!" Vanessa was vehement. "I don't care what anyone says. Roger is totally innocent."

"We are not entirely in agreement about all the possible suspects," Uncle Walter interjected; "and there are a surprising number of them. That is why we have come to you, objective outsiders who can ignore our prejudices and find the truth no matter whom it indicts. I do hope you will take the case. There will be much more detail forthcoming should you agree to help us. You will find that there are ample leads on which to exert your very logical mind, Ms Nosemitt, whether one would have thought them all enemies or not."

"Who is Roger?" Nosemitt asked.

"The man my mother wished to marry."

"Out of the question," Uncle Walter said quietly.

"I thought you included him as a suspect," Sniffle said, now absentmindedly sketching a jacket and sprinkling it with tiny spots. Fortunately, Vanessa could not see it.

"Her marrying him was out of the question. But I believe our half hour is up and the cab driver should be waiting. We will be at the Tapton until tomorrow noon; I hope to hear that you accept this case and will come to St. Edwards within a very few days. I am prepared to pay all your expenses plus a considerable fee if you find the guilty party."

"And if we do not?" Nosemitt asked.

"Then all your expenses and a reasonable fee," he said smiling.

"Is there some pretext you have in mind to explain our being in St. Edwards?" Sniffle asked. "I gather you do not wish us to announce that we are investigating the case."

"Indeed, discretion is of the utmost importance. I do have a small stratagem to offer: we are holding a memorial service on the fourteenth, next Sunday afternoon. It would be more than reasonable for Vanessa to have written and invited two old friends from Harriette's school days to come to the service. We would make arrangements for you at the Edwardian Arms until after the service; then it might be more convenient for you to move in with my niece. May I assume you will not need any additional pseudonyms?"

"Nosemitt and Sniffle will do," they both said; "and," Sniffle added, "we think of them as first names. No need to say 'Ms Nosemitt' or 'Ms Sniffle'."

"Are we really contemporaries of Ms. Kettle?" Nosemitt asked. "I am sure we are at least a decade or even two older."

"Not a difficulty," Walter Wrothwell assured them; "Harriette attended the college on a part-time basis for a while and had friends of many ages over the ten years she took to achieve her degree."

"And you say poisoning?" Sniffle asked. "There is no blood in the case?"

"None," he said, almost smiling and shaking their hands as he asked if this meant that they already knew they were taking the case. They needed only a glance at each other to know they had come to the same rather surprising conclusion: yes, they were taking the case, even though it was far beyond anything they had envisioned for themselves. As the four walked to the door, the old man touched Nosemitt on the arm and said, "Quench an old man's curiosity. What does the 'v' in 'vpi' stand for?"

"Very," Nosemitt said.

"Ah, excellent, excellent. Discretion is guaranteed if you are very private investigators."

"Perhaps you inquired after the wrong letter," Sniffle suggested. "We are not private investigators. Ah, your cab is here. I've written our phone number here; we'll expect a call from you before you leave, giving us whatever information is necessary, including of course the directions once we reach St. Edwards."

"Not private investigators? Not– ," Vanessa was saying as they walked to the cab.

"Never you mind, my dear," he assured her; "it will be all right; and though I am in the dark, I am not at all surprised." He turned back to tell them to expect his call that same evening at seven. Nosemitt nodded and waved goodbye, but Sniffle was already back in her studio.

In the cab, Vanessa expressed the opinion that they were very peculiar investigators. The driver couldn't help looking at her hat.

They met Walter Wrothwell that same night in the dining room of the Tapton. Vanessa did not join them, pleading fatigue, but in fact Uncle Walter preferred to hold this conversation without her. There were many details he could provide that would be needlessly painful for her to sit through but that would indicate several possible directions for the two women to investigate. His first goal was to give them an outline of the family tree, and he was quick to mention Marvin Kettle and his mother, the late Fredricka Portcullis Kettle of the Portcullis fur fortune.

"I never heard of a furry portcullis," Sniffle whispered in an aside to Nosemitt as Walter searched intently for a paper in his briefcase; "perhaps that was the trim on Vanessa's hat."

"Ah, here we are," Walter said, handing them three sheets of paper, one a precise map of St. Edwards highlighting several specific spots and red-lining a route to Harriette's home, the other two containing a carefully drawn but not very complete genealogical chart of the Kettle and Wrothwell families. "I have had this taken back only two generations; more would be unnecessary and less would be impossible. I am particularly interested in all who stand to benefit from Fredricka's will."

"How does that have anything to do with your niece?" Nosemitt asked.

"You see here on this chart," he said, not hearing her question, "that Fredricka Portcullis married Horatio Kettle, who, incidentally, came from a relatively poor family with more ambition than ability. They had two sons and two daughters and another son by adoption, but I have not put him on the chart. Marvin, the second natural son— full name Horatio Marvin Kettle II— married my niece, Harriette Wrothwell. Their children, you see here, are Dustin and Vanessa. Harvester Kettle, the oldest of the four Kettle offspring, married Portia Lockett and they have a son Fredrick. Obviously they hoped to curry favor with Fredricka. Despite this ploy, Harvey was not a favorite, nor was Freddy for that matter."

"I thought we were dealing with your niece's murder," Nosemitt tried to interject again. Walter remained oblivious.

"Fenton never married but remained in his mother's home, really quite dutiful but always feeling cheated. I would be surprised if he felt otherwise now. The last of the sons was Rodney, but he was committed

14

to an asylum in his mid-twenties, sleeps about ninety percent of the day, and probably is unaware of the death of his mother, not to mention Harriette's. I believe he is safe from all suspicion. Albina and Marie married twin brothers in the diplomatic corps and are both in Europe. I believe we also may safely doubt their involvement."

"I fail to see any connection to your niece," Nosemitt tried to say again. "Are you suggesting that a member of her ex-husband's family murdered her? What motive could they possibly have? She wasn't even in the family any more."

"When did Fredricka die?" Sniffle asked.

"Six months ago," he said. "And yes, they could all have the same motive. Despite the divorce, it was made known to the entire family that Harriette was to receive Fredricka's jewelry, gems valued some years ago at more than a quarter million dollars and certain to have appreciated since then."

"Why Harriette?" Sniffle asked.

"Fredricka loved her and thought Marvin a fool to divorce her. She was disappointed in all her sons, and she thought her daughters had deserted her. She did admire Portia but did not think highly of her intellectual capacity, and Fredricka was quite furious about the deterioration of her gene pool. She was somewhat of a fanatic on that point."

"She approved of Dustin and Vanessa?" Sniffle asked.

"Not really," Walter said with a tinge of embarrassment at the question. "It was Harriette herself she valued most, thought of as being most truly her daughter. Harriette's children did not interest Fredricka greatly. They were not of the desired caliber either."

"So, what happens to those jewels now that Harriette has died?" Nosemitt asked. "Does Vanessa stand to receive them? Do you think she is in any danger?"

"I hope to learn soon if the will was specific on that point– or changed, and to know in whose estate the jewels now belong. They had never yet come to Harriette; I think none of the terms of the will has been carried out. There may in fact be a contingency clause, and I intend to try to learn more about that myself; but it is my present assumption that Marvin might well have believed that he could make a case for the jewelry to pass to Dustin. There is no way he could get them directly himself, nor any way that his vapid new wife could be the intended Harriette. Harriet the lesser, as I choose to think of her, was not even born when the will was first written."

"He married another woman with the same name?" Nosemitt asked. "This adds to the confusion."

"For Marvin that would be as good a reason as any for doing it," Walter said bitingly. "At least the two names are spelled differently."

"Why Dustin any more than Vanessa?" Sniffle asked.

"It is an understatement to say that Marvin is not close to Vanessa," Walter said; "he and Harriette were divorced when Vanessa was two–which is why the family was all the more offended that Harriette was still the beneficiary. Dustin lived with his father; Vanessa lived with Harriette, always has, even to this day. Well, you know what I mean–until now. Mother and daughter were very close; in fact, Vanessa was Harriette's personal assistant at the newspaper. Marvin has remarried twice since then, and I give poor odds on this one lasting. My great-niece has little contact with that man." He spoke bitterly and made it clear that he had no more to say on the subject of Vanessa's father in that role.

"Earlier you seemed to be implicating– what was his name? a man named Roger? Yet you have painted quite a detailed motive for Marvin or some member of the Kettle family," Sniffle observed. "What would Roger's motive be?"

"Anger at her refusal to marry him," Walter answered immediately, "and jealousy. He was insulted by her reason for rejecting marriage and did not want her to see anyone else, although I am not aware that she was seeing anyone else. I suspect him of no financial motive."

"And what was her reason?" Nosemitt asked, feeling as if they were having to ask the most obvious questions while he talked fulsomely on other points. She kept having the feeling that he wanted to test them; yet, at the same time, she felt that his mind, obviously immensely capable most of the time, was experiencing lapses now and then. He saw small details and had keen insights but missed slightly larger details and overt facts. It was stress, she decided. After all, the man was also in mourning. Periodically that became all too evident. Now was one of those times, and he looked at her in a confused way.

"What was your niece's reason for refusing to marry Roger?" Nosemitt repeated gently.

"Oh," he said, rubbing his temples. "His name. It was in part his name. There were other reasons of course, but there was that impossible name." The women waited for the name. "So you will take the case?" he said vaguely and stood up to shake hands with them. "All this ado about names. Double names and secret names and names that stand for other names." He seemed exhausted suddenly and left the dining room. They noticed a falter in his gait that had not been there earlier, and they wondered how much they could count on his statements. Perhaps, they hoped, the trip to Sunford had taken more out of him than he had anticipated; and, once back in St. Edwards, he might become again the strong, energetic, clear-thinking man they had met at noon.

"I suppose we're adding to the confusion too," Sniffle said sadly.

"Are we ever going to tell him what the P in VPI stands for?" Nosemitt asked, "speaking, that is, of names."

"Possibly." In fact, she doubted.

Thursday, January 11

"Shall I drive?" Nosemitt asked, gritting her teeth unnecessarily since Sniffle knew the correct answer.

"I'll drive; no problem."

"It's only three hundred and seventy-five miles; you won't be tired? I could take over once we get off a major highway."

"That appears to be the last four miles," Sniffle said, studying the map. "I think I can handle the entire drive if you promise not to go on a rampage if I ask you to check something on the map and you cannot find it immediately. You may not shred the map." There was no answer. Sniffle looked up from the map to repeat her demand, but Nosemitt had remembered another book she wished to take along and was not there. Sniffle folded the map, incorrectly as usual, put it next to her suitcase, and went to find the cache of chocolate bars that she kept hidden for emergencies. Actually she had two caches, but one was already packed. This second one was kept for long drives, specifically to placate Nosemitt when her highway phobia and her preference for many stops along the way conflicted with Sniffle's eagerness to pass every car on the road and get everywhere first. Inevitably someone who encountered this trait in her would suggest that she learn to stop and smell the roses; but she knew that she had spent her daily life doing so for years and had thousands of paintings, dozens of manuscripts, and prolonged sneezing bouts to show for it. Often she would stop to see the scenery, especially canyons and waterfalls. She would willingly get out of the car to see any view. Right now, however, her mind was geared to reward. Frequent stops played havoc with her goals when they were on flat or dry land, but chocolate bars had proved to be a worthwhile investment. She had a dozen bars ready for the trip, surely good for three hundred and seventy-five miles, perhaps enough for part of the return trip as well. She had put them in a plain brown paper bag and had taken them out to the car, hiding them carefully under the driver's seat. Now she looked contentedly at the back seat, which held the four small paintings that she had selected to accompany her, never feeling quite comfortable away from her work for any length of time. If she could not be painting or writing, she at least liked to be near her pictures. In touch with reality, she called it. "Your security blankets," Nosemitt said.

Nosemitt came downstairs with her luggage, double-checked the windows and back door, patted the light timers affectionately, and came out to the car.

"Where's your purse?" Sniffle asked. Nosemitt borrowed Sniffle's key, went back for her purse and returned, making sure she had both sets of keys in her right hand, and carefully closed and checked the door. It was locked.

"I wonder what else we are forgetting," she said, a determined smile of good cheer frozen to her face. "It is a beautiful day for a ride." In the silence that followed, each of them knew what the other was thinking and it related to the euphemism *ride* for a more than eight-hour journey. Sniffle backed out of the garage, reached the street, paused for a car to pass, and then took off. There was silence in the car all the way to the interstate, a distance of some seven miles.

"So what do you think of Uncle Walter?" Sniffle asked, seeing a heavy stream of traffic ahead on the highway and hoping to divert Nosemitt from panic. "Can we have any confidence in his opinions of Marvin?"

"Marvin is a bastard," Nosemitt declared, teeth clenched for the upcoming knot of cars.

"Is that metaphorical, or do you think Fredricka did not much care for Horatio Marvin the first?"

"I think any man who cuts off contact with any of his children is a bastard," Nosemitt said; "watch that driver on your left; I think he is drunk. And perhaps if we got off at the next exit and had a cup of coffee or something, this traffic would die down and we could travel a little more comfortably. We don't have to get there today."

"We're fine," Sniffle said. "I can't make up my mind about Walter. He obviously is very fond of Vanessa– he practically twinkles when she is nearby– and I get the impression he was equally fond of Harriette."

"I think he has been under a great deal of strain and has prided himself on handling details. I think he does not have as firm a grasp of everything as he imagines– or as much as he would have had in slightly younger days. We certainly can understand that. Watch that blue car!"

"That blue car is at least a quarter of a mile ahead."

"Only for the moment. You'll be passing it any instant."

Forty-five minutes into the trip, as they passed exit five, Sniffle was silently congratulating herself on getting so far without a bribe when Nosemitt suddenly said, "Are we driving straight through? Aren't you planning to stop at all?"

"We've only been on the road forty-five minutes," Sniffle said. "How about stopping at exit fifteen? That's at Yincon and there's a diner there that you liked once before."

"Exit fifteen! That's two hours from here! I am not a camel, but suit yourself." Nosemitt's voice was still fairly calm, a good sign, except for that slight taint of martyred resignation. Sniffle continued driving, going on the assumption that Nosemitt would probably accept a compromise at exit twelve but might feel a little bad about suggesting exit seven or eight. The exits were getting farther apart now that they were in farm territory. In fact, it was exit twelve that was two hours from here; fifteen was considerably longer off. It was sometimes good that Nosemitt did not enjoy reading maps.

"What do you think Roger's name might be?" Sniffle asked at exit seven, hoping to get them an extra fifty miles if the conversation went anywhere.

"How would I know?" Testiness was edging in, a danger signal however unintended it always was in this situation. The two women exchanged a few basic character traits once they were in a car and especially when state or federal pavement was involved.

"Well, I can't believe a woman would reject a man she apparently loved just because of his name."

"Perhaps it is Roger Belch," Nosemitt suggested. "Or Roger Puke. Or Roger –"

"I get your drift," Sniffle said, "but would Harriette have been too offended to marry him? These days, she wouldn't have to take his name anyway."

"Walter did seem to imply that there were real reasons, deeper reasons."

"And then he disappeared right out to the cab," Sniffle reminded her. "I wonder why he doesn't like Roger."

"But Vanessa does. Exit nine seems to have disappeared; I bet you passed it," Nosemitt complained. "I don't think we should wait for fifteen. How about ten?"

"Twelve?" Sniffle countered. Nosemitt grimaced but shrugged and they drove on, coming to exit nine thirty minutes later.

"We've gone nonstop for two and a half hours," the passenger complained. The driver hummed a little tune and smiled. Exit ten came into view three hours into the trip. "We have to stop now!" Nosemitt insisted. "I am stiff and sore and thirsty and hungry, and I am tired of hearing you try to sing. 'I Am Honking to Pretoria' is not amusing the first time, let alone the twentieth time."

"Well, it's a good time to fill up the gas tank anyway," Sniffle conceded. She took the ramp for exit ten and pulled into a Petroco station. Nosemitt hurried off to the restroom and came back almost immediately, before the car could be serviced at one of the available pumps. She looked outraged and could barely speak coherently but did finally manage to sputter, "Do you know what the attendant said when I inquired about toilet paper? Do you know? I cannot believe it. We have to go to the next exit; I will not stop here. That idiot informed me that they didn't stock toilet paper because people just 'used it up'! Used it up, he said. Of course they use it up. That's what it's for. He offered me a rag! A greasy, dirty, oily rag! Said they were about to throw it out anyway! If you had stopped back at a decent exit… !" but then she became too indignant to say more.

It was clearly time, and Sniffle did not lose a minute. "Here!" she happily offered. The chocolate bar had melted only at the edges when a strong blast from the heater had attacked it. "Thank you very much," Nosemitt said with a meek voice as she delicately removed the foil wrapping. She nibbled at the soft corner and closed her eyes. Sniffle smiled at the thought that she had gained at least twenty more minutes of driving time. Then in a more emphatic voice Nosemitt said, "but this will not be enough. We are stopping at the next exit for a real lunch and some time to stretch and walk. And that exit is in five miles; do not zip past it. It had better have clean restrooms!" She did eat the whole candy bar without fear that it might spoil her appetite.

As they sat in the booth at Korner Kupboard #34, now finished with their BLTs and enjoying a second cup of coffee, Sniffle again brought up the Kettle family. "What do you think of Walter's clear suggestion that some member of the clan is the guilty party?"

"I guess I keep thinking that he doesn't like them and is prone to thinking one of them is guilty; but you do have to admit that all that jewelry makes a very strong motive."

"And that makes you think that it cannot be the true one, let alone the true solution?'

"Of course I think that. I am too loyal a detective story fan to think that he would hire us if he had the answer already. There's no story in it. There must be more or I will be very disappointed, and you as a writer would be too."

"But I don't like detective stories. I want them solved at the outset to avoid the unpleasantness. I would make all detective stories very short and there would be no victims of violence– an occasional minor inconvenience, a lost item, a missing person who turns up befuddled but lovable– no foul play and certainly no one murdered and left in a gutter."

"Then it's good that you don't write them. Anyway, I still don't like Horatio Marvin Junior; and, by extension, since he prefers Dustin, I don't like Dustin either. Perhaps I will change my mind once we are at St. Edwards, but I begin by regarding the son as a bastard too. How could anyone not love Vanessa?"

"Perhaps her father sets a different standard in dress," Sniffle suggested. "Not everyone would share our admiration of her very unusual wardrobe."

"I still don't know about that hat," Nosemitt said, happily sipping her coffee. "Can we just sit here a while? Traffic might be getting lighter in an hour or so." But Sniffle, accustomed to that phrase, was already putting her coat back on and getting change to leave a tip. All those cars were getting far ahead; there were miles to go before she'd consider stopping again. She let Nosemitt bask in the booth while she took the car to the pump and paid extra to get full service so that they would check under the hood. The car had been ready for five minutes when Nosemitt sauntered out, stopping to look in the window of the service station. At last she got slowly into the car.

"See any cans of oil there that caught your fancy?" Sniffle asked. "Shopping for brake fluid?"

"Very funny. Well, what are you waiting for? Let's go." Clearly more relaxed after the infusion of lunch, Nosemitt began humming and singing. One particular refrain kept going through her mind, although she could not quite get back the words. "It's a lengthy ditty my father used to love," she kept saying. "'Can you imagine…' and then I don't remember the words, only the tune. Oh well, it will come to me if I keep on humming it." After ten minutes, Sniffle reached under the seat and got herself a chocolate bar but continued rummaging under the seat. "Watch out for that turn!" Nosemitt said mid-hum; "don't look for things while you're driving."

"Can't find them anyway," Sniffle muttered, knowing full well that she kept earmuffs under there somewhere. Nosemitt went on humming, clapping her hands lightly in time to the rhythm of the forgotten refrain. "I think it might have been a patriotic song," she said. Sniffle accelerated only slightly.

While one or the other was humming, singing, nibbling, and alerting the driver about distant or phantom hazards en route to St. Edwards, Vanessa was steeling herself for the upcoming memorial service. She had tried to assure Uncle Walter that he had no need to stay with her until Nosemitt and Sniffle's arrival; she insisted that she was a capable adult and could handle things, but he insisted with even greater determination that she should not be alone at this time. He settled himself in a guest bedroom on the second floor, the room that had been Dustin's when he was very young. Exasperated, Vanessa finally threw up her hands and stalked off to her own room where at least she had a phone of her own. Someone she called was extremely sympathetic to all her complaints and must have been happy that Vanessa was home again. She hung up the phone feeling considerably better.

Walter, meanwhile, was on the other phone line in Harriette's study, making additional arrangements for Sunday's service. He had put off calling Marvin but now he could delay no longer. It required an almost unintelligible conversation with a babysitter who seemed to have a negative IQ, interrupted by the arrival home of Harriet (lesser), followed immediately by a forced stint of saying hello to Tabitha, their four-month old daughter, before Marvin came to the phone. Uncle Walter, not disposed toward infants anyway, regarded this encounter as yet another reason to detest most of the Kettle family. Eventually he was able to notify Marvin of the time of the service and to request that Dustin be given this information as well. Marvin expressed disinterest in the entire matter but grudgingly indicated that he would see if Dustin wished to attend.

"Two o' clock Sunday at the University Chapel. Please make sure that Dustin wishes to attend." He did not mean it to sound like a threat, but Marvin chose to hear it that way.

"Don't think you have any power here, Walter." The phone clicked and the old man slowly put the phone back in its cradle. He made one more call to the minister to confirm the time on Sunday afternoon and was greeted with the news that the minister had been called out of town on a family emergency and might not be back in time. A replacement had been found, and he had already been given the time and place.

Walter sat back in Harriette's chair, and it squeaked as if to tell its occupant he did not belong there. "I'm getting all too fanciful," the man said out loud, and the chair squeaked its confirmation. He ran his hand over the arm and drew his finger along the seam of the upholstered cushion. Harriette, his beloved niece, had worked here. She had read thousands of letters at this very desk and answered many of them here as well. The walls were filled with photos and newspaper clippings and one small framed watercolor by a young Vanessa and a crayon scribble by a toddler Dustin. Slowly her absence seeped in and he cried softly for her, though he never once allowed himself to picture how she had looked in the scatter of snow. Others had been called to identify her, and he was grateful to have been spared. The chair squeaked.

He noticed little details now– a white enamel-framed photograph of Roger on a boat, a cluster of political buttons magnetized to her paperclip holder. Had she been interested in politics? He thought he had known all there was to know about her; she had been more like a daughter, but he was unaware of any particular attraction to political buttons. He reflected on the impossibility of fully knowing anyone, though he had certainly tried– tried more than the objects of his great interest and affection had ever welcomed. He knew he had come to be regarded as a busybody, he who had always been so large-minded, so community-minded. He was a generous and kind philanthropist in his own way, having accumulated a comfortable fortune that he was always quite willing to share. Smallness, even the accusation of smallness, nettled him; gossip interested him only for the information he could glean between the lines.

His eyes were drawn to the in and out baskets at the corner of the desk. Work to be done that would never be done, at least not by Harriette, Ms Ettikettle of *The Edwardian Times*. How she had hated that trite name that her editor had insisted upon! And it was Walter who had encouraged her to use the excuse of Roger's laughable name to spare him the real reason for her refusal to marry him. He, Walter, knew all about that. Marrying Roger had been, as he had said, out of the question. But now he idly lifted the top letter from the pile in the basket and casually skimmed its contents. He could not believe that Harriette had had to read such drivel for all these years.

Dear Ms Ettikettle,
My mother-in-law is coming for a lengthy visit, and I am quite determined to make her stay a pleasant one. I have already bought many of her favorite foods and also new towels and sheets. I have arranged to have someone come in and clean the house even more thoroughly than I do myself, and I bought some new furnishings for the guest room and will have fresh flowers on the table. I am so worried that I will say or do the wrong thing. I got some etiquette books from the library, but they are due back soon and I haven't even finished the first chapter.

Walter started to put the letter back in the basket, irked as he was by the tone and the triviality of the letter– in fact, he suspected that people enjoyed making up outrageous letters and sending them in– but something made him continue. Possibly it was his need to have completion. Despite himself, he was drawn to know about the person behind the letter.

It wouldn't be so bad, Ms Ettikettle, if she were coming to see the children or me but she will only want to see Joe. I never had the courage to tell her that Joe left last summer. It was the fourth of July and we were down at the river to see the fireworks. When the smoke and noise cleared,

Then he had to stop, depressed beyond his present limits by this unexpected turn in his awareness of the human condition. Again he wondered how Harriette could have endured all the years of letters, though now it was not for their triviality but for the pain masked by the ridiculous. He was all too familiar with pain and all too familiar with ridiculous. In his times of strength he was fascinated, but this was not such a time. He dimly felt that he was betraying the writer, but he needed what strength he still had to cope with the crises in his own family. Joe's disappearance in the smoke and the noise could not distract him now; he needed to be there for Vanessa.

He heard the other phone ring in her room and so he just sat there in Harriette's chair, studying Harriette's walls, replaying his memories of his niece when she was a child who loved to visit him. He would take her to the zoo, read to her, show her his office in the old Winchell building, let her play on his secretary's typewriter. Her father had died when she was quite small, and Walter had taken seriously his role as guardian and godfather. He remembered how proud he had been of her scholastic success, even though it had been delayed in coming, and her decision to become a journalist, although he had been even more disappointed than she when the newspaper insisted that she take over the etiquette column. She had wanted to do more investigative work, had wanted more challenging assignments. Behind the scenes, under a more sensible name than Ettikettle, she did a great deal and wielded quite a bit of influence; but unlike Nosemitt and Sniffle, she never liked having to resort to pseudonyms. She too had had her secrets, but they had never given her pleasure.

Walter sat and pondered these facts and came to no conclusions. He sensed once again that he had been drawn to the two women vpi's from Fondue at some level beyond any rational thinking, drawn at an essentially psychic level. He knew that their use of those silly names was fundamentally not silly at all, that for reasons too deep within his soul to fathom he respected their integrity all the more. Perhaps it was that they honestly said, "Our lives must be our own." He removed his glasses and wiped them carefully with a methodical, deliberate, and customary pattern: first the right lens exterior, then its interior, then the left in the same order. He held them up toward the light and searched for spots. He wiped the frames gently and then, oddly, he casually tossed them on the desk and rubbed his eyes. Slumping there in the gray upholstered chair, he dozed but he did not dream.

Vanessa's call had been from Herbert Molecott, her mother's editor at the paper. He was already pressuring her to take over the column but was also upset that she had been away without telling him. "Things are piling up here," he had said; and she was angry that he would expect her to go on as if nothing had happened. "You know the police have been here several times. They found a stupid note that they think I have something to do with. I need you to clear me. Get over here first thing in the morning."

She had refused, pointing out to him that she had a great deal to do before the memorial service and she needed rest as well. "The newspaper will just have to wait," she had said firmly. Herb was not used to an assertive Vanessa, nor did he like this change.

"You be here at eight-thirty or else."

"Or else what? I will not be there. Am I supposed to think that I need to take over the column because it would be convenient for you? I don't want the job. Perhaps I will see you Sunday at the service but not before then," and she had hung up quickly before she could relent. She liked this change in herself and so would Roger.

She made one last call that evening, checking in with Sergeant Bradley of the small homicide department that doubled as a kind of domestic and civil violence unit. Normally they had very little to do– perhaps an occasional fight to break up, sometimes a wild party that was brought to their attention, most often teen vandalism in the park or behind the little league fields. Sergeant Arthur Bradley and his colleague, Detective Lesley Anne Duke, were the entire team; and until now Duke's most serious and only unsolved crime was a serial bird murderer who periodically took out his or possibly her rage or dementedness on the pigeon population with a foray into sparrows or doves for variety. Sometimes a rash of pet murders occurred, and the assumption was that the same person was responsible. St. Edwards had little in the way of other overt violence; and, despite the ironic circumstances of Harriette's murder as depicted by a few callous members of the media, the town's residents were genuinely shocked. Bradley and Duke hoped that they could solve this, their first human murder case. They had asked Vanessa to keep in touch with them regularly, and she had complied. Their supervisor had been irate when he learned that they had let the victim's daughter and uncle leave town, but they had assured the chief that neither Walter nor Vanessa could have been the guilty party and both would definitely return. Chief Bigguns had chewed them out loud and long. "Don't be taken in by anything!" he had stormed. "Suspect everyone! That is a detective's only motto." So Bradley breathed a happy sigh of relief when Vanessa called in to report her return and confirmed that Mr. Wrothwell was safely back too. The chief would think that meant nothing, but Bradley and Duke needed a little reassurance.

They had worried at first that there would be too little to go on, but their gradual accumulation of evidence had produced an incredible number of people with motives. Every letter writer was a potential suspect; but, more realistically, the list included those of Harriette Kettle's colleagues at work who were jealous of her real power; her editor, who seemed to have written an incriminating memo; a few members of her family who were involved in some shady dealings that Harriette was in a position to expose– all had significant interest in removing Harriette from their respective spheres. Bradley and Duke were excited at first by every new suspect and every new fact; but then, as the trails led in upon themselves and remained in the realm of conjecture, they felt overwhelmed. Long days of tracking down small clues were followed by long nights of sifting words on reports that soon became meaningless. Their minds were numbed by the amount of work they faced; but had they known of it, they would have been extremely hostile to Mr. Wrothwell's suggestion that he needed the services of two very private [?] investigators, post-middle-aged ladies who were steadily maneuvering closer and closer to St. Edwards at that very moment, travel-weary women sick of the tune that Nosemitt still could not quite remember the words to and down to their last four chocolate bars.

Late that same Thursday night

Sedately they were escorted to their room at the Edwardian Arms. Like Sandburgian fog on stealthy cat feet, they silently followed the bellboy down the plush carpeted corridor, observing the heavily embossed velvet patterns on the wallpaper and the large potted artificial plants at odd corners. The bellboy indicated the path to follow to obtain extra ice and left a room service menu in clear view on a bedside table. Nosemitt passed him a feasible tip, and Sniffle collapsed on the bed nearer the window. Her muscles were stiff, her mind a tired jumble except for the insidious wordless tune that drove itself round and round on a turntable in her head. **Duh** duh da **duh** duh da **duh** duh duh... She fell asleep fully dressed and Nosemitt went out for ice.

A moment later, or what seemed like a moment later, Sniffle was awakened by a knock at the door. Assuming that Nosemitt had gone out without the key, she went to the door and called out, "Is that you?"

"Of course it's me," a rough male voice answered, "but who are you? It's Mel, but Jeez, I musta went downa wrong hall. You sure ain't Chick."

"Quite right," Sniffle muttered and went to brush her teeth and go back to sleep. Five minutes later the sound of the door opening proved that Nosemitt had not forgotten the key at all. She had gone to check out the menu in the restaurant and had been in time to get a couple of chicken sandwiches before the kitchen shut down for the night. She had stopped for two cans of soda on the way back.

"Here's a sandwich for you, no mayo," she offered. "What's the matter? You look perturbed."

"Nothing, I just was awakened very abruptly by some man named Mel looking for Chick, whom 'I sure ain't.' It's nothing."

"You'll be pleased to know that tomorrow night's special is shrimp." Now that Nosemitt had been off the highway well over an hour, she was back to herself. She looked around the room as she munched on her sandwich and tried to guess where Sniffle would hang her own paintings. It was a sure bet that the thick oil painting of a longhorn steer would soon be on the floor facing the wall. Why a painting of a longhorn was hanging in a room with flocked red wallpaper was beyond her– and she said so.

"Perhaps 'flock' is the secret link," Sniffle suggested, almost half awake now. "Maybe the decorators thought that steers traveled in flocks rather than herds. Conversely, maybe they think that the correct term for flocked wallpaper is 'herded'. On the third hand– "

"Go back to sleep," Nosemitt ordered. Sniffle was surprisingly compliant, and Nosemitt finished both sandwiches. After all, there was no refrigerator in the room.

Friday morning, January 12

Sniffle awoke the next morning at nine to the sounds of the shower running and Nosemitt once again at work on the song. The wordless tune echoed off the steamed walls and hung in the vapor. While she waited for the shower to become available, Sniffle began rearranging the walls. As predicted, the longhorn painting was the first to fall. The imitation Utrillo Paris scene found itself in back of the dresser, and a mauve floral that clashed painfully with the red wallpaper went into the closet. In their places went three of the four misty cosmoscapes she had brought. She remained undecided about the fourth and simply left it standing against one of the chairs. She heard the shower stop, though the tune lingered, and she gathered clothes to wear that day. Nosemitt emerged wearing a royal blue sweat suit and bunny slippers. She sported a fluffy red hotel towel around her head. "You know, this room isn't right for your paintings either," she said.

"I know," Sniffle agreed, "but I can block out the walls more easily than I can block out the steer." Just as Sniffle was adjusting the shower temperature, there was a knock at the door. Sniffle, in the clothes she had slept in, went to the door and demanded sternly, "Are you Mel again?"

"I never was Mel in the first place," a surprised female voice answered.

"Me either," a husky male voice assured her. Sniffle looked at Nosemitt, who looked back with a mixture of curiosity and mild apprehension. Who could know they were there?

"Probably another wrong room," Sniffle said. "Who is it? Who are you? Whom are you looking for?"

"We're looking for, uh, Nosemitt? and Sniffle?" the male voice said, doubtful about their names.

"I am Detective Duke and my partner here is Sergeant Bradley. We're from the homicide squad. Walter Wrothwell sent us." That was the female voice, and it sounded both professional and friendly. Sniffle, more than incredulous, kept the chain on the door but opened it a crack. Both officers handed in their identification; and after shrugging and motioning for Nosemitt to make the decision but getting no immediate response, Sniffle let them in.

"I don't understand," Nosemitt said, coming to the door too. The two officers entered the room.

"We're just coming from a meeting with Mr. Wrothwell," Duke said. "He said he had invited the two of you here and that you would be staying with Vanessa."

"Why did he need to report that?" Sniffle asked.

"Excuse us for being confused," Nosemitt said, "but the whole point of our being here to investigate the crime was that we would be unknown. He stressed discretion and the importance of blending in as old friends of Harriette. Why would he have told you?"

"Investigators?" Bradley said, shocked. "He did not tell us you were investigators. He just said you had known his niece in the past and that you might be staying a while."

"He suggested we wait until after the memorial service if we had any need to ask questions, but we saw no reason to wait," Duke said.

"So much for our discretion," Sniffle said. "The very first thing we do is expose our roles here. Great omen!" She was so depressed that she almost sat down on her painting by the chair.

"Great painting," Bradley said. "That almost looks like a Nigel."

"You've heard of Nigel?" Sniffle asked, astonished. Bradley came closer to study the painting and saw that it was in fact a Nigel painting. He smiled serenely, then noticed the other three on the walls. He was diplomatic enough not to say that they did not go with red flocked wallpaper.

"Where did you find these?" he asked. "The gallery dealer I like to drop in and talk with every now and then says they're hard to come by."

"You buy art?" Sniffle asked, awed.

"No, but someday maybe. I got acquainted with this artist's work last year when there was a benefit exhibit. I was asked to moonlight as security guard, so I had plenty of time to look at all the work. There were three or four artists whose work I liked, and Nigel was one of them. I don't know anything about him, and neither did the gallery owner."

"He's a she," Sniffle said. "I own the largest collection of Nigels in the world, although I often wish that I didn't."

"You do?" he asked; "how did– ," and then a slow flush of happy understanding spread across his face. "You're Nigel?" he asked, and it was his turn to be astonished, "and you are also a private investigator?"

"Well, not exactly a private investigator," she said. "Right now I guess you'd say we are quite public and inept investigators. Painfully public, at least to the police; painfully inept to ourselves."

"This is quite a pleasure," he said, shaking her hand exuberantly. Sniffle glowed, genuinely happier and more pleasantly startled and amused and flattered than she had ever been in her life, with the possible exception of a single occasion in the Grand Canyon, but that was long ago and definitely of no interest to the visitors. This was now.

All of this conversation was of no interest to Duke, except for the revelation of the unexpected roles of these two rather odd women. Nosemitt still had the towel around her head and her reading glasses on top of the towel. "It seems very strange to me," Duke said, trying to divert Bradley away from the paintings, "that Mr. Wrothwell would have pushed us in this direction if he wanted to have them here in an anonymous role."

"Obviously we have no information at this point other than what Mr. Wrothwell has supplied us," Nosemitt said, suddenly aware of the towel. She removed it, forgetting that her hair was in a wet tangle, and hoped that her appearance had improved a bit. Her glasses fell to the floor. Sniffle made no comment, only sent her a telepathic message to put the towel back on, but also realized that she herself looked equally bizarre in her sweatshirt that declared *And I Am Marie of Roumania.* The fact that she had borrowed it from Nosemitt to drive in when the car heater stopped working for a while would be unwise to state and basically irrelevant. It would be compounding the problem to try to explain why she was holding two tubes of toothpaste and wearing a strand of dental floss as a necklace. Besides, she didn't know why she was holding two tubes of toothpaste.

"I guess we might as well be going," Bradley said, "but here's our number at the station, and let me add my home phone number to this card. If you learn anything helpful, give us a call."

"Let me add mine to that," Duke said.

"Are we allowed to come discuss any of your findings?" Nosemitt asked. "We're still pretty new at this."

"Within limits," Duke said. "We aren't too experienced at murder cases ourselves." Bradley scowled at her, knowing what Chief Bigguns would say if he heard her.

"Will you allow us to keep our secret?" Nosemitt asked.

"We really are just amateurs," Sniffle assured him. "We shouldn't get in your way."

Bradley smiled sourly and nodded; Duke knew enough to worry about amateurs who had no intention of getting in the way but assured them their secret was quite secure. They had no interest in a lecture from the chief.

After they left, Sniffle hurried to shower; then they both left for breakfast, then off to explore the community of St. Edwards. They traced the route to Harriette's house; they found the public library. They drove past the high school and the University, locating the chapel, and searched out likely restaurants. "You know," Nosemitt said, "I keep feeling that I know someone who lives here, have at least heard of someone who lives here. I wonder who it might be. Nothing is coming to me. "**Duh** duh da **duh** duh da **duh** duh duh…. Why don't you try humming it? Maybe if I hear it wrong, I will remember the words suddenly."

Sniffle groaned. She tried humming as close to the same tune as she could manage, but it sounded more as if she were simply hitting a hard surface with her hand, trying only for the rhythm of the thing. She refused to keep humming and changed the subject. "I don't know anyone here. Did you ever make contact with a gallery owner for me? I still can't believe that nice sergeant knew my painting."

"Something about 'a sorry sight' or a 'sorrier sight' I think, now that I hear you trying to hum it. 'Could you ever imagine this sorry sight …?' Oh, well, it will come back. Anyway, I don't recall ever

contacting any gallery owners here, but he said a benefit exhibit.
Someone could have donated a painting he or she had bought from
you. We'd have no way of knowing that. Who told me about a relative
living in St. Edwards? I just can't think."

They stopped around two to buy lunch and took it to a scenic
overlook at the nearby state park, but it was too cold and it started
to get very cloudy. They spent the rest of the day at the library,
developing a background as schoolmates of Harriette Wrothwell Kettle.
Working in separate areas of the library, Nosemitt became something of
an authority on the cultural opportunities in St. Edwards while Sniffle
studied the university catalog and found in the microfilm department
articles in old newspapers from thirty years back. She realized with
some concern that they had not learned exactly how old Harriette
was, so she read up on several years. Nosemitt discovered a dozen
old high school yearbooks and had a good time recalling some of her
own school days. She did find the one that Harriette was in and so
she knew her activities. She studied the formal photograph and knew
that she would have liked this woman very much. Her eyes were clear
and straightforward, intelligent, alert. She looked kind without being
sentimental, handsome rather than pretty, certainly not cute. There
was some faint resemblance to Walter, or perhaps Nosemitt was just
imagining it. Harriette had been active without being into everything;
she had been involved in sports. She had shown an early interest in
writing and in community affairs. She did not appear in the popularity
poll, nor was she ever a prom queen or cheerleader. Nosemitt read and
re-read the quip someone had selected to characterize her: *A word from
the wise.*

Harriette was now a friend.

In their comparison of notes and their creation of a history
with Harriette, they managed to overlook some basics and to think
mistakenly that they had fully covered others.

Sunday, January 14
1:30 pm

The morning had turned colder, dreary, hinting of freezing rain,
which was holding off for the moment. Nosemitt drove to the campus
and found a parking space in the lot near the science building. The
chapel would be about a quarter of a mile walk from there, and Sniffle
complained. "Why are you complaining?" Nosemitt asked her; "you at

least aren't wearing heels."

"No, but I don't enjoy any walking in cold weather and you do," Sniffle answered. They crossed the main quadrangle and then cut off to the west, glad that they had stopped the day before to locate various points of interest. The sidewalks were lined with stark old trees that housed too many nests to count. Pigeons and crows and a squawk of grackles fought in the berry bushes clumped nearer the buildings; and an occasional cardinal flashed past, the only note of color in a bleak day.

The women drew their coats more snugly around themselves and walked as quickly as they could, coming at last to the chapel where a crowd of black coats seemed to imitate the birds, although the people were quieter. A few of the men carried umbrellas; a few stood off to one side and smoked. Their conversations were muted, sedate. Only the birds were raucous. At ten minutes before two, all of them entered the chapel and silently meditated on death. Death was sober, earnest, real, austere, and not to be encountered without solemnity and awe.

2:00 p.m.
University Chapel

"Dear Friends, we are brought together at this solemn moment to pay tribute to a life that gave so much to so many." A well-dressed young man tried to step past Sniffle to take a seat. Uncle Walter in the front row placed his arm lovingly around Vanessa's shoulder. The two vpi's could detect nobody fitting their image of Marvin and Harriet the lesser. A gentleman in back of Vanessa might be Dustin, or it might be someone from the newspaper. The minister waited for the rustle in the assembly to subside. Several people coughed decorously. The young man kept turning anxiously to look toward the back of the chapel. Nosemitt conjectured that he was impatient to get on to some date. Sniffle wondered if he had come with someone else and the driver were having trouble parking. There was quite a crowd in the chapel, and they all seemed unwilling to subside fully. The minister continued on pause for two full minutes but then could contain himself no longer. He raised the volume two or three notches:

"In person so charming, as I have been told, not having the great privilege of direct knowledge" – there was a flurry of whispering then– "and yet not perfect, for who among us is perfect? And would not an etiquette columnist eschew the idea of perfection as but a goal and never a realized human accomplishment? a sublime dream? a pattern to hold before the world with which to lift it to God? I think so!

"Was she demanding? I had the distinct honor to speak with her former husband, who I am pleased to number among my friends and who told me that some have called her so. Perhaps it was only a feminine stratagem, one of the clever little ploys the fair sex has developed to near-perfection in its struggle to uplift the rougher gender. But was she rigid? Not really."

Nosemitt was visibly offended; Sniffle had been having a terrible time keeping from embarrassing herself by laughing out loud at yet more examples of the absurdity that does surround us. It was only for Vanessa and Walter's sakes that she managed to keep some control, although her lip was already bleeding and her eyes were watering.

"Who? we ask, who? could so foully murder this dear friend to some among you, taskmistress to others of you, sage by some accounts, and model of elegance both personal and expository, as apparently everyone does agree? Who?"

"Who is this fool?" Nosemitt whispered a little more loudly than she had intended; and that was the straw that unhinged Sniffle. She broke into hysterical laughter, followed by a prolonged wheezing, coughing fit, and had to creep out of the chapel and into the cold winter air. "Who?" she croaked to a passing pigeon, but it did not speak the language. It fluttered weakly past, landed feebly, and flopped over. Sniffle was instantly sobered and returned quietly to the service.

"All of us have known the bread of sorrow…"

"In this case, also the crumbs," she could not refrain from softly whispering to Nosemitt, although she felt terribly unkind. There was once again a need for a ministerial pause as everyone turned to see what was making the terrible disturbance halfway back in the chapel. It seemed to be two women, unfortunately in mid-pew, presumably overcome by grief and memory. Walter and Vanessa did not turn around, a bit too confident of what they would see. The vpi's excused themselves out of the row and the chapel and would have missed the highpoint of the eulogy, had Nosemitt not dropped her purse near the end of the aisle and been stopped by the clergyman's next words:

"I would like to read to all assembled here a letter that so fully and wonderfully captures the essence of what the deceased meant to her far-flung admirers in numerous counties in this state– the faceless multitude who, whether they knew her personally or not, sought her wisdom and counsel through the pages of any of fourteen, nay fifteen, daily or weekly publications. She cast pearls of sanity and was rewarded with necklaces and bracelets and rings of gratitude. Hers was a difficult job, demanding taste and tact and a love of people even in their worst aspects. I am reminded of a funeral at which I officiated recently, a funeral for a shoe salesman. I said then, as I say now, who but someone who genuinely loved people could tolerate being a shoe salesman? And who but someone who loved people could daily deal with the endless problems large and small that plague the masses? Here is an example, though, of that gratitude I have mentioned, a little ring of pearl.

'Dear Ms Ettikettle' [and I interrupt here to remind you that so she was known to her public],

I want to thank you for the good advice that you gave me last month. Perhaps you remember me; I wrote to ask if it was proper to chew gum at a wedding feast and, if so, was it okay to put it on the bread and butter plate or should I look around for an ashtray. I wanted to do it right and not embarrass the bride who is my dearest friend– or was anyway. You said it would be best to leave the gum at home and asked if I might be trying to make a statement with the gum. I thought a lot about that, and I finally figured out what you meant. So I did take the gum, because then if I wanted to make a toast or something, the gum would help me concentrate. And I did and it did, and now my snooty friend and her dumb husband aren't talking to me anyway; but I don't like them and I don't care. I stuck the gum under the table afterwards, but I don't think my old boyfriend and his new stupid wife even noticed. Shows how smart they are. Thanks a lot, Ms Ettikettle, I would never have made a toast if you hadn't suggested it. I'm really glad I wrote."

'I ask you, dear friends and family, could anything express us all better? Thanks a lot, Ms Ettikettle, wherever you may be now. We trust it is in Heaven. Let us stand."

Vanessa left the chapel sobbing and many commented on the depth of her loss, although a few were disturbed at her mourning ensemble that included the unfortunate fur hat and a black mid-calf skirt that had been noticeably let out, topped by a black t-shirt over which she had draped what seemed to have been a magenta and taupe piano shawl with a tiny border design of yellow music notes. Uncle Walter escorted her to the door and asked her to wait there for him. Then he turned back to find the minister and deliver a sermon of his own. Every fiber of his being felt assaulted; Reverend Fibble would know it, and Marvin would hear from him as well.

As friends and relatives and business associates came to pay their respects and express their condolences at home, Nosemitt and Sniffle discreetly mingled. At first, to anyone who asked her connection with the deceased, Nosemitt uniformly indicated that she and her companion across the room there had known Harriette quite well back in high school days and had predicted back when they worked together on the St. Edward's *Yerebooke* and the school paper, *The Megaphone*, that Harriette would certainly amount to something in the journalistic field. She was placidly recalling those simpler days to a woman in a dark floral dress and a black hat.

"Yes, who could have predicted such a violent end for such a lovely person? It is odd that I do not remember you at all," the woman said, frowning in puzzlement. "I know my memory has not been so good lately, but I was very involved in the paper. Not the yearbook, but the paper. Are you sure you worked on both? And the school, so small and all, surely we would have many memories in common. You must excuse my appalling forgetfulness; Gerard has been telling me I should see a specialist, and I fear he may be right. Oh dear, this is so embarrassing." Nosemitt felt terribly guilty and worked her way across the room to ask Sniffle for suggestions.

"We didn't allow for real high school friends," she whispered furiously. "I feel caught in a dreadful trap, and I may be responsible for needless brain surgery."

"High school friends?" Sniffle repeated. "We agreed that we met Harriette in your sophomore year at the university. We worked for the same political causes. I was a graduate student."

"Oh, dear," Nosemitt sighed. "It all flew out of my head after that horrible service. I was thinking we had agreed on high school."

"I am quite sure that we agreed that college is safer, especially since I am a few years older. Harriette didn't take ten years to finish high school," Sniffle said. Nosemitt unhappily sidled off to mingle and was soon immersed in another conversation.

"You say you knew each other in high school and were college chums?" a tall, distinguished gentleman was asking.

"Well, mostly in college. We were not in the same high school class. We learned at the university that we shared quite a number of political sympathies and a love of theatre. Youth was a wonderful thing."

"Quite peculiar," he said, scratching his silver hair. "Harriette Wrothwell was quite famous on campus for getting her degree in her mid-forties, not quite a decade ago. How is it that she never let anyone know that she had attended our school in her youth?"

"Now that you mention it, I do believe she left after that first year or two. Perhaps she did not want her previous dropping out known to all," Nosemitt said, vowing never to get into such a situation again. A fine fishiness of Kettles, Sniffle would later say of this whole day.

"Just finished ten years ago?" Sniffle repeated when Nosemitt related her latest faux pas. "Oh, dear. Well, I suspect we can be safely chalked up as a couple of loons who just wanted to hobnob with a syndicated celebrity in the county newspaper line. Just keep nibbling and get overcome with emotion if more people keep asking how we knew her. Ask them questions instead."

"Dammit, I am getting increasingly tempted to get a loudspeaker and announce that we are here as private investigators," Nosemitt said. "I have never had any problem with our choosing to go by other names, but we cannot be forced to enter into these elaborate lies. I am not at all happy. We could just be here in a more natural way, as people who knew of the death and came to express our sympathy."

"Private investigators?" Sniffle repeated. "You know better, but I don't like the pretense either. I described Harriette to her own sister, who wondered why I wouldn't know who she was. Still, remember, the point was to give a reason for our being invited to stay here after today, not to account for our presence at the service. By the way, that skinny little woman over there next to the unpleasant-looking young man with the blonde mustache is Harriet the Lesser. And the young man himself is Dustin."

"How do you know all that?" Nosemitt demanded, irritable with one and all.

"Exceptional mingling talent; remember it for my own eulogy. That phrase and the music of *The Grand Canyon Suite* constitute my only requests so far. Oh, and no Reverend Fibble or anyone like him or I will haunt you mercilessly."

"Too many occasions like this one and I'll be haunting you first.

No bones about it, I'll haunt you." The comment was pure vintage Nosemitt, and Sniffle grinned. "Oh," Nosemitt said, hearing herself, "no question about it. No question. Forget about 'no bones'; you know what I meant." She moved off to the other room, hoping no one would approach her; but a few minutes later, Sniffle walked casually past and overheard her partner saying that she had known Harriette somewhat in high school and had run into her again when she and her older friend in the navy slacks that had a bit of copper paint on the knee were taking some courses years later at the university. "But really we came here mostly for Vanessa whom we met in entirely different circumstances." Her listener, a pale woman in a black dress and a dark floral hat, smiled blandly and said how nice. Her husband murmured some pleasantry about Vanessa and went looking for a refill of the glass he was holding.

same Sunday, about 5 p.m.
post-mortem post-mortem

Nosemitt had had to cleanse herself of her part in the dismal day by a long soak in the tub before she felt able to discuss her feelings. "There is no way we can do this again," she moaned. "I am not at all up to the level of sham required. I hate it, hate everything about it."

"Then it's agreed for all future cases, if there are any, that we will not be part of any act. We will be ourselves, apart from the obvious name business. I'm for that. This other is exhausting, not to mention potentially dangerous," Sniffle said.

"It is downright humiliating, but you seemed to be enjoying it," Nosemitt insisted. "I was the one getting in all the trouble."

"Not so– you just missed the good parts I got myself into. I didn't tell you how I learned who Dustin is."

"Oh? This sounds promising. I hope it is really awful!"

"Fear not. I expressed my incredulity that Harriette's own son would have lived all these years with a man like Marvin."

"You didn't! How good of you! Thank you. But why did you need to say anything like that? And to whom?"

"I did, and you're welcome. And I said it in response to some nice gentleman who had already whispered contempt for Marvin, but then all of a sudden there was this Dustin fellow right there. So this is my own objection to what we agreed to do for Walter– here we were, trying in desperate little ways to convince people that we knew Harriette and were naturally close to Vanessa so that we could reasonably be invited to stay with her– as if we needed any excuse before the fact– and we felt driven to become people we're not. I'm not denying that I have very definite opinions about people, but I don't generally go around expressing such criticisms, least of all to strangers. You know I think people will be who they are and, what's more, are entitled to be who they are. I hate the role I played. It came to a head with Dustin, leaving me feeling not merely like a fool but a petty, ugly little person. I did learn a few things, but I don't think they were worth it."

"Oh? What things?"

"Dustin must be very heavily in debt. And, no, before you even ask, he did not say, 'Now here's a woman who says what she thinks. I admire her for that. I will tell her I'm in debt.' I overheard him cornering Walter and asking for money, a lot of money– said he would pay him back if his grandmother's will ever got settled but that he needed to repay someone else very quickly."

"I didn't learn a damned thing," Nosemitt said irritably. "At least you got somewhere. Now we know Dustin certainly has a motive."

"Yes, but I don't believe he did it," Sniffle said. "He seemed quite upset, though admittedly more at the timing than the fact of Harriette's death. He told Walter that his mother had promised to help him as soon as her royalty check arrived. However, I definitely got the impression from Walter's intensely angry response that Dustin is involved with drugs. And please don't forget that you invariably find our solutions, not I."

"Perhaps he just wants Walter to think that he's upset," Nosemitt suggested, ignoring Sniffle's last comment. "What did he say that implied drugs? And was Marvin there? And do you think that Harriette wrote books of her letters? Or maybe she did other writing more to her liking."

"I didn't hear all of what Walter said, but I did hear something about not supporting his habits. I had thought that Marvin might have been the slightly graying middle-aged man who avoided Walter entirely. He stayed in the far corner of the living room with that young man who sat next to us at the service. At the house, that younger one kept staring at Vanessa. At first I wondered if he was Dustin, but definitely no. So I think he may be the cousin, Freddy Kettle. I know that Portia Kettle was here. But the older man is the one who made the comment about Marvin, so it doesn't take even my mingling talent to deduce that he isn't Marvin."

"Well, it could be gambling as easily as drugs. But, tell me about

Portia– was she the one in the flowered dress and black hat?" Nosemitt was forgetting that the husband had said his wife been a classmate of Harriette's as well as that it was a black dress and flowered hat.

"No, Portia was the snowy-white-haired lady with the cane. I now know that Portia Lockett was seven years older than her husband, who died five years ago prematurely. 'Prematurely' is her word– I think he was only fifty-nine, so it really was too soon. It just seemed an odd word. I can tell you quite a bit about Harvester; she showed me a picture of him four times, unaware that she had done so before, although she speaks quite intelligibly. I kind of liked her. You know, I think we're all just batty enough that nothing that happened today will be remembered."

"We can hope! I probably will remember that awful minister. *'Was she rigid? Not really.'* 'Rigid? Not really!' What a terrible thing to say at a funeral."

"No bones about it," Sniffle agreed, chuckling.

"So, what next?" Nosemitt asked, ignoring the remark, still tired and not at all sure that they had gotten themselves into anything they should have.

"We wait to be invited to stay with Vanessa, I suppose, and then we get better acquainted with the Kettles and their assorted motives. I don't suppose we can rule out Vanessa entirely yet. Her choice of clothing does her no good, except to make us admire her for her individuality, but that magenta and taupe thing makes me wonder about her state of mind. Is she needing to prove something, or is this her permanent style?"

"Old photos will tell," Nosemitt said. "I am going out for a walk to clear my mind of the ridiculous conversations of this afternoon. If it's too cold out, I will be pacing the halls. This morning, when I asked the housekeeper if there was a good place for walking around here, she said many of the guests like to get some exercise and suggested the eighth or ninth floors as popular spots– fewer rooms and fewer guests to bother. She said the view is nice from the windows. I didn't tell her I hate heights."

"Watch out for Mel," Sniffle said, hunting for her sketchpad and a couple of pencils. Nosemitt left and Sniffle found the pencils but no paper. She opted instead for a nap and was just turning on the television to lull her to sleep when the phone rang. "Room 274," she answered.

"Ms Nigel," a choked voice asked.

"Sergeant Bradley? Are you all right?" The phone went dead. Twenty minutes later, Nosemitt returned to find Sniffle wide-awake and definitely upset, staring at the television screen and drumming steadily on the bedside table where the phone was.

"What's going on?" Nosemitt asked. "I've never known you to be interested in pork belly futures."

"You can turn that thing off; I haven't heard a word of it. Either something is wrong with Sergeant Bradley, although that voice was not anything like his, or someone has learned more about our names and is trying to scare us, or I don't know what."

"Slow down. What are you talking about?" Sniffle told her about the call. "Well," Nosemitt said, "are you sure the person asked for Ms Nigel? Maybe it was a wrong number and the name was similar to Nigel. Maybe it was nothing at all." Sniffle looked very dubious.

"The voice asked for Ms Nigel; that was definite. Look in the phone book, please, and see if other Nigels are listed. That might help." Nosemitt got the phone book but there wasn't a Nigel or a Nivel or a Niggle or anything close that she could think to check. Sniffle looked more upset. "Who could have found out another of our names?"

"Consider how Bradley and Duke found out that Nosemitt and Sniffle were here to investigate. Walter Wrothwell put them onto us and we told them outright who we are. Why would you have to ask? For all we know Bradley went to tell his gallery friend that he knows who Nigel is. There, that could explain it. The gallery owner was just checking it all out. You said you thought it was the sergeant. You answered his question."

"And the caller just hung up? Why?"

"He had nothing to say or to ask. He just wanted to know if you were really Nigel."

"Maybe. If so, remind me never to send paintings here again."

"We don't remember sending any here before. Let's go get some dinner."

When they returned, there was a light flashing on the phone and Nosemitt called the front desk for the message. It had been from Vanessa, presumably to invite them to move over there. Nosemitt returned the call and Sniffle finished the last of the packing. "No! No!" Nosemitt was saying. "That's terrible. No, it would be no problem, but are you sure you want us to come over? We really could stay here. You're sure? Do they know anything yet? Of course not! We'll be there as quickly as possible. All right. Yes, goodbye."

"What was that?" Sniffle asked.

"Walter has been taken to the hospital. Probably an anxiety reaction but they can't rule out heart attack. From what I could make out of Vanessa's jumble of words, he was found slumped over the phone, clutching his chest."

"And Vanessa actually wants us there? Why?"

"I think she may be a little afraid. We may offer some sense of security."

They carried their luggage out to the car and then came back for the paintings. It was difficult for Sniffle to put the longhorn back on the wall but she did. Then she double-checked for items under each bed and scanned for Nosemitt's purse, finding her own sketchpad instead.

"I have it on my arm," Nosemitt said, "but where are my glasses?"

"Aha!" said Sniffle, finding them next to the phone and handing them over. "I believe we're actually ready." Nosemitt drove, while Sniffle scuffled with her own purse, looking for her own glasses. She finally found them under the car seat, right next to the earmuffs.

"Do you think we should telephone Sergeant Bradley about that scary call?" Sniffle asked. Nosemitt shrugged and suggested they wait and see if there was any follow-up. In five minutes they reached the house and were greeted immediately by an unusually animated Vanessa.

"I'm so glad you could come right over," she said to them. "I just had a call from the hospital. Uncle Walter's heart is fine; he was just overwrought. They're keeping him tonight, but now every little sound is making me jump."

"We're glad to be here," Nosemitt assured her, "but who took your uncle to the hospital? I was surprised you would still be here."

"It's hard to believe, but my father did."

"Marvin?" Sniffle said. "How did you come to call him?"

"I didn't. He had come over to see Uncle Walter, which I don't understand, and I was upstairs in my room when my father called to me to get an ambulance and said that he had been waiting while my uncle had been on the phone and then there was a thud. Uncle Walter had collapsed. When the ambulance arrived, I was told to stay here and wait for news– that I would just be in the way if I went along. You know, I'm so tired of being treated like a child; but right now it's just fine. I really didn't want to go with them."

"But he's fine, you say?" Nosemitt asked. Vanessa nodded.

"And you're sure you want us to stay?" Sniffle asked.

"Definitely, but let me show you where to put your things. This house was built for a large family; you have a choice of rooms."

They went upstairs where Nosemitt selected a pleasant dark blue-and-white wallpapered bedroom facing the street. It had white curtains and an antique white quilt and suited her need for simplicity. Sniffle chose a room painted pale gray with soft mauve carpeting. It suited her paintings. It faced the backyard with its winter-bare bushes, its ghostly flowerbeds, and its dead brown grass. The room seemed to need her paintings too. Each room had a simple chest of drawers, a small closet, a chair, and a lamp. Nosemitt's had a phone on top of the chest. She thought it was odd that anyone wanting to use it would have to stand–its cord barely stretched two feet.

Downstairs the doorbell was ringing, and somewhere in the house another phone was ringing. Vanessa did not need all the commotion, Nosemitt thought, and went down to see if she could be of any help.

Detective Duke was waiting in the living room while Vanessa was on the kitchen phone. Nosemitt greeted the policewoman and asked if she would be in the way, offering to leave. Duke insisted that she had been hoping to speak with her and Sniffle too, that she was happy to find them there. Nosemitt filled her in on Walter's condition while they waited for Vanessa to finish on the phone, although they could hear her voice getting louder and more agitated. Finally they heard a slam of the receiver and a mild little shriek of frustration. A minute later Vanessa came composedly into the living room and Sniffle arrived too in order to find out what the shriek was. Now they were all together, hoping for some sort of explanation. Vanessa calmly waited for Duke to ask questions; and as it became quite clear that the phone call would go unexplained, the detective did indeed get out her notebook that had all kinds of unintelligible scribbles covering several pages. Code, Nosemitt thought. She likes to draw, Sniffle assumed approvingly. Oh, god!, moaned Vanessa.

As it turned out, the homicide squad, putting its two equal heads together, had not come up with many questions but were afraid to appear inept. Vanessa was relieved to be dismissed after giving Lesley Duke the guest book from the funeral parlor and indicating which of the many names belonged to family, which to friends, and which to business colleagues or acquaintances of Harriette. There were quite a few that were unknown to Vanessa. Duke did not mark in the book but made several more cryptic notes in her notebook, which Sniffle recognized as meaningless and Nosemitt thought absurd. Vanessa did not care and left as soon as Duke thanked her for the information.

"Now, to why I really came," the detective said to the vpi's. "We are hoping you learned something at the memorial service or afterward. We were at the chapel– out of uniform– don't know if you saw us– but could not find out much; but you had a chance to talk with people at the house. Get anything?"

It seemed more than a little strange to Nosemitt and Sniffle that police in a small town could be anonymous in any situation and, even more, that the two visitors should be expected to find out more at what was basically a sad social function. Still, Sniffle did mention the possible reference to a drug involvement for Dustin. She hurried to add the fact that she believed Harriette's son was distressed by his mother's death but did not mention that it seemed to be the timing that bothered him more than anything. She had not been able to think about that too much; it disturbed her just below the surface and she was not willing to let her imagination run on it.

"Did you happen to find out anything about Marvin Kettle?"

"We don't even know what he looks like or if he was present," Nosemitt said. "His wife was there, so he probably was. We thought for a while that we had picked him out, but we were wrong."

"Blonde hair, balding slightly. Tall, somewhat on the heavy side but not really fat," Duke said, mentioning as many details as she thought would be helpful.

"I did learn that he was not the gray-haired man of medium height and average build. I was definitely wrong on that guess," Sniffle said.

"Sounds like you are describing Roger Lescouth," Duke said.

"Really?" Sniffle asked. "And I was talking with him and never knew."

"Lescouth? Lescouth? What a perfect name!" Nosemitt said. "Surely she could have married him with that name," and she could not suppress a delighted smile. "Oh, she really should have married him."

"Then you do know something about him?" Duke said.

"Not much– just that he wanted to marry Harriette and that she refused for reasons we do not know. That she used his name, which we did not know until now, as an excuse, hardly polite for an etiquette specialist and seemingly very out of character. Do we know anything else, Sniffle?"

"That Walter seems strongly opposed to him and may even have been a factor in keeping them apart. We obviously did not know what he looked like."

"I can fill in a little more," Duke said, whipping out the notebook and adding *WW-link to RL?* "Let me see what I have on him." She flipped through several pages, saying names out loud as she went and Nosemitt was impressed that the notes appeared to be in alphabetical order. "Kettle, D; Kettle, F; Kettle, H; Kettle, H again; Kettle, M; Kettle, V; Kettle, W; ah, here we are– Lescouth, R G."

"What does the G stand for?" Sniffle asked.

"I don't have that," Duke said, "but I do have some things. He's a publisher, which may be how Harriette met him in the first place. She was interested in doing some serious research and got in touch with him. We don't know if that was the first contact or not. He likes boating. He was married before– first wife died ten years ago– has children, including a son who lives here, but we haven't gotten around to any of them. We haven't had time to get much more; we've been concentrating on the Kettle family first."

"Even though Roger was possibly the last person to see Harriette alive?"

"He was?" Duke asked Sniffle, getting her pen out again. "Where did you learn that?"

"Vanessa and Walter said they had dinner together that night, just before she was found."

"They never mentioned that to us," Duke said irritably. "I clearly remember we asked whom the deceased might have been with that evening, and they said they did not know."

"Perhaps at the time they did not," Nosemitt suggested, not willing to implicate anyone she liked.

"Perhaps you should not have used the word 'deceased'," Sniffle muttered.

"I think we are overdue in checking out Mr. Lescouth," Duke said, still nettled, as she got up to leave. "One or the other of us will be checking in with you regularly, and it will probably be me. You have been a help already. Let me know if you learn much about Herbert Molecott."

"Who is Herbert Molecott?" Nosemitt asked, feeling that the whole world was becoming involved and that she and Sniffle were in well over their heads.

Duke seemed pleased but merely said as she left, "May have been plotting to get rid of her. Talk to you soon. And, I almost forgot, would you tell Vanessa that the lab reports are due back tomorrow?"

"'Molecott' has quite a villainous sound to it, don't you think?"
Sniffle said. "Perhaps my vote goes to him, whoever or whatever he
is."

"It doesn't ever work that way!" Nosemitt said vehemently. "You
have to learn the rules of the game."

"I see no reason to," Sniffle said. "I'm too old to start now with
rules. We could save Walter a lot of money and ourselves even more
embarrassment by clearing this up right now."

"I think not," Nosemitt said calmly. "We don't have the solution
yet."

"Clearly we want Vanessa exonerated out of our affection for her
style; we excuse Roger on purely romantic grounds. Walter, though
frequently strong and brisk, is not in fact capable of the exertion.
Besides, he is paying us. You have proclaimed Marvin and Dustin
bastards and thus given them the inclination if not the motive; and I
now offer Herbert Molecott as Dustin's long-abandoned fraternal twin,
eager for revenge and angry that he was changed at birth from a Kettle
to a Molecott while Vanessa got to live with Mommy and Dustin was
Daddy's favorite and Grandma didn't give two cents for him either, let
alone a quarter of a million dollars."

"Stick to painting."

"No, I think I am onto something. The name 'Molecott' suggests a
definite relationship to the Portcullis fur. Yes, he was adopted into the
grandmother's family. It's tidier than I like, but it's quick."

"Is she gone?" Vanessa asked, peering down from the middle of
the staircase. "Is the detective gone?"

"Yes," Nosemitt said, motioning the young woman down to join
them, "and so, for all practical purposes, is Sniffle. Tell us, who is
Herbert Molecott."

"Mother's editor at the paper."

"Aha! I am not surprised," Nosemitt said.

"That's his public persona," Sniffle insisted. "How old is Herbert
anyway?"

"About my father's age, I would guess," Vanessa said. Nosemitt
looked triumphant.

"So I had the wrong generation as twin brother. His real name is
Horatio Herbert Kettle and he was not ever recognized by anyone, not
even Harriette, his sister-in-law/employee, an irony that established an
ongoing love-hate relationship. Quite sad." Vanessa looked more than
puzzled; but Nosemitt assured her that Sniffle was simply in one of

those moods, was impossible really, best left ignored. Vanessa nodded.

"The only difficulty," Nosemitt said, "is that every once in a while she turns absolutely psychic in these moods and invents the most impossible scenario that turns out to be true. I think we're safe this time, but you cannot always separate the chaff from the chaff from the chaff from the wheat from the chaff." Sniffle declared that she had a higher percentage going for her than that. "Are you feeling at all up to giving us some help right now?" Nosemitt asked Vanessa. "We have a bunch of fragments and nothing solid. We've looked at the informal chart your uncle gave us." She fetched it and put it on the coffee table.

"I'd like to see it too," Vanessa said. "I don't know a lot about my father's family."

"There isn't a whole lot there," Sniffle said.

They set the chart on the coffee table and managed to arrange themselves so that they all could see it fairly easily, although Nosemitt thought that tea would help calm them and Vanessa went searching for cookies.

Sniffle looked at the chart and turned it over. Oddly, all the dates were on the back, making it inconvenient to keep turning the paper over to check anything. She jotted down a few dates on a separate piece of paper for easier reference. Nosemitt and Vanessa returned with tea and snacks, and they studied the meagre information.

Vanessa looked at the names for a few minutes, pointing out that Uncles Fenton and Rodney were not on it but finding little that she did not know, except for the death of a cousin, Albina M. She had never heard of her. "She must have died very, very young because I would have known her otherwise. Fred is Dustin's age, and this sister apparently was younger. Of course I know Fred, but I wonder why my mother never mentioned that there was a girl too."

"I think she was two," Sniffle said, reporting from her random notes, mentioning the probable year of her death.

"When did you learn that and how?" Nosemitt asked.

"Someone after the service was whispering about the tragedies in the family and someone else recalled a mysterious death of a two-year-old back some twenty-plus years ago. I didn't know the child's name and am just assuming now that the little cousin must have been the one. I wrote it down and ignored it until now."

Nosemitt turned back to Vanessa. "Perhaps if the girl was your age, your mother thought you would be frightened. Or maybe it was difficult for her even to talk about," Nosemitt suggested.

"Well, I've heard of the rest but don't remember Aunt Albina or Aunt Marie very clearly. I think they may have spent one or two Christmases here years ago. I don't remember ever meeting their husbands at all, but I think that the two brothers were mid-level diplomats for most of their careers. I think one of them might have become an ambassador before he retired. But if this little cousin died when she was two and the year is correct, I would not have been born yet."

"Do you have old photos?" Nosemitt asked. "Not so much for the aunts and uncles, but we still don't know what your father looks like. Sniffle saw your brother and your father's wife, but I think it would help if we could visualize some of these people." Vanessa left to find photos and came back with two shoeboxes and three albums. The three women huddled together on the couch so that all could see the pictures. Vanessa picked out two early photos of Dustin, one as a cheerful but mischievous-looking toddler and another with his arm around cousin Freddy. Marvin was kneeling down next to both of them, smiling as if the three had just shared a little prank. In fact, Dustin was making a discreet obscene gesture at the tender age of three, and Nosemitt was placidly sure that Marvin had taught it to him for the purpose of the photo. Sniffle noticed that Marvin had his hand behind his back and was willing to assume that he was making the same gesture.

"Here's one of Grandmother, taken a year and a half ago," Vanessa said, pulling out a formal portrait from one box. "Can't you just tell she was regal?" That was not quite the word that had come to the minds of the investigators– disdainful, perhaps; snobbish, yes; always proper by her own definitions. "Here's one of me with Mother," Vanessa said, skipping past a whole clump of snapshots.

Dressed that way even then, Sniffle thought, looking at a ten-year old Vanessa in a floor-length blue denim skirt and a black taffeta bolero jacket over a green striped blouse. She wore a Robin Hood cap with a red feather. Harriette had on jeans and a plaid shirt. "Were you going somewhere special?" Sniffle asked.

"Just grocery shopping with Mother," Vanessa answered. "I think that she always thought she could encourage me to dress more normally if I saw myself objectively in photos. She kept the camera handy and would pounce on anyone to take our picture if my outfit particularly distressed her. She never caught on that I needed to be different from her. The more photos, the better. I have mementoes of some great outfits in these boxes and albums."

"Maybe she enjoyed them and wanted a scrapbook of your choices," Sniffle said, knowing that that is how she herself felt.

"Did your grandmother show more approval?" Nosemitt asked, feeling sure of the answer. Vanessa just laughed.

"Roger is the only one who ever showed he appreciated the way I dressed," she said wistfully. Nosemitt and Sniffle looked at each other, wondering the same dark wonder. Was Vanessa jealous of her mother's relationship with Roger? Did Roger return the interest? He had been the last one known to see Harriette. They had not anticipated this possibility and were not willing to pursue it just then, and yet it bothered them both.

The phone rang and Vanessa took the call in the kitchen. While she was out there, Nosemitt and Sniffle looked at each other and worried in whispers about how to proceed. What would happen if they confronted this innocent-looking and somewhat fragile-appearing young woman with having a strong motive for conspiring with her mother's friend– lover? – to kill Harriette? "Unthinkable!" Sniffle insisted, not wanting to picture it.

"But not altogether impossible," Nosemitt said against her own will. "We need to do some active research tomorrow. I wish I knew what." Sadly she wrote a memo in her notebook to look into this unexpected connection.

"We need to find a reason to talk with Roger Lescouth," Sniffle said. "He is a publisher. I think that's the way we approach him. I will say his name came up, which it did, and that I am interested in learning what kinds of work he publishes, as I am. I'll mention some of my manuscripts."

"That might be the way," Nosemitt agreed. Out in the kitchen Vanessa's voice was rising. Nosemitt was closer to the doorway and could make out some of the words and all of the shrill, angry tone.

"What?" Sniffle asked. "What is she saying?"

"Something about 'I'm not covering for you' and 'just take care of yourself' in an angry voice."

"It doesn't go with that soft adoring voice she had when she mentioned Roger, does it?" Sniffle asked.

"Not much goes together yet. We have a tangle of suggestions and nothing clear at all. Talking to Roger about publishing sounds more and more like a reasonable next step."

"Yes, but it would help to know whom she's speaking with now. As investigators, surely it is not unreasonable to ask?"

"No need," Nosemitt smiled, her ear still leaning toward the kitchen. "She just said, 'Don't call me again, Herb,' and hung up. I'm glad we don't have to ask."

"You see, she too thinks it is Herbert Molecott."

"Who knows what she thinks?"

Monday, January 15

While Nosemitt fixed coffee and toast, Sniffle looked up publishers in the phone book. There were three: AAAOK Publishing Company, a name that struck Sniffle as more than a little redundant and certainly unnecessary in a small community– so it probably was not a local outfit; Gladiolus Press; and Self-Made Success (You Write It, We'll Do The Rest- We Do Our Best For Your Success). "I certainly hope that Gladiolus is the one," Sniffle said. "These other two sound more than a little shaky."

"I have never liked gladiolas," Nosemitt said ruefully; "funeral flowers. I was so predisposed to like this man for Harriette's sake that now I'm angry with him without any solid evidence, except that Vanessa clearly loves him too. What an ironic reason for suspecting someone, when you think about it."

"There is another problem," Sniffle said, closing the phone book but leaving a napkin as page marker. "I found a man's bathrobe in my closet."

"And you're just first telling me?"

"I found it this morning. I didn't put anything into the closet until this morning. Anyway, it's long. It would be way too long for the gray-haired Roger of medium height."

"Well? What are you suggesting now?"

"We still don't know what Herbert looks like; maybe he is tall and likes bathrobes. I don't give up my theories easily. Also, there is an ashtray in my room, which still has faint traces of cigar stench. I had to put it outside on the windowsill. We need to know who smokes."

"Walter was staying here, but I've never seen him smoke and he is not tall," Nosemitt said.

"I doubt that I would have been put in Walter's room, especially since he's coming back today. Besides, there were no other clothes. I wonder if Uncle will be up to any conversation this evening."

They ate quickly, wrote a note to Vanessa saying not to expect them before five, and left to find Gladiolus Press on Berkeley Street. It was closed. "Library?" Nosemitt suggested. It was closed too, making them feel a bit conspired against until they saw the generic sign, CLOSED FOR NATIONAL HOLIDAY. "Oh," Nosemitt said; "I forgot that it was the fifteenth. Well, where can we go to learn anything?"

"The police station?" Sniffle suggested. "The lab report should be back."

Nosemitt drove more slowly than usual, distracted by the number of children out of school and in the streets. According to their town map, the easiest way to the police station was through the Axel Louis Rodbender Memorial Playground, past the pond, then out at the second gate. City Hall had been built right there by the gates in 1919, before there had been a playground, and had been rejuvenated by funds from the same family. In a stirring ceremony just last fall, the plain old city hall had become the Axel and Rosamund Rodbender Municipal Complex. Plans were on the drawing table for a community sports facility and small theatre. A citizens' group was clamoring for a new bingo parlor, but so far the town fathers and lone town mother had successfully fended the group off by diverting their attention to the shortage of good solid family radio and television programming and offering to make the group en toto the advisory committee on cultural uses of local media. None of this was known to Nosemitt or Sniffle.

Nosemitt pulled into a parking space at the station, backed out and pulled in again, and checked her purse for notepad and working pen. "Do you have some questions in mind?" she asked. Sniffle thought for a while but was undecided. "What about this?" Nosemitt suggested. "I think we need to take the questions about Roger slowly and carefully. I think we should just start with the lab findings and see where we go from there. But I will want to ask about Herbert. I wonder how he wants Vanessa to cover for him."

"In fur," Sniffle said. "Portcullis mole. The much more difficult question is Why."

Sergeant Bradley greeted them with a big smile and offered to get coffee or soda as he ushered them out of the line of sight from the chief's office. Nosemitt accepted black coffee; Sniffle requested decaf with extra sweetener. Lesley Duke joined them and left again to get some new file folders. They all went into the homicide squad's small cubbyhole with its two scarred wooden desks, its four uncomfortable vinyl chairs, and its lonely file cabinet. "So, what do you have for us?" Bradley asked. Duke opened the file cabinet and got out one thick folder from the K section, hoping to be able to add to it after this visit.

"We don't have much," Nosemitt began; "but we realized that we have never been told the actual cause of death, although poisoning was presumed."

"Presumed incorrectly," Bradley said. "The black crumbs all over Harriette's coat and upper body were definitely full of Rodex, no doubt about that; but there was no evidence that she had ingested even a speck of poison. She died of suffocation." He pulled the autopsy report from the folder and skimmed it before handing it to Nosemitt to see. "Definitely suffocation." He smiled at Sniffle. "Been doing any painting?"

"Hardly," she said, disappointed that this young man who had astonished her so pleasantly by knowing of her work would now sound so patronizing. She let Nosemitt do the talking.

"We have been wondering about the Herbert Molecott connection," Nosemitt said. Bradley looked surprised that they had been wondering anything relevant, and even Duke noticed his changed attitude since their visit at the hotel. She moved her chair slightly away from his and toward the women's chairs. They noticed and were both amused and appreciative. "We have some very slight and very dubious evidence to intimate that he just might have both a motive and a desire for help from a very unlikely source in 'covering' himself," Nosemitt continued.

"What kind of evidence? And what do you mean by 'covering' himself'?" Duke asked before Bradley made any put-down type of remark.

Nosemitt mentioned the fragment of phone conversation they had heard. "It was the mention of not covering for him that is the slight, dubious evidence. We really do not know the context at all."

"And the motive?" Bradley asked.

"Well, we've been through a number of conjectures," Nosemitt said, reddening, "but my strongest suspicion is that it may have to do with behind-the-scenes wrangles at the newspaper. Sniffle wonders if there might be more personal motives."

"I see," Bradley said.

"What?" Sniffle asked, rapidly coming to lose all of her initial regard for him. "What is it you see?" She managed not to sound hostile.

"We do have some information on Molecott," Duke hurried to say. She was getting to like these two women, whether they helped the investigation or not, and resented on their behalf Bradley's arrogance. She suspected he was trying to impress Bigguns and was not about to let any outsiders help. This might be the opportunity for promotion he had been wanting but only if he solved the case. Duke wondered if he had kept any information from her. In fact, Bradley was reacting to the chief's anger when he had learned from the sergeant that Wrothwell had hired outside investigators– women, no less; amateurs both and one an artist. The insult was pure Walter. Bigguns and Wrothwell had been at odds for years, ever since Walter had served a term on the police board and had been the sole vote to fire the chief. Bigguns certainly did not wish to have outsiders show up his department, more especially if they had any connection to that old thorn in his side. Now Bradley found himself needing to please his boss; that was the only information he had withheld from his partner. He didn't really mean to sound any particular way, but he could tell from the women's responses that he had offended. He wasn't sure what they were reacting to, though, and so made no effort to change his style again.

"We don't have anything our friends here would find useful," he said. All three grated at 'our friends.'

"Sure we do," Duke said, scowling emphatically at him and flipping through the pages of her notebook. "Herbert Molecott is the feature editor at the newspaper. He and Harriette were having a battle over a major policy decision, and Harriette seemed likely to get her way."

"Enough to kill for?" Nosemitt asked.

"Not the surface battle," Duke said, "but we do know there was probably much more to it. There is evidence of a scam of some sort that Harriette wanted to expose and Molecott wanted suppressed. We found memos in Harriette's files that only lead us in that direction but nothing is named, no person is named, no specifics are to be found. We don't even know the sources. We turned this information over to our chief, and he has others working to track it all down. But you are right that it may be both professional and personal, and he is not someone to dismiss."

"I think we can rule him out," Bradley said. I would think that 'covering' simply meant he wanted Vanessa to do some of his work."

"So Harriette did do work besides the etiquette column?" Sniffle said, ignoring Bradley. "And why would the feature editor care?"

"They both were advisors to the editor-in-chief on major stories," Duke explained.

"But you two can worry those pretty heads about other matters," Bradley interjected.

"Young man," Nosemitt said, "our heads are neither pretty nor turned. They also are not stupid. You may not take us seriously, but at least have the decency not to let us know it. Subtlety is a lovely gift, improved upon by silence."

"Just ordinary respect will do" Sniffle suggested.

"Hear, hear," Duke said softly, and Bradley looked amazed. He threw up his hands in mock submission and reminded them of how much he respected Ms Nigel's paintings.

"I'm not here as a painter," Sniffle said; "and if we are not typical investigators, may I remind you that you are not exactly the typical homicide detectives yourselves. I noticed that your files are practically empty, except for the K and the B sections. Have you had only one other case? Even the B's are slim."

Bradley was unwilling to admit that they had had no other case and did not want Duke saying so. He pushed the file drawer closed with his foot and said that they did not have all the files in this room, only present and unsolved ones.

"Come off it," Duke said. "This is the first murder in St. Edwards in years, except for all the birds, which accounts for the B files having anything in them at all."

"Odd that you should mention that," Sniffle said. "A pigeon fluttered past me outside the chapel and fell dead. I wonder if Rodex is involved." Bradley stared at her; Duke stared at her. Nosemitt looked pleased.

"Perhaps a little meal of crow may be in order," Duke suggested to Bradley. "We never made any connection."

"Whether Rodex is involved or not, I think I have just learned something," Bradley said. Duke did not know if he intended an apology toward the other two but chose to take it that way. In reality, Bradley just meant that he was going to have to keep some of his sources to himself; otherwise, the chief would be furious.

3:30 p.m., same Monday

With Roger unavailable at the Gladiolus office– assuming he did not own an anonymous or unlisted publishing company– and the library closed and their desire thwarted to get acquainted with the Bureau of Vital Statistics for the fun of it, the two women arrived back at Vanessa's quite a bit earlier than they had intended. They were startled and embarrassed to hear giggling in the kitchen as they came into the front hall. "We're back," Nosemitt called out loudly. Vanessa came out to greet them, followed by the tall handsome young man who had sat next to them at the service. He definitely could wear that robe, Sniffle thought.

"We're having company for dinner," Vanessa said gaily as the young man wrapped his arms around her waist. "Nosemitt, Sniffle, I'd like you to meet Roger Lescouth."

"What?" Nosemitt said, confused.

"Who?" Sniffle asked.

"Junior," he said, coming forward to shake hands. "We have met but not by name."

"Very, very happy to meet you," Nosemitt said, thrilled to learn that Vanessa's Roger was not Harriette's Roger and even more thrilled that they had said nothing to Bradley about this suspicion. Later she would happily cross off a few items in her notebook.

"Does Uncle Walter know about you?" Sniffle asked; "and how is he? Where is he?"

"No, Uncle Walter does not know that I am more than my father's son. He'd be quite unhappy to know I have been his nephew for the past three difficult weeks."

"Uncle Walter went to rest at Aunt Emmaline's, thank goodness," Vanessa said; and though they heard her, they were still taking in the news that Vanessa and Roger were married.

"You didn't object to the name Lescouth?" Sniffle teased.

"Are you kidding? I love it!" Vanessa said.

"When I first saw Vanessa, dressed in gray fake fur shorts and an orange silk blouse with a cape, I knew I had met my true love," he said, beaming at his wife. "I knew my name would not matter one bit, even though her mother made such a point of it. It was the only thing about Harriette my father ever spoke bitterly about."

"I'm delighted to hear all this," Nosemitt said. "Another theory bites the dust, where it should have been kept in the first place."

"Now, now," Sniffle said, "it isn't over yet. You are the one who always insists on a surprise element."

"No, no, I refuse to let this little romantic interlude be spoiled."

"Do you smoke cigars?" Sniffle asked; "not that it really matters, but it would solve one small mystery and that might do wonders for us."

"Only rarely," he said, grinning. "Like when I make a huge commission on the cars I sell."

"You are a car salesman?" Nosemitt asked, more openly dejected than she felt was acceptable.

"For the time being."

"It doesn't make him dishonest," Vanessa said. "I don't expect stereotypes from you two of all people."

"A little crow for us too," Nosemitt said.

"I see there are five place settings at the table," Sniffle said. "You say Uncle Walter is at his sister's; who is the fifth?"

"My father," Roger said. "Tonight he learns that Vanessa, at least, accepted the name."

"Will that bother him?" Nosemitt asked; "or will he be glad?"

"I don't know, but now we can tell him and have to do so. It isn't right that others know and not Dad. You're almost the first people we've told, and that's only because I just couldn't resist."

"Dinner will be ready at five-thirty," Vanessa said, "unless Roger keeps interfering."

"Why don't we leave you two alone?" Nosemitt suggested. "We could use a long walk."

"I guess we could," Sniffle reluctantly agreed. "Or I could take a nap."

"Walk," Nosemitt repeated. "A long walk, and tomorrow we'll go pay our respects to Uncle Walter for as long as these two would like."

"'Subtlety is a good thing,' I thought I heard you say, or was that my imagination?"

As they were about to leave for their walk, Sniffle turned back and said, "Why did you want us to come here? You certainly don't need us around."

"I thought Roger was leaving on a business trip," Vanessa said, blushing. "And he is, after dinner. Feel free to visit Uncle Walter tomorrow but not on our account and do please stay here for as long as you'd like."

"I didn't know car salesmen had to travel, but what do I know?" Nosemitt said.

"I don't sell to individuals; I sell company cars to corporations," he said. "I spend too much time traveling, and I'll be looking to change that now."

The two aging investigators talked in little puffs of steam as they walked briskly along the narrow sidewalk. Nosemitt's stride was longer than Sniffle's and she kept getting slightly ahead. "Slow … huhhuh… down …huhhuh… please," Sniffle begged after five times around the same block. They were now three doors past Vanessa's yet again.

"This is a good healthy pace," Nosemitt called back, but then she stopped and waited.

"Thank you. What were you … saying about … Roger?"

"Just a minute. Is someone waving to us from that window there?" she asked, pointing. Sniffle looked, but at the wrong window, and saw no one. She didn't care, glad as she was to stop. A minute later, the front door of the house opened and out came a wiry little woman with thinning brown hair, pink harlequin glasses, and a rumpled tweed coat.

"Yoo-hoo, yoo-hoo, wait a minute," she called to them from her front porch in a voice more piercing than they could possibly have expected. She was still waving strenuously. When she reached them on the sidewalk, she pumped Nosemitt's hand. "I don't remember your name but we met after the service. I was so interested to know of your devotion to the culinary arts while you and Harriette were at the university. I pride myself on my cooking, and you did show some interest in getting some of my recipes." Sniffle glared darkly at Nosemitt, who looked blank.

"I don't recall your name either," Nosemitt said. "It's …?"

"Olga, Olga Berlin. How is darling Vanessa? Is she eating?"

"She seems to be holding up quite well, considering," Nosemitt said.

"And is being sustained by friends as well," Sniffle said pointedly. It was Nosemitt's turn to glower.

"Oh, is that nice young man there? She has him to lean on, doesn't she?" and she winked almost lewdly. "I keep seeing all those new cars and I ask myself, Olga, why would a nice young man have to have so many new cars? Not that I think there's anything wrong with having them, but why? I just have to keep asking myself, Why? Is Vanessa getting enough food, do you think? I was planning to bring a little something in the casserole line over in a while. Cooking is a delight to me, but then it was ever so. My sister and I would create recipes by the hour, by the livelong day."

"By the gross," Sniffle suggested. Nosemitt was not happy with her.

"That too," Olga said. "Our record was over a hundred ideas one day. It was rainy."

"Well, we have to be going," Nosemitt said, "but I do happen to know that dinner for tonight is well in hand."

"Perhaps you could save your casserole for next month, when things have calmed down here and people are not all rushing to help. I'm sure she would welcome being remembered then," Sniffle said.

"Indeed, indeed, but a little casserole in the freezer is worth half a dozen down the block, as my sister and I are fond of saying in instances such as these."

"Really, the freezer will be filled to overflowing any minute," Sniffle said, making motions to start walking again.

"And how is that handsome beau of poor late Harriette?"

"You know him?" Nosemitt asked.

"Oh, not well. Well, not. Oh, I have seen him often enough." Sniffle began humming *How Much Is That Spyglass In the Window?* but fortunately no one knew her private wording. Olga was twisting her gloved fingers nervously. "It gets a little lonely here, what with everyone and all. But then, we always have our little friends in the kitchen to keep us happy. Our pots and our pans and our jelly jars. My husband says no one can whip up a better batch of rutabaga-carrot chutney than his little Olga." Sniffle nearly gagged.

A light suddenly dawned in Nosemitt's mind as a familiar voice from home came in strong and clear; and finally she knew who it was who lived in St. Edwards, the person she had heard of but had not known— and damn it all, this was that person. Her sister Helga had been the cooking teacher in a pasta class Nosemitt had taken. It was Helga who had referred frequently to her sister in St. Edwards, her partner in many a recipe that was inedible even by Nosemitt's generous standards. Pastapus had been the supreme blow to her digestion. She joined Sniffle now in wanting no part of any casserole made by either sister.

"Cucuracha Olé is such a simple dish, warm, nourishing, and festive without being inappropriate at times like the present. And the beauty of it is that it is so adaptable; I have even made it in dessert form. Your main dish requires a great deal of ricotta cheese, a handful of black olives— such a good source of protein and partly the ingredient that suggested the name— pimiento and celery and dyed mushrooms and a swirl of noodles with a generous portion of cinnamon and dill. Do they know what killed poor Harriette?"

"Food," Sniffle said grimly.

"They had suspected poisoning at one point, but that is probably not the case," Nosemitt said, pushing Sniffle on toward a walk. Sniffle was glad of the opportunity, said a hasty goodbye, and trotted on.

Nosemitt was unable to catch up because Olga was intent on describing several other delightful recipes to her and had a firm grip on her sleeve. At the corner, Sniffle looked back and knew without a doubt that her best friend was thinking strongly of the photo of Dustin and Marvin making their separate gestures and transmitting one of them psychically to Sniffle. She considered it wisest not to be offended and walked a little way on extremely slowly, sending back only the kindest of thoughts and the sincerest of wishes for a speedy getaway. She pictured Olga volunteering for Meals on Wheels and was glad they lived almost four hundred miles apart. She was as yet unaware that the potential for Olga to visit Sunford was great, but Nosemitt had no intention of keeping her in the dark.

After slowly and coldly moving three new blocks on, Sniffle began the return trip. She met up with a steaming Nosemitt at the second corner and did not risk a word. She would pay one way or another before very long; she half hoped it would be at dinner. Public revenge could be milder, limited perhaps to a few embarrassing anecdotes. She did not know what she might expect otherwise, but there was fire in Nosemitt's eyes and no immediate forgiveness in her heart. They returned to the house in silence and in silence went to change before dinner. Vanessa was finishing preparation of a salad, and Roger was looking for wine glasses. Roger Senior was due any minute, and Uncle Walter had called twice to make sure that his niece was all right without him. He was relieved to know that his Fondue friends were there.

It was not so quiet at dinner as Sniffle had feared, although she had almost dreaded the initial meeting with Roger Senior. He arrived on time, pale and quiet, dressed in charcoal slacks and a medium-gray sweater that matched his hair over a blue shirt that matched his eyes. Lines of strain around those eyes suggested a great deal of crying, but he was calm now. His voice hoarse and his strength on ebb, he still conveyed social ease and pleasure in being with people. He smiled gently as he was introduced to Nosemitt and Sniffle and immediately offered to help Vanessa in the kitchen. His son followed him out to the kitchen where the news must have been shared. All the vpi's could detect was a brief silence, a pleased yes, really! from young Roger, a demure thank you from Vanessa, and then the sound of a cork. It must have been acceptable news, for the trio came out with the bottle of wine and two extra glasses to share in the happiness. And Roger Senior did indeed seem happy. His eyes now were gleaming softly; and the lines of strain disappeared into other lines more crinkling, more like the lines of joy. "One way or another," he said, holding his glass up to his son and daughter-in-law, "we have Vanessa in our family." Nosemitt was close to tears and Sniffle was over the edge. They just knew he could not have murdered Harriette; neither of them would allow it.

No one alluded to the fact that Vanessa might have become young Roger's sister, even though not by blood. They all helped carry food from the kitchen to the dining room. Roger Senior clearly felt at home there, knowing as well as Vanessa where everything was. He went to the pantry for a platter for the roast and rooted in the back of a cabinet for a tray for the little glasses of tomato juice. He knew exactly how long to wait for the water to turn hot in the tap before rinsing one spoon that had fallen to the floor. "Company coming," he said pleasantly. "My mother used to say, 'Fallen fork fetches fellow.' I think she had some other saying about a spoon bringing a woman guest, but I don't remember the words."

"In our family it was just, 'Next person to ring the doorbell will be a woman," Sniffle said. "I don't remember that it was true more than half the time."

"I hope no guests at all until after dinner," Vanessa said, looking at how the roast had shrunk.

"Always room for one more," Roger Junior said, his arms again around his wife.

"It should always be more, never be less," the father said, and yet it was not said for sympathy; he managed to make it sound warm. Nosemitt kept wondering how they would ever be able to ask this gentle wounded man any difficult question at all.

At dinner the conversation flowed quietly. In his low, hoarse voice Roger described for Sniffle the kind of publishing he did; and though her work would never fit any of his categories, she knew she would like the subjects he chose. "High quality," the son assured them. "Always the best materials and the best quality photography and the clearest typefaces for the project. Dad's books do not fall apart."

"I love the mountains and the oceans," the father said, "but I wanted to show that the Midwest has its own grandeur too– prairies and rolling hills and forests and rivers, deep lakes and tiny ravines, wildlife. And then I do look for work relating to native cultures of the Midwest and try to bring out a pictorial book on one of the tribes every few years. Harriette was working to get a grant so that she could research the role of women in four different tribes. She was going to leave the newspaper; we planned to produce the book together. Everything was starting to come together." He stopped and looked away, and no one said a word.

They were almost through with dinner when the doorbell loudly rang. "Company, as I predicted," Roger Senior said, grateful for the interruption. "We'll see if Mother was right. She never lied."

The son insisted on answering the door, assuring them all that he was as capable of dealing with door-to-door salespeople as he was of selling. "Vanessa will buy to get rid of them; I promise to come back empty-handed. Be right back."

"Please sit down, Rog," Vanessa said. "I will demonstrate my strength of character that you have maligned. I am quite capable of answering a door without buying anything." Rog sat down.

"Make sure you ask who it is first," he said. Vanessa snorted.

All smiled as they heard Vanessa ask who was there; they smiled as they heard the door open and smiled a third time as they heard, "Thank you. Yes, thank you, it is very kind of you." Then all but Sniffle smiled as Vanessa said, "Really, it is too kind. No, we are already eating. In fact, we're in the middle of– ," Then only the older Roger looked pleasant as Vanessa said, "Yes, perhaps it is a tad warm for winter, but a chilled casserole will be lovelier in the summer. Oh, it's dessert? How original. Your sister's conception but you adapted it? Cucuracha Olé? I see. Well, thank you for– no, I haven't spoken with any of the other neighbors. We are eat– Oh? No, I never see them."

"You see?" Rog said. "She may not want a knight in shining armor, but I'm riding into that fray anyway."

"It's such a pleasure to have a romantic in the house," Sniffle said. Roger smiled at her and said that not every woman liked that these days. He had thought she would be more of a feminist. "I don't know that I could be married to a knight," she said; "I just enjoy seeing one as an occasional antidote. It's nice to see people want to help each other out."

"Indeed it would be nice to see that more," Nosemitt said quite pleasantly, although there was an edge detectable to her partner. Roger failed to understand Sniffle's embarrassment. All three listened to Rog in the drafty hall.

"Hello there," he greeted the guest warmly; "nice to meet you, and I am so sorry to cut you short but we have an emergency. Vanessa, I have no idea where you keep the mop. How do you do– yes, pleased to meet you too. Yes, I hate to usher you out so abruptly; but we could have quite a flood. Good night." And then they actually heard the door close.

"And I thought you said he was honest," Nosemitt teased when the two came back into the room with the icy casserole.

"He did not lie," Vanessa said. "Had I stood there another minute, there really would have been a flood. Excuse me."

"You were very wrong, Roger," the father said.

"What do you mean, Dad? I didn't mean to do anything wrong."

"But you promised us you would come back empty-handed and look at yourself, standing there with a dessert casserole called Cucaracha Olé." Rog took the dessert out to the kitchen, Vanessa returned, and Nosemitt described the contents of the main dish format and mentioned a few of Olga's other recipes.

"I fear there may someday be a book in them," Sniffle said.

"I'm awfully curious now about this dessert," Roger said. "Son, spoon some of that stuff up for all of us."

"None for me, thank you," Sniffle said emphatically. "I predict Mexican jumping beans in yogurt with a little cinnamon and dill."

"She is haunted by food," Nosemitt said casually; "I think it stems from a traumatic experience in her youth." Here it comes, Sniffle thought; revenge. But Nosemitt said no more, figuring correctly that it would be more deadly to keep the suspense active.

"Are you going to tell the ice cream story?" Sniffle whispered sharply. The words had just slipped out; she had not meant to suggest anything.

"I? Tell the ice cream story? I wouldn't think of it." To both women's surprise and to the relief of one, no one thought it appropriate to inquire further. Vanessa went to the kitchen to get four parfait glasses for the dessert and returned with two filled glasses. Rog followed with the other two. One glance at the contents and Sniffle was almost under the table. The others took cautious little spoonfuls.

"Sour cream," Vanessa said, face puckering.

"Chocolate malt balls," Roger junior said, scraping the sour cream away from the lumpy brown globules. "Raisins too."

"Cinnamon redhots. You were partly right, Sniffle," Roger senior said, offering her a second chance at a taste by shoving his glass toward her.

"Not one infinitesimal bit of it, thank you!"

"Red and green maraschino cherries, my favorites!" Nosemitt said, pushing her glass away too. "And overchilled. The edge of the sour cream is scarred for life."

"That won't be long now," Vanessa assured them, taking the bowl of Olé directly to the garbage can.

After dinner, Vanessa refused help in the cleanup from all but her husband. She sent the others off to the living room, suggesting a fire. Both Nosemitt and Sniffle wondered if they would be able to ask Roger Senior anything about Harriette. They did not know if he was aware of their purpose in being there. He left the room for a few minutes and came back with several small logs and some kindling and immediately set to building the fire. They sat back and watched, admiring this skill that neither of them had. When he had the fire going, he turned and said in that soft strained voice, "You'll be needing to ask me some questions, I assume."

"Then you do know how we came to be here," Nosemitt said gently.

"Yes, my son told me. I was prepared to dislike you both. It will become unavoidably clear that I regard Walter Wrothwell as the enemy of my personal happiness. He certainly loved Harriette, but his other interests made him put a lot of burdens on her and, to an extent, on Vanessa. His hiring you made you his agents. In person it is quite difficult to dislike you; and I would like to believe that you are interested in the truth, no matter at whose expense. If so, I have nothing to fear from you, although I blame myself for not being with Harriette. If I had stayed, it would not have happened."

"What can you tell us?" Nosemitt asked, her voice matching his– low and tense, barely above a whisper. "We hardly know what to ask about that last night."

"Harriette and I had a late dinner. She had worked until ten, getting well ahead on her columns so that we could have some time together. I picked her up at the newspaper office and drove to our favorite restaurant."

"Which is that?" Nosemitt asked.

"A little place called The Wild Truffle."

"And what was Harriette wearing?" Sniffle asked.

"She had on a gray wool suit and a kind of teal blouse. I called it teal; she insisted it was blue. I think it was teal. Why?"

"What kind of jacket or coat?"

"She had on a heavy poncho, black with a dark blue fringe and a weird pattern on the sleeves. I teased her about it, said that I thought Vanessa could really make something out of it. She privately loved her daughter's style but was always so worried that people would underestimate Vanessa, never seeing beyond her way of dressing. I was always trying to encourage her to lighten up. Vanessa is going to do as she pleases." Sniffle made a few notes on a piece of paper she had left on the coffee table the previous day.

"Did she have a gray windbreaker?" she asked.

"Not that I ever saw her wear. I kept one here, but it was blue. Why?"

"She was found in one," Sniffle said. "You did not see her, I take it."

"Vanessa was called to identify her. I did not see her until later." It was very difficult for him to speak, and he looked away.

"So you had dinner?" Nosemitt said.

"Yes," he said, taking a deep breath, "and finished around eleven-thirty. I drove her home and then went to my own house. I got home a few minutes before twelve. I should have stayed with her."

"Do you have any witnesses who might have seen you leave?" Nosemitt asked.

"I don't know. The waiter at the restaurant could probably remember when we left there, but obviously no one has come forward and said he or she was watching us here from their window. If someone saw me leave, I would be happy to have him or her say so."

"Vanessa was not at home?" Sniffle asked.

"No, and now we know why, don't we?" he said, almost smiling. "I wish Harriette could have known our kids got married."

"She would have welcomed the news?"

He spoke carefully, perhaps in the hope that by choosing words slowly his emotions would remain in check. "There were so many factors, things that may or may not all come out in the open; there are so very many. For now, suffice it to say, I know she would have been relieved that Vanessa broke free of all the restraints on her and followed her own heart. And yet, there were complications."

"Might Harriette then have chosen to follow her daughter's lead?" Nosemitt asked, praying that she was not overstepping the boundaries. Roger looked away then and contemplated all the separate shoots of flame playing blue and golden in the logs. His eyes remained on the flames for a long time, and then he turned back to look at these two women sitting here and asking him these questions that to his inner self made no sense at all.

"The restrictions were not exactly the same, but as to marrying, she had done the same already," he said quietly. "I was not going to say so, but your questions I see will keep pushing me to the point. No one else in St. Edwards knows, and for now they must not. It is extremely important that no one knows. Possibly all will come out despite me, but you'll have to accept my word that it does matter. There are too many secrets in life, but sometimes they are forced upon us. We were married two years ago."

"Well, we're glad for you. It never made sense to us about her refusing you for your name."

"No, that was the public fiction, and I acted my part of resentful resignation. I hope it won't disappoint my son that he is not the only one who has had a romantic secret, but he will be pleased that Harriette was not the petty woman she had to appear to be. She was anything but petty, and we both despised the need for the charade. It's Walter I blame for that, but you'll have to get his reasons from him, not me."

"Believe me, we both can understand your feelings about the charade," Nosemitt said. "We are having the same reaction about the pretense we are going through. We hate it."

"We heard of some sort of scandal at the newspaper that Harriette wanted to expose and her editor wanted to suppress; is he involved in all of this?" Sniffle asked.

"Still trying for Molecott?" Nosemitt said. Sniffle shrugged.

"Herb Molecott and the suppressed story may have something to do with Harriette's death, although I don't really believe he himself is tied that closely to any criminal element. He has nothing at all to do with the reasons our marriage had to remain secret or why it was so difficult to accomplish in the first place." His voice was all but gone from the strain, and yet he looked a little bit relieved that at last he had been able to acknowledge to someone that he and Harriette had married.

"And so Vanessa was your daughter after all?" Nosemitt said with a smile, recognizing that there could be no more unbearable questions for now. Roger just nodded and wiped a pair of tears. "She has needed a father all along, I gather," Nosemitt said. Roger said nothing.

"Won't you at least be telling your children now?" Sniffle asked.

"No, they must not know yet. The right time will come, but I have to have your word that you will tell no one unless I come and tell you it is all right."

"It seems such a simple request, and of course we will honor it," Nosemitt said, glancing at Sniffle to make sure she spoke for them both, "but it does complicate our own job. As I said, we are having quite a bit of trouble balancing our own need for discretion and all the restrictions on what we can know and can discuss without breaking a promise or hurting people. It would be much simpler if we were just out and out investigators."

"But then I would not have told you," he said, smiling ruefully.

"Just as an example," Sniffle added, "we have heard in more than one way about some sort of scam or scandal that the newspaper is onto and may be suppressing. How, as alleged friends from out of town, can we go looking for information or asking people anything? It was ridiculous from the start that we came in that guise, and we blew it right away with Sergeant Bradley and Detective Duke. None of us thought it through in advance. There just was not enough time to plan carefully."

"It does seem that you will have to work something different out. I see that," Roger said, going over to prod the tiny flames back into the charred logs. He knelt in front of the fire quietly, wishing he could come up with a plan that would help them without giving away any more of his own secrets. "Definitely the police team knows why you are here. Walter hired you, and Vanessa was with him. Now Roger and I know your role. Does anyone else?"

"We don't think so, but we don't know," Sniffle said and told him about the mysterious phone call she had received at the hotel, a little unanswered question that had never left her mind.

"I think I can give you a new cover," he said after a while. "It still involves a pretense, but it would also be basically true." They were interested. "I know that I must be available to the police, but I cannot tolerate the calls I have been getting from others. There have been some very ugly anonymous ones; and there have been quite a few from Harriette's friends and associates, some just wanting to share their grief but some who have been called on by the police for questioning. They want me to help them, and I don't want anything to do with any of them. If it would suit you, I can get word out gradually that I met you both after the … the memorial service." He paused, briefly distraught at the word 'funeral' that he had started to use. "The service," he continued; "and that I have taken advantage of your offers to be of assistance by asking you to try to find some answers for me. It is no lie to say I want to know who did it. You can openly do all the investigating you want, and no one will know that Walter hired you, and I can tell you the names of some of these people who are calling."

"A very interesting offer," Nosemitt said, "too valuable to refuse."

"But what will Walter think of our doing that"? Sniffle asked. "He wanted us to not to be out in the open." Nosemitt had to agree with that, but Roger wasn't so sure.

"Whether or not you go public, I think I can still suggest a few other people you might want to think about, people who are not calling."

"For example?" Sniffle asked.

"Carleton Blackburn, the owner of the paper. He's the one who made the decision to suppress the story you mentioned."

"We don't even know what the story is," Nosemitt observed.

"My voice is not up to that one tonight," he insisted, "perhaps tomorrow; but I think you ought to know about Frank and Louis Waldo, the owners of the automobile agency where Roger works. I'm glad he's looking for another job, but I am confident that he is quite in the dark about his bosses' activities." His voice was more like a soft scratch by now, and he excused himself to go get water, asking if they would like anything.

"What do you think?" Nosemitt asked, after Roger left the room.

"I think father and son are too good to be true, but I like them both," Sniffle said. "I still don't think anyone is going to be interested in telling us anything just because Roger has asked us to see what we can find out. We've learned what we always knew, that we're not at all cut out for disguises and pretense. Pseudonyms may well be our limit. I wonder if we're up for this kind of work at all. I miss painting and writing."

Tuesday afternoon, January 16

Nosemitt was putting on her gloves and Sniffle was looking for hers when Vanessa came downstairs with a sheaf of papers in her hand. Nosemitt smiled and mentioned that they were off to see Walter. Was there anything they could do, any message to deliver, any stops on the way home they could make?

"I have to take these over to the newspaper," Vanessa said. "Herb insists that the column keep going, so I found several letters that my mother had answered for future columns. We have plenty of food in the house; tell Uncle Walter hello. I can't think of anything else."

"How about if we deliver those for you?" Sniffle suggested. "That way we can have a chance to see this infamous Herbert and maybe talk to a few others on the staff." Nosemitt immediately seconded the motion, and Vanessa had no objection. Sniffle found one of her gloves and decided that she had looked long enough. They left to go visit Walter, Sniffle driving and Nosemitt back to humming the tune for which she still had few words.

They were greeted by Emmaline, a frail woman with thick glasses and an apparent aversion to speaking. More accurately, the door was opened by Emmaline; she smiled and motioned them in, managing to indicate that her brother was waiting for them in that room toward which she was pointing. She disappeared, but Walter called out for them to come see him there in the little parlor through the double doors.

They went through the doors into the dark room, its curtains an ancient bronze floral brocade sagging against the almost black wallpaper with its dark green intricate print. Huge pots with rubber plants and ferns looked cemented into every corner, and the old worn Persian carpets were threadbare in spots and rewoven with bright contemporary yarn in others. For reasons completely unaesthetic, the yarn was a brilliant orange. Perhaps, Sniffle thought, the infamous hat had never been Portcullis fur at all. Perhaps Vanessa's tastes were a genetic curse. Or blessing.

Walter was sitting in a purple velvet chair, though he did not look kingly at all. He looked very tired but quite pleased to see them, eager to hear what they might have learned. They each found a seat several feet from Walter, the chairs being randomly placed in the room without regard to conversation but more with respect to covering holes. What, Nosemitt wondered, had lived there?

"So tell me," he said; "tell me. Have you gotten anywhere?"

Sadly they feared they had not. "We are planning to talk with Mr. Molecott this afternoon," Nosemitt said. "We want to see what we can learn about the suppressed story that Harriette wanted to run."

"Ah, then you have learned something," he said, pleased. "I did suggest to Sergeant Bradley that a look into Marvin's affairs was in order, especially in connection with that story. I am delighted that you at least share my concern and see that there might be a lead there."

"We still don't know a single thing about the story itself," Sniffle said, "including how Marvin is involved or how anyone at all is. We only know there is a story."

"Oh, Marvin is involved all right. By the way, before I forget, I owe you an apology, Ms Nigel."

"What?" Sniffle said, startled.

"Yes, I'm afraid I was overcome with severe chest pains just as I called you the other night. I thought at the time that it would be a discreet way to greet you because I was expecting Marvin at any moment and did not wish him to know of our connection; but as things turned out, I imagine you must have been quite frightened. I assure you, I am most sorry."

Sniffle said nothing, but Nosemitt acknowledged the insecurity the call had caused and expressed great relief for both of them that it had come from him.

"Marvin had just arrived but was not yet in the room; and frankly I am glad he did not get to hear the invitation to move to Vanessa's. It would have seemed to him one more example of interference coming from me, I think."

"Why was he there?" Sniffle asked, not as comfortable yet as she would have liked. Somehow the news that Walter had been the source of that call was a relief, and yet it felt unsettling still. She wondered why it bothered her, but it did. Maybe it was that choked-off sound. It had stirred some other memory, but she did not know of what.

"On Dustin's behalf, I imagine– what else could it be?" Walter said in answer to Sniffle's question.

"The will and the jewels?" Nosemitt asked.

"Possibly, although Dustin is quite capable of asking for himself. No, I think we will not understand Marvin's actions unless we get to the bottom of the story you know only a bit about. I myself have been trying to get to the bottom of it for many months and have made some progress. I suspect Marvin knows that I have been poking about in his business and his son's and called to come over to warn me off."

"This business of Marvin and Dustin's," Sniffle asked, "has to do with a drug habit?"

"So Dustin would have me think," Walter said. "No, life's stories are even more complex than a soap opera at times. Wheels within wheels, lies within truth, secrets and fables and all kinds of disguise– the human mind is capable of astounding productivity. It would be easier if it were not, but then it would also be quite a bit duller. You know, I have thought all along that I was drawn to the two of you because you hide your identities so well – and for no reason I can discover. I may know the names 'Sniffle' and 'Nigel' and 'Nosemitt' but not your true identities."

"There is only one reason, and it is simple," Sniffle said. "It amuses us. We decided when our lives came together from our different pasts that we each would take on a humorous identity for ourselves. We remain the people we were, still the same in every respect but one; but that one has changed everything. It started as a joke but became very appealing. In Fondue we became Nosemitt & Sniffle, and the events of our lives seem to hang on those names. They have added a dimension that was not there before. I suppose some could think it might make for an interesting psychological study, but mainly it is fun. And now it is useful as well."

"Reasons as sensible as any I've ever heard," Walter said, "and infinitely saner than most. But to me it suggested that you would understand the capacity of individuals to hide for a variety of reasons, some of them honest and some not; some of them probably criminal and others not at all. I assumed you would not pass judgment on someone just for having a secret– because who does not?"

"You assumed correctly," Nosemitt said. "But, to get back to the subject at hand, we need more information about Dustin and then about the Waldo brothers."

"You see, you know more than you told me. You let me believe you know nothing, and then you say matter-of-factly, 'we need more information about the Waldo brothers.' Yes, you do live up to my expectations. Frank Waldo bought what used to be the Blackburn agency before Carleton became owner of *The Edwardian Times*. There was a great deal of pressure on Carl to give up the agency or the paper, especially whenever questions were raised about the finances of the two organizations. Other car dealers did not like that Blackburn had free full-page color ads while they paid heavily for much less; but that was the minor issue. The agency has been indicted on a whole slew of charges, acquitted of all; and a number of people think the power of the press had everything to do with the jury's decisions.

"Eventually Carl sold his agency to his wife, Yvonne, but that brought on new outcries. In came Frank Waldo, seemingly an outsider, to take over the car dealership. What the city really needed was someone from outside, new and ideally not corrupt, to buy out the newspaper, because whether Carl owns anything of the agency on paper or not, he is still part of all their doings, whether he likes them or not. And their doings have grown."

"Does everyone know about this and it goes on anyway?" Sniffle asked, thinking about Roger Junior and his father's conviction that he was unaware.

"Not everyone even believes there is anything going on at all," Walter said. "First, all those acquittals mean a lot to some people. Then, the Waldos are pretty good at hiring young good-looking salesmen with clean records who probably haven't the slightest idea that they are being used."

"We understand that a son of Mr. Lescouth is one of their young salesmen," Sniffle said, looking for a reaction.

"So I've heard," he said calmly, "but I have no interest in him. As for Marvin and Dustin, however, I do have a great deal of interest. I believe Marvin owns a part interest in the agency and is fully aware of what is happening. I suspect that Dustin is one of the active engineers of the plan. If you are asking my opinion of the young Lescouth, it is that he probably knows nothing about the agency's actions."

"What plan? We still haven't a clue. What is this plan?" Nosemitt asked.

"Here is what we think is going on, not that we have conclusive proof yet: various salesmen are sent around the country to call on corporate clients. They really think they are selling a fleet of cars; but, in fact, the clients have all prearranged to pay the Waldos for some specified number of cars which are delivered with significant additions."

"Drugs smuggled inside the cars?" Nosemitt asked.

"That's what we are convinced is happening. The salesmen move on to other leads; and, oddly enough, the same cars that went to Mr. Smith now arrive at the corporate garage belonging to Mr. Jones. The salesmen, as I say, never see that aspect of the transaction. They think they make sales; they receive their generous commissions. What do they know? What do they need to know? Nothing."

"Why does the agency bother with the salesmen?" Nosemitt asked.

"It gives the appearance of legitimacy and creates all the necessary paperwork when there is an investigation. It is worth the cost and effort to all concerned."

"How do you know all this?" Sniffle asked.

"I've worked behind the scenes here for most of my life, and I've fought this particular kind of thing ever since illegal drugs started coming through St. Edwards. It started as minor stuff and grew rapidly. Soon we had hints that big-time dealers were funneling their goods through this community. Those of us who care about such things, and there are several of us, have formed a small society of our own. We are variously regarded as pompous and self-serving old men or as civic-minded philanthropists; but very, very few have any idea of what we really do.'"

"Which is what exactly?" Sniffle asked.

'Monitor the likely sources of the drug trade and work at whatever speed we can to destroy it. For quite a few years now, when I've received word of some possibly criminal activity, I've passed it on to Harriette and let her do more of the investigative work. I still have a few young spies, however, who are my legs and ears and eyes. But I'm sure you see that if Marvin and Dustin are as involved as I think they are, there are more substantial reasons than Fredricka's jewels to make Harriette an obstacle to their success. It is primarily for Vanessa's sake that we refer first to the jewels. She has no idea that Marvin and Dustin are suspected of engaging in drug traffic. I see no reason to tell her. Also, the value of the jewelry makes them a real factor anyway."

"You did not mention the jewelry in Vanessa's presence," Sniffle pointed out. "You told us about them in the dining room that first evening."

"But that is the motive she assumes," he said.

"Vanessa is not a child, and didn't you say she was Harriette's assistant?" Nosemitt said.

"I suppose that to the world she is not a child, but to me she is; and being her mother's assistant did not mean that she was brought in on this kind of story. I don't believe she ever was. I believe in protecting our young people from unnecessary evil."

"Doesn't it seem reasonable that Vanessa would see herself in greater danger if the jewels were the only motive?" Sniffle asked. "If her mother was a target because of her power in the community, then Vanessa would not be an equal target. It is only the jewelry that might make her seem threatened."

"That is an interesting angle," he said, thinking it over. "My own opinion is that Vanessa is not interested in the jewelry and would feel that anyone who wants it is welcome to it. She would not see herself as a likely victim. Besides," he said smiling, "the style is far too conventional for her. She would never wear any of it, except perhaps her grandmother's ornate tiara. "

Emmaline entered the room with a tea tray far too heavy for her. She stepped gingerly over the familiar creases in the carpets and tottered a bit as she tried to set the tray on a rickety mahogany table. Nosemitt tried to help but Emmaline whispered her away. "No need, no need, my pet." The tray, vibrating and clattering and threatening to cause an avalanche of tea and sugar, managed to land safely on the table. Only a little hot tea splashed onto the well-spotted carpet. Emmaline insisted on pouring, an arduous and nerve-wracking experience.

"Cake?" Walter asked his guests, leaning forward to pick up a plate that had slices of pound cake surrounding a small dish of strawberry preserves. Extra plates and forks were passed; napkins went around. The cake was moderately stale and the tea was anise, a flavor Sniffle found unpleasant in tea. She set her dish and cup down. Emmaline picked them up and carried them off to the kitchen. She did not return.

"What kind of spies do you hire?" Sniffle asked.

"Ones with an ability to keep secrets," he said, smiling, not noticing the slightly sheepish look on the faces of his very pleasant investigators. "Sometimes I need intelligent spies, such as yourselves; sometimes I need a spy to whom information means nothing. Mostly I need the latter because that is safest. But I want to know what other 'nothings' you have learned. I feel sure you have acquired many pieces of information, and I may be able to put separate bits together for you."

"Perhaps there will be such information after we meet Herbert Molecott," Nosemitt said. "Right now we really know very little."

"Of course," he said, sipping his tea. Emmaline arrived to show them out.

Sniffle played with the single glove as Nosemitt drove to the newspaper office. She absentmindedly counted the fingers and came out of her semi-trance when she reached the number six. "Where have you been?" Nosemitt asked.

"Thinking about spies with little intelligence," she said, choosing not to mention that she had counted six fingers on the glove. "You know, he did not answer all our questions. He is very adept at ignoring what he wants to ignore. I'd like to know more about those agents of his. I have a new theory about Mr. Molecott, you'll be pleased to know."

"I will not. I am beginning to be bothered by all the commotion with names in this case. Walter expressed it the other day– 'double names and secret names and names that stand for other names.' You cannot make Molecott both a spy and a fortune-seeker on the basis of his name; enough already."

"I think we should find a reason to look at cars while we're here. I hope we don't find Roger Junior involved in this mess," Sniffle said to change the subject.

"Walter skipped away from him fast enough," Nosemitt said. "It occurs to me that he might well be one of the young spies, despite Walter's disclaimer."

"I wonder if that puts him on the side of the good guys or the bad guys," Sniffle said. She dropped the glove on the seat beside her and stared long and hard out the window.

"You aren't going to tell me that you think Walter really did murder Harriette? They seem to have been a team."

"No, I don't think Walter wanted to get rid of his niece. I just have this sudden image of a network of little spies he has set up, not all of them knowing about each other, some of them more than a little stupid perhaps. Walter sees safety in such stupidity, but to me it compounds the danger."

"So, after we drop these papers off at the newspaper office, where do you see us heading?"

"I don't know. Not yet to the car agency. Maybe we need a fuller picture of Harriette first. Who could tell us about her from an unsuspecting and unsuspected point of view?"

"How about Portia?" Nosemitt said.

At the offices of *The Edwardian Times* they asked to be directed to Mr. Molecott's office. The young woman who was substituting for the regular receptionist looked harried but did call her superior to ask how to put all the phones on hold, then got up from her desk and led them down the hall, up the elevator to the third floor, through a large open office area, around the water fountain, past the utility closet, and into a small office. "Visitors for Herb," she said to the secretary. "You can show them how to get out of here."

Ms Barnaby asked if they had an appointment, knowing that no one did, and took their names and asked the reason for their visit. She disappeared into a slightly larger office and came back saying that Mr. Molecott was quite busy and asked that they simply leave the columns with her, thank you very much.

"Vanessa was quite emphatic that we give them personally to Mr. Molecott," Sniffle said. Ms Barnaby looked offended.

"Oh, it was not out of any feeling that you would not give them to him," Nosemitt managed to manufacture.

"No," Sniffle agreed, "she must have had some feeling that Mr. Molecott might let her think he had not received them."

"I see," Ms Barnaby said coolly, though in fact she did. Herb Molecott would let them all think that. He was always playing one staff member against another and managing to duck responsibility for everything. "I'll see if he will step out for a moment." She disappeared again and came back with Mr. Molecott irritably in back of her.

"Thank you," he said crisply, reaching for the envelope.

"We would like a receipt," Nosemitt said, pleased that she had thought of it.

"A receipt? What nonsense. Tell Vanessa I have them," he said and started back into his office. Nosemitt and Sniffle followed after.

"A pen?" Sniffle said, offering one. Angrily he scribbled and then initialed acknowledgment of the delivery.

"While we are here, Mr. Molecott," Nosemitt said, "I want you to know that we sympathize with your own loss here at the paper. Everyone's heart goes out to Vanessa of course, but you have to be suffering and feeling Harriette's absence very much yourself."

"Why, yes, thank you. We have taken up the slack naturally, but we will miss her. The burden does fall on the top dog, so to speak."

"An interesting image," Sniffle said. "Could we burden you with a few questions? We have been asked to look into a few matters by interested parties who are unable at this time to take a detached view themselves."

"What kind of questions? Who has asked you? I am quite busy," he said, not prepared at all for this sudden change. He did not invite them to sit down, nor did he sit down either. He started to walk toward the door to usher them out but was stopped by a very softly spoken question from Nosemitt.

"Vanessa's refusal to cover for you– surely you understand that?" Nosemitt had no idea of what she would say next and simply had to hope for the best.

Molecott, at the door, closed it and came back to his desk. Now he did invite them to sit, but he himself stood at the tiny window with his hands in his pockets. "You know that I asked her to cover for me," he said. "No wonder the police have called twice– she must have used that phrase to them too. What a ridiculous mess. I asked her to take over the column; I said I needed that column to continue because it has been one of our most popular features. That was how I asked her to 'cover' for me. I needed a replacement quickly."

"And yet," Nosemitt said, looking at her own small notebook, "the police seem to think there is more than that. An incriminating note was mentioned, I believe. I hasten to add that that information did not come from Vanessa."

"That damned note again! There is no 'incriminating' note; there is only a memo suggesting that Harriette reconsider an opinion. There is nothing unusual about an editor suggesting to one of his writers that she reconsider an opinion."

"How strongly was it worded?" Sniffle asked. "Might an outsider think it was a threat?"

"Malarkey!" he said, pounding his fist down on the window sill and almost cracking it. He looked at them. "You haven't seen the memo, have you?" They conceded that they had not, that they had second-hand knowledge of it. "Well, you look at it and then tell me that it's a threat. If anything, it was a friendly warning. I told her it was dangerous to take the stand she was taking and wanted her to have more regard for her own safety and that of her family. I am not the source of danger."

"Well, Mr. Molecott, you do have to agree that those words could be seen as a threat," Nosemitt said.

"I take it she never changed her opinion?" Sniffle said.

"No," he said, looking out the window. "But I repeat that it was not a threat from me; it was never a threat from me." He had no more to say. Ms. Barnaby escorted them back to the receptionist.

On the way out, they asked to see a phone book and were taken to an empty desk. It was not Harriette's desk, but it made them think of her again. Nosemitt had grown to consider the woman a dear friend and wanted for many reasons to help solve the crime. She felt now that she needed to know more about Harriette in all kinds of ways. Portia might be an ideal source. It was her address and phone number they now looked up; then they called to ask if they might visit.

They approached the house slowly, trying to keep in mind the few things Walter had told them. They expected a modest home, probably from the implication that Harvester and Portia had not met Fredricka's standards and so had not done too well in life. In fact, Harvey had always been more industrious and more intelligent than his mother had recognized and had created a thriving little factory that made pet houses and carriers– bird cages and dog houses were his biggest sellers. Before he had died, he had made Portia the executive of the business, knowing that his son would have no interest. Unfortunately, Portia had little interest as well and was trying to sell the company. Ever since she had broken her leg in a fall three years back, she had never been able to walk well again. She had no energy for business.

Now Nosemitt and Sniffle found themselves on the circular drive of a large home, not quite an estate, with professionally maintained lawn and extensive gardens and lovely woods all around the house. Even in January a visitor could tell that the place would be a delight in the spring and a shady oasis in summer. The only jarring note was the vast number of doghouses scattered about the lawn, though all were beautifully painted. A few had names and dates over the little doorways, leaving Sniffle concerned that these were small mausoleums.

Portia was leaning on her cane, waiting to greet them at the front door, and smiled at the two unknown guests. They followed her to the winter porch, a glassed room that looked out to the woods but was warm and luxurious to be in. Plants were elegantly placed and the furniture was tasteful as well as comfortable. Family photographs rested on a long, low, handsome chest against the inside wall, and a pair of small sculptures of schnauzers flanked the photos. Three miniature doghouses seemed out of place but they were nestled among the sculptures. The three women sat in the sunniest part of the porch, and Portia brought out coffee on a rolling cart that she managed with some difficulty. Though she had seemed a bit vague after the memorial service, she did not seem vague now at all. Perhaps, Nosemitt thought, it had been the stress of the occasion.

"You said you wished to speak of Harriette?" Portia began. "I assume you mean the first?"

"Yes, although we're willing to hear about the second one too," Nosemitt said.

"I don't like Marvin's new young wife," Portia said; "he's always been such a fool. I did like his first Harriette, though. All of us did."

"Then does anyone have any idea of who would have wanted to hurt her?" Nosemitt asked.

"Oh, my, I certainly don't. I imagine people are wondering if Marvin did it; but for all one can say against him, I just would never believe he would kill anyone. He might want to scare a person, but he's all words– a bit of a bully."

"Why would Marvin want to scare her?" Sniffle asked.

"The jewelry, I suppose. You do know about the jewelry?" They nodded. "It is my opinion that Fredricka wanted to punish Marvin for divorcing Harriette; but Marvin would not do anything so obvious, so clumsy, so stupid, and so pointless as killing Harriette."

"Why do you say so?" Nosemitt asked.

"For many reasons. The main one is that the jewels would not go to Marvin under any conditions, so he could not hope to profit by Harriette's death; but outsiders would not know that. That's why I say people might be thinking Marvin did it."

"You know for sure that he couldn't have had the jewelry?" Sniffle asked.

"I saw the will. Fredricka made sure all of her children and their spouses saw it. The jewelry was to go to Harriette five years from the date of Fredricka's demise; and in the event of Harriette's death before the five years were up, the jewelry was to be sold by an outside agent with the proceeds going to a scholarship fund at the university. Knowing Harriette, I think she might well have done the same anyway. She did not want the jewelry, knowing how some members of the family felt."

"I don't suppose there is any individual at the university who personally benefits by Harriette's death," Sniffle said. "The school does but I don't think we need to pursue that line of thinking, do you?" Nosemitt did not. "We can always come back to it if all else fails," Sniffle said.

"This is very helpful," Nosemitt said to Portia. "We had been wondering if there were such a contingency clause as you described. This removes the jewelry as the motive for the murder, or it seems to anyway– but then I'm back to wondering why Marvin would want to scare Harriette."

"He is just mean enough to want to make her uneasy. I think he never stopped resenting her. You know, in the beginning he really loved her; and then she did such a wonderful thing and he never saw it right. He thought she had ruined their life together and robbed Dustin and himself of her time. He was not a man for sharing her."

"What do you mean?" Nosemitt asked.

"Why, I mean when she adopted Vanessa– such a darling little child and so in need of a family, especially a mother. But Harriette really should have asked Marvin first; she should not have made the decision without once talking it over with him."

"Does Vanessa know this?" Nosemitt asked, shocked.

"I haven't any idea," Portia said, sipping her coffee and looking out somberly to the woods. "I lost my own little girl more than a year before Harriette adopted Vanessa; and although she and I were always on very good terms, we never discussed the little girls. I think Harriette knew how difficult it was for me."

"May I ask, how did it happen?" Nosemitt asked.

"We found her in those woods out there," Portia said, her eyes tearing slowly. "It might as well have been last week or this morning. We never knew for sure who did it, and I think I never wanted to know. Such a sweet child. She would have been such a comfort to me now. I often wonder if I could ever move away from this house, but then again I wonder how I can stay and see those woods. They haunt me and they hold me." She changed the subject and no one returned to it.

On their return to Vanessa's, Nosemitt decided on the spur of the moment to stop at the police station again to see if Lesley Duke was available. Going through the park, she passed a parked black shiny Mustang with a couple tangled inside and a pair of little boys in parkas and mufflers laughing and throwing pebbles at the car. Sniffle watched as a young man rolled down the window to moon the boys, who ran off immediately. "The course of young love is running about as usual," she said to Nosemitt, who shrugged and began singing *Hello, Young Lovers, Wherever You Are.* "They're right there in and out of the car," Sniffle assured her.

The detective had just left, but Sergeant Bradley was there. "We're still trying to make a connection with the bird murders, but until an hour ago all had been quiet on that front for a few days. No sightings."

"I just saw a live loon," Sniffle said, "but I guess that doesn't count."

"Loon or moon?" Nosemitt asked without expecting an answer. "What happened an hour ago?"

"A woman called and said she was with her son at the school playground where the boy found six sparrows."

"Rodex?" Sniffle asked.

"Lesley's on her way there to collect evidence."

"Any new information on the auto agency?" Nosemitt asked him, catching him off guard by the sudden switch.

"The auto agency?" he repeated.

"Yes, the suppressed story, the possibly criminal activity involving drugs that Harriette apparently wished to expose but Molecott did not. The car agency formerly owned by the current owner of the newspaper. The auto agency."

"You have been busy," he said. "We have not read the reports that our colleagues have turned in," he said, dismissing the subject.

"From what we have gathered so far, it does not sound like work for the local police; it sounds like a federal case," Sniffle said.

"Perhaps that is why we have heard nothing down here then," he said blandly, adding belatedly, "if it is a federal case."

"Last I heard, smuggling drugs around the country was not left for the local police in their spare time," Sniffle said, still annoyed with him.

"No, if that's what is involved," he said, again conveying a very

79

slight jeering tone which neither Nosemitt nor Sniffle could quite account for. They still did not know Chief Bigguns or his style of dressing down a subordinate who was making little progress, let alone the chief's absolute determination that his people, not outsiders, would solve this case. With Duke out, they had no inclination to stay and ask more questions. They went back to Vanessa's, hoping to have some time alone with her for quiet conversation about her relationship with her mother. Did Vanessa know she had been adopted? They thought not. Could they ask directly? They were not sure that the time was right or that it would ever be.

They were quite surprised to find Duke there and even more surprised to discover that she had been interrogating Vanessa quite extensively on her whereabouts on the night of the murder. Bigguns apparently had chewed her out as well and had demanded a more thorough accounting of every possible suspect. "Why," he had shouted "is there no record of the daughter's whereabouts? Where was she and with whom, if anyone? Don't you think it's pretty odd that the daughter is always there except this one particular night? Doesn't that strike you as more than a little unusual? And what is this about Mr. Lescouth being 'probably innocent'? No one is 'probably innocent' unless proven not guilty. In the courtroom maybe it works the other way, but not in the mind of the police. Get out there and get some hard information, and don't be so worried about hurting her feelings. This is murder you're dealing with, not a tea party. Manners don't matter. Facts matter. And the fact of the matter is neither you nor Art is looking too good on this case." Duke had swallowed hard and left. She had stopped in the schoolyard long enough to find and collect dead birds, drop them at the lab, and then had gone to Vanessa's.

"I tell you," Vanessa was saying just as Nosemitt and Sniffle came in, "I was staying at a friend's place. Isn't it enough that I am willing to tell you her name and you can check with her? You don't need to know who else knows if I was there or not."

"You may think it is unimportant, but it may make an enormous difference," Duke said. "I need the names of any witness to prove that you were at Ms Park-Jackson's apartment. You have already told me that she was out of town."

"Yes, as a matter of fact she was out of the country," Vanessa said. "I was looking after her apartment while she was gone. What kind of witnesses would I have?"

"If you were looking after the apartment, why would you need to stay there overnight?"

"If you lived at home with your mother, wouldn't you occasionally want to get away?"

"Yes, but doesn't it seem a little odd to you that the one night you were away, or say you were away, your mother was murdered?"

"It seems very odd to me that my mother would be murdered under any conditions at all," Vanessa said, eyes reddening.

"Vanessa," Nosemitt interrupted, "is it still so necessary to keep all the secrets? You do have a witness who could testify to your presence."

"You know about this?" Duke asked, tossing her notebook aside with a gesture of frustration. "I don't care what the chief says– you two might as well take over the case. We keep struggling for information that somehow you already have gotten around to."

"Perhaps it's all in how you ask," Sniffle said.

"More likely in how you two do and don't ask," Duke said.

"It's Nosemitt's sympathetic ear and my unsympathetic eye," Sniffle explained.

"You're underrating yourselves," Duke said and then turned to Vanessa. "So who is the witness, and why are you hiding him or her? It's not helping you at all. You might as well know that the chief thinks you are the prime suspect, and I don't believe it. I'd like anything that would support your case."

Vanessa was not at all sure she believed Duke. She looked at Nosemitt and Sniffle, then down at her bare hands. She stared at her left hand for a long time, then finally reached into her pocket and pulled out her wedding band and put it on. "My friends, Sarah Park-Jackson and her husband, thought that the nicest wedding present they could give me was a place to have a secret honeymoon. She joked that it was a great bargain– for the price of a trip to Europe she got a free gift for Roger and me. She knew we could not leave town, and she knew that our wedding was a secret from everyone else. I hope you won't need to break this confidence. You can check at city hall and confirm that Roger and I got married; please do not check with friends and relatives– none of them knows, and some would have a fit."

"Roger?" Duke repeated, making the same assumption that Nosemitt and Sniffle had.

"Junior," Nosemitt said. "Roger Lescouth, Junior. I assume his middle initial is also G, but we never asked."

"The G is for Gladley," Vanessa said with a tiny smile. "I too am gladly Lescouth. It's another little joke we have."

"Aha!" Sniffle said, "is that the source of the Gladiolus Press?"

"Yes, the family has a mock crest with three sprays of gladiolus kind of strewn across a field of weeds. I love Roger's whole family." Nosemitt and Sniffle were not surprised.

"This is all fascinating of course," Duke said, "but why all the secrecy?"

"I don't understand why, but Mother told me a few years ago that there was a trust fund established for me years ago and that I was not allowed to marry before I was twenty-five unless I was willing to forfeit the money. I assume my father set it up instead of child support, but I don't know why the condition was set down. All I know is that I didn't see any reason to announce that I was married and I still don't. I don't even know who is in charge of the funds. I'm willing to wait until I'm twenty-five to find out, and then we can have another wedding. Or go ahead and give up the money."

"You're planning to keep your marriage a secret that long?" Duke asked.

"It's less than two more years," she said. "Roger travels a lot and I plan to stay here anyway until he gets another job and we can be together all the time. It doesn't seem impossible."

"Have you ever asked your father about that fund?" Sniffle asked.

"No."

"Do you have any expectation of receiving your grandmother's jewelry?" Nosemitt asked. Duke again looked surprised.

"Grandmother's? Not at all. It was very clear to me that it went to Mother eventually or to no one."

"I am surprised your uncle did not know that as well," Sniffle said.

"The Kettles don't like Uncle Walter," Vanessa said simply. "Why would they tell him?"

"Wouldn't your mother have told him?" Nosemitt asked.

"I guess she didn't. You know, Uncle Walter always kept track of so many things about us, kind of like a guardian angel, and Mother got pretty tired of it. I am not surprised that she didn't tell him. Sometimes you get to feeling as if the only way to have a life is to run away and hide. That's sort of what I am doing."

"I think that's what a lot of people do," Sniffle said.

Duke had the sense to realize and appreciate that Nosemitt and Sniffle were asking their questions in her presence not to upstage her but to get Vanessa to give necessary information. She made many notes and was inwardly happy that Vanessa seemed to have a legitimate alibi for her absence from home. Not that she couldn't have hired someone, but what was the motive? There was none apparent. She herself intended to go after the ex-husband and the son; she had not ruled out the jewelry as a motive for someone.

Wednesday, January 17

Nosemitt came down to get coffee and found Sniffle making a list. "Going shopping?" she asked her.

"In a manner of speaking," Sniffle said, sipping her cooling tea. "I think I have too many little voices clamoring for attention. It's time to hit the federal highway again. I don't suppose you want to come along to the state capital?"

"In spite of the road, I would like to; but I think Walter is expecting us back today. I don't think we should ignore him."

"Why don't you go there with Vanessa while I go try for a little research? I was thinking we ought to split some of the names on the list and see what we can find. You can learn just as much about Dustin and Marvin here in St. Edwards. I am getting more curious about Vanessa herself and Roger and maybe a couple of others as well. There might be something of interest at the Bureau of Vital Statistics."

The idea suited Nosemitt, and Vanessa had already indicated her intention of visiting her uncle anyway. Sniffle left around nine and planned to be back sometime after lunch. Nosemitt went back to bed to read until she heard Vanessa come out of the shower. The two of them had breakfast together and agreed to go see Walter at eleven. Until then, Vanessa suggested, why didn't Nosemitt get better acquainted with Harriette through some of her columns. She brought out a large stack of clippings, along with dozens of unanswered letters that had rough draft replies attached to them, and got Nosemitt settled in Harriette's study.

At first, Nosemitt was amused at the content of so many of the requests– how best to eat tomatoes if one detested tomatoes, how to dress for a company picnic when one's spouse was hoping for a promotion, how to tell the boys from the girls when one's child lived in a coed dorm; but then they got a little more serious: how to postpone indefinitely a visit from an old friend with whom one no longer had anything in common, how to shop for a baby shower when the mother-to-be already knew that the baby would not survive but had not had the strength to tell her friends. Like Walter before her, Nosemitt was horrified at the kinds of situations that people confronted daily; and, like him, though she had known her own share of absurdity and pain, she was always interested. But could she have taken a daily onslaught of strangers' anxieties and dilemmas? Could she have offered them any help at all? Harriette had taken on the task and had done so with humor and sense; yet Nosemitt could not help noticing that the responses to the most painful questions remained in draft stage. For some questions there simply could be no answers.

Nosemitt got up from Harriette's chair and took about thirty letters with her to the couch. She turned on the lamp and sat down, wanting to stretch out and read leisurely but there was no cushion or pillow for her head, and the couch arm was hard. She went to ask Vanessa if there was a pillow she might use, and Vanessa looked puzzled. They went back to the study and Vanessa frowned. "There were always two blue cushions here. Mother liked to read the letters lying down too; she said answers came to her more clearly if she could be relaxed." She looked under the couch and under the desk but found nothing. "They were a blue nubby fabric, not big but quite plump. Two of them. They were always here." All Nosemitt could think of was that Harriette had been suffocated, but until now it had never occurred to her– and certainly not to Vanessa– that Harriette might have been murdered right there in that room. Vanessa broke into sobs, and Nosemitt hardly knew what to say. She did, however, call Lesley Duke, who came right over. Sergeant Bradley came with her.

"Two blue cushions, you say?" he repeated, writing down the description. "Nubby. How big?" Vanessa could only make a rough shape with her hands. "About ten inches, you think?" She nodded.

"By the way," Nosemitt said softly, "the jacket she was wearing was not hers. Whoever did it must have put it around her when he took her from the house."

"How odd," Duke said.

"Why didn't you report this sooner?" Bradley asked.

"We never noticed it until now," Vanessa said. "Nosemitt called you as soon as we realized."

"You search the house," Bradley said to Duke; "I'm going to check outside. Maybe down in the creek too." He went out.

"I really don't expect we'll find them here," Nosemitt said.

"No, probably not," Duke agreed, "but if you knew our chief, you'd know why Art has been so obnoxious. We've kind of taken a beating. It's hard to become a homicide squad overnight. We're not used to thinking the way we ought to. In some ways I'd rather go break up a quarrel or find a lost puppy, but we have been wanting more work with a challenge. Now we have it and we're not up to the kind of work involved. I mean, we can't even track down the birdman." All three women went through the house but found no sign of any blue cushions. Outside, all along the creek and in the sewers and under the shrubs, neither did Art. But then he didn't see Olga either, hiding behind her curtains and pondering a new recipe for which she had only a name, Mystery Mousse. Blueberries would do for the police and something quite tart for that littler woman visiting. A cottage cheese or sour cream base, probably. For the taller one who was so pleasant she would happily throw in a half pot of honey. Her recipes, she reflected, had so much greater depth than most. There was always a story line to them. How could she represent Harriette in the mousse? She would have to think about that; it would come to her.

Bradley went back to the house to get Duke and to tell her they needed to obtain at least one search warrant. It was painfully clear that things did not look good for Roger, the last person known to have been with Harriette, the last person in the house with her, the owner of a windbreaker that he thought was blue. But, as Nosemitt remembered, he and Harriette had differed on how they described blue. The poncho he claimed she was wearing that night was in the hall closet and was indeed black but the fringe was not dark blue; it was a medium gray with a slight tinge of green.

Duke and Bradley left, and Nosemitt tried to go on reading while Vanessa remained in her own room for quite a while.

Sniffle arrived at the State Building and thought about how she wished to proceed. In the past she had prided herself upon appearing publicly competent. She would not have stooped to the feigning of stupidity or absentmindedness to attain a goal. As time had passed, she discovered two disturbing facts: first, that she was becoming more successful if she did act incompetent and, second, that she sometimes was genuinely absentminded and did not have to act at all. The extent of her unhappiness at these realizations varied from day to day. On this particular morning she was resigned to be willing to accept bumbling and fumbling as a strategy if it proved helpful. She locked the car without forgetting her keys; she walked laboriously up the ridiculously long flight of marble steps, not stopping to rub her throbbing knees until she got to the top; and she opened the heavy doors with some real effort and some false timidity. She peered in and scanned the marble halls. A pair of uniformed guards chatted against one wall, their gun holsters prominent and their walkie-talkies making a periodic staccato buzzing at their belts. There was an information booth in the center of the main corridor, but no one was stationed within it. Sniffle looked for a directory but found none. She still had not decided on her strategy when a very efficient-looking woman in tailored suit and crisp hairstyle entered the building, looked around for a directory too, and then went straight to the pair of guards to ask the way to the lieutenant governor's office. The guards went right on chatting. The woman gave up and walked on.

"So, that's the way it is," she muttered. She walked slowly down the hall toward the guards, looking confused and worried. She fumbled for a handkerchief in her purse, dropping everything. She said, "Oh, dear, what next?" quite pathetically and dropped everything a second time.

"Need some help, little lady?" both guards hurried over to ask. One picked up the purse and its contents; the other inquired after her destination. She inwardly bridled at the 'little lady' but gave no outward sign, merely dusting imaginary specks from her coat and thanking them for the purse.

"I need to inquire about a, a, birth certificate?" She was extremely competent at being vague. "What department would that be? Births? It isn't mixed in with deaths, is it? So depressing. And adoptions? Are they treated the same way? I'm just not sure."

"Vital Statistics is what you want, ma'am– fourth floor, turn right. Got that? When you get to the fourth floor, get out of the elevator. Turn right immediately and go about twenty feet. Doors. Go through the double doors that say Bureau of Vital Statistics. Someone there can help you."

"Thank you so much," she said. "Double doors. 'Vital Statistics.' That is such an appropriate name for something so important as birth and death– and you say adoption too? How convenient."

"Yes, ma'am. Have a good day." They grinned at each other as she turned in a complete circle before heading tentatively in the right direction.

All the way up in the slow elevator Sniffle replayed the idiotic conversation and grew more and more indignant on her own behalf. "They have no idea how insulting it is to be allowed to succeed only by caricaturing oneself. After all these years, women are still punished for being capable. 'Fourth floor– got that?' Yes, I got it ages ago. 'Get out of the elevator.' Thanks for that tip!"

She got out at the fourth floor, turned right, went through the double doors determined not to insult herself again. The young lady at the counter was filing her nails while talking on the phone about her date the previous evening. Sniffle tried to get her attention long enough to ask where she needed to go to get information on births, deaths, and adoptions; but the woman just glared at her and turned away. "And this is what will perpetuate the attitude toward us," Sniffle said to herself. She looked around for someone else who might be able to help her, but there was no one. Again she looked for advice on walls or signs or anywhere, but there were merely some job advertisements and a dozen placards for missing people and wanted people. "Well, both categories apply in this case too," she said. "Where is anybody? I just want a little information."

"So, what can I do for you?" the young lady finally asked. She set her nail file down next to the phone and turned bored eyes on Sniffle.

"I need to get some information on a birth, an adoption, and on two or three deaths. How do I proceed?"

"Do you want to fill out a request for assisted research or do you want direct access?" the woman asked robot-like.

"Direct access, if that means I look through the files myself."

"Yes, it does. I need you to fill out these forms and this one and this one and sign on that one twice."

"What would I have to do to get help?"

"Fill out these forms plus two others and come back for the results in six to ten weeks or when you receive notification that the data is either ready or not available."

Sniffle filled and signed and dated and affirmed that she was the person she claimed to be. She shook her head as she was asked if the signature she had just signed was in fact her own. "You just watched me sign it," she said softly. "It has to be my own."

"Not necessarily," the woman said cryptically and then asked for identification.

"You have a point," Sniffle said to her.

She motioned to Sniffle to follow her and led the way to a huge room crammed with file cabinets, shelves of free-standing boxes, one row of microfilm machines, and in the far corner two coin-operated copying machines. "Used to be you couldn't come back here, but now you can. If you need official copies of anything, you need to see one of the registrar's clerks. Births, deaths, and adoptions, you said?" Sniffle nodded, surprised that the woman remembered. Perhaps this woman was also more competent than she appeared. "Birth information in those sections on the north wall; adoption records may be with birth certificates or may be in a separate file over there– see?" she pointed. "Adoptions from out of state locations will be in the separate files. All death records are on the south wall. Recorder of Deeds is down the hall if you need more specific information." She said all this rapidly and mechanically and then went back to her place behind the counter and, since no one else was there, made a phone call and once again picked up her nail file.

"At least she thinks I understood all that," Sniffle said, taking a deep breath and wondering where to start. "With Vanessa," she said out loud. "Let's learn about that adoption. Then I'll move on to the others."

At four that afternoon, Nosemitt and Vanessa returned from both visiting Walter and attempted shopping. They found Sniffle sound asleep in the living room with a heap of notes on the floor next to her purse and shoes and a chocolate bar wrapper. "Looks like she found out quite a lot," Nosemitt said, sorry she had not gone along. The visit with Walter had been virtually useless. He had been very happy to see his niece but too tired to talk. Emmaline's tea had been some peculiar flavor that seemed to resemble tree bark dipped in bleach, and Nosemitt's eyes were still burning. She and Vanessa had gone together to do some grocery shopping but the shelves had been depleted earlier in the day. Dinner tonight was going to depend on what might be in the freezer. Maybe she ought to go see what the choices were; no need to sit around waiting for Sniffle to wake up. She went out to the kitchen to help Vanessa but found her on the phone. Restless, Nosemitt went out for a walk.

Mistake! She had walked for all of a minute when Olga came hurrying out to her, waving again and calling to her to wait. She waited. "Hello, hello, hello again," Olga bubbled. "I want your opinion on my newest recipe in memory of my dear neighbor."

Nosemitt braced herself for the worst. How many people in the world would honor a murder victim with a new recipe? Why did she have to bump into that one person? "Oh?" was all she managed.

"Yes, indeed! It was going to be a mystery mousse, a delicate little ripened cheesy custardy thing with fresh blueberries and honey and lemon, but I could not think what to put in for Harriet, but then I knew: rosemary for remembrance of Harriette. Well, there it is. But you know, it almost sounds like a wedding recipe. Something old and ripe, something new and fresh, something borrowed since I don't have any honey on hand, and something blue. So perhaps I will save it for a wedding; maybe Vanessa will marry one day. I still need a mystery dish. I wonder if crumb cake would do as a base."

Nosemitt, shocked by the allusion to the crumbs, expressed horror at the very idea of such a thing, but Olga merely looked puzzled. "Crumbs," Nosemitt repeated. "Crumbs would be the most horrible reminder. I cannot imagine a more devastating dish."

"I haven't the slightest idea why," Olga said, hurt. "Crumb cake makes a lovely start for some of my best breakfast creations and a number of unique salads."

"Please find something else," Nosemitt said, realizing that Olga did not know how Harriette had been found. For some reason she had imagined all the news reports carrying that awful detail. She hurried away, leaving Olga upset at the reaction to her wonderful recipe but also relieved that she would not need any honey after all. A quart of cold water would do.

Nosemitt walked rapidly to clear her head; she was very curious about what Sniffle had found but would not ask while Vanessa was present. On her second trip around the block, she was surprised to see Sniffle coming out of the house. She even had both gloves and her earmuffs. "You're willing to walk?" Nosemitt asked, pleased.

"Yes, but not toward Olga's."

"No problem. What did you find out? I could hardly stand the suspense."

"Well, you were half right, as is half usual," Sniffle said. "Usually you are completely right of course."

"Of course. What?"

"There is indeed a bastard in the family, but it is not Marvin or Dustin; it is Vanessa. I have never thought of women as bastards, though. Is there another word?"

"I don't know, but the news shouldn't be a total surprise. I assume she was born out of wedlock to some poor woman."

"And to a well-off father. All of the twinkle in Walter's eye should have tipped us off. Vanessa is Walter's daughter."

"I guess I am surprised a little; but now that you say it, it fits. It's not a shock at all. I suppose Harriette knew that he was? And Marvin, do you think?"

"I don't know. We have a troublesome conversation ahead with

Uncle Daddy, I fear."

"Well, how does this affect anything? It makes it less likely that Walter is guilty, but I never thought he was. It just adds to the layers of secrecy."

"Funny, I thought it cleared up one or two layers. If, as Portia said, Harriette took Vanessa in without ever discussing it with Marvin, it suggests that she did so at Walter's request. And it confirms the general impression everyone gives us that Marvin hated Walter. At least now Marvin seems vindicated at least somewhat."

"Yes, but now we have to wonder if it was a request or a demand from Walter. He seems to have exercised enormous power, whether others liked it or not. We have to wonder if Walter is the source of all the restrictions on Harriette, although I think it's a safe bet that he is the source of the trust fund that prevents Vanessa from marrying. He wants to keep her his little girl."

"Well, all that is fine but I found some other very interesting information. For starters, don't you find it a little strange that Portia never wanted to know who killed her daughter?"

"Yes and no. You aren't going to tell me that Portia is the prime suspect now?"

"Not at all. But Albina Marie Kettle, aged two, died of poisoning."

"That was over twenty years ago; are you assuming that there is a link in these two murders? That's stretching it quite a lot."

"Harvester Kettle, aged fifty, was found dead in his office, poisoned. In a town that claims to have no murders or serious crime, don't you think it more than a little strange that three people in one family would all be poisoned, even though the deaths span a twenty-year period? Odder yet, the crime is not even in the files or known to the so-called homicide squad."

"Very strange, but was it listed as a suicide? Anyway, Portia is the common thread. Perhaps insanity. Perhaps she lost her child to an unknown murderer and, as time passed, came to hate her husband. Perhaps she harbored resentment toward Harriette and Vanessa all through the years and finally acted out her revenge."

"A possible scenario," Sniffle conceded, "but then are you the one accusing Portia? I don't think she dragged Harriette out of her house and deposited her in a gutter somewhere. She has trouble enough walking on her own. I think we need to find out whether Harvey Kettle was considered a suicide or not. The death certificate states poison as the cause but not by whom."

"And what else did you learn while I was sipping the vilest tea ever made?"

"You'll be relieved to know that Roger's first wife did not die of poisoning. She had a rare liver disease."

"Yes, it is kind of a relief, isn't it? For us, I mean."

"And you'll also be happy to know that Roger junior and Vanessa really did get married a few weeks ago. It's duly and newly recorded."

"And Roger and Harriette?"

"Nothing listed. Do we want to ask about it or let it go? Does it matter?"

"Credibility. Wouldn't you say it matters for that? He needs it more than ever."

"Oh? So you did learn something after all?"

"I almost forgot after all your news. We think we know the weapon, and it doesn't look good for Roger. Two blue cushions from Harriette's couch are missing. No one had noticed until today."

"Two are missing? I wonder why two."

"Do you get the same feeling that I do, that whoever did it had some paradoxical sort of concern about her? Why put a jacket on her if she was suffocated in her own home?"

"Well, is that definite?" Sniffle asked. "Maybe she went out for a walk after she got home."

"And was attacked by someone with two of her own cushions? It's one more detail that makes me wonder about Roger. We know he cared for her; but no matter how we feel about him, he is strongly on Sergeant Bradley's radar now."

"I can more easily accept that she was attacked by someone waiting when she got back from a walk. I don't like thinking about this at all. It was slightly easier when she was found in a remote street. To contemplate it being done right there in her home by someone who knew her, not to mention someone who loved her, is too much. No, I can't deal with that."

"Roger senior is coming over again tonight for dinner," Nosemitt said. "We can at least ask him about the marriage. If he sticks with the story that they got married anywhere in the state, we know he's misleading us, to say the least."

"What if Vanessa stays in the room? We can't ask him unless she leaves."

"One of us can get her into the kitchen. That's the least of the concerns."

They completed the third circling of the block, changing the subject and mood by the description of Mystery Mousse, and then they went back to the house to help Vanessa with dinner. Plans to speak privately with Roger had to be postponed; Uncle Walter had been brought over to join them for dinner. Emmaline had dropped him and a roast off. It was clear that of those present he was the only one happy about being with them.

"I told Aunt Emmaline that tonight was not convenient," Vanessa whispered to Nosemitt while cutting up lettuce for a salad. "She looks so meek and the next thing you know, you have been bulldozed. And I hope you can eat leather.'"

"I know that bulldozed feeling," Nosemitt said, avoiding thoughts of eating leather. She got out tomatoes and carrots to slice for the salad and was looking for dressings to set out when it suddenly occurred to her that Emmaline might know quite a bit. Possibly she would know about Vanessa's adoption, which might or might not be of relevance; and, even if not, she could give them a greater insight into Walter. Roger had made it clear that he would not speak for Walter's actions. When they took Walter back, perhaps they could arrange for one of them to speak with his sister.

Roger arrived and was not pleased at all to see the old man. He managed to nod curtly in Walter's direction and then went out to the kitchen to offer to keep Vanessa company. Sniffle suggested that Nosemitt detain all the others in the kitchen as long as possible so that she could let Walter know that they were aware of his true relation to Vanessa. Nosemitt thought it better to wait until after dinner, which would be strained enough as it was. "Perhaps this will terminate it," Sniffle suggested. "He might wish to leave."

"And if he doesn't? Then what?"

"Then it's a little more strained." Nosemitt thought about it and finally agreed, provided there was one change. She preferred to be present too and suggested that she simply tell Vanessa and Roger that they needed some time to speak with the uncle alone. At last the plain truth was the easiest solution, and both women were relieved. They also agreed that they needed to make it clear to Walter that they were not against him.

Walter was pleased to have them come sit with him in the living room, although his pleasure quickly faded when they reported their findings. He smiled weakly as he assured them that they were indeed continuing to live up to his expectations. "But I would be happier if you were making headway in finding the murderer," he said. "I had not anticipated having my own secret revealed, but I assure you it had nothing to do with the crime in question."

"No, we are not at all trying to make such a suggestion," Nosemitt said emphatically.

"Still, it does provide you with a motive, which the police will probably question you about," Sniffle pointed out. "That is our present concern, that they will see a motive."

"What would it be?" he asked.

"Since you did not know that Vanessa could not inherit all the jewelry," Nosemitt said, "they will possibly conclude that you saw a chance for your daughter to come into a great deal of money."

"I've no need to be concerned about that," he said calmly. "There is a substantial trust set aside for her."

"With conditions that might be difficult for her to abide by," Sniffle said.

"You know of that too?" he asked, surprised again. "Who could possibly have told you that?"

"The important thing," Sniffle said, ignoring his question, "is that the police will see a motive, whether you do or not."

"Yes, I imagine they will."

"It is an odd restriction to place on a daughter," Sniffle said softly. "Did you need to tie her to you so tightly?"

"No, there you have misinterpreted my actions," he said, sighing heavily. "I made those restrictions for her safety, not to tie her to me. Vanessa's natural mother became very seriously ill during the pregnancy and died within a few weeks of giving birth. I learned that the odds favored Vanessa's developing the same disease, a painful but quickly progressing disorder that is commonly called polyfatalis– a grim name for a disease in which any of many symptoms could be the cause of death. It does not show up until one is in one's early twenties; and if she does have it, the odds of her children having it increase. I did not want her to marry without knowing if she had it or was a likely carrier."

"But she knows nothing of any of this," Nosemitt said. "Shouldn't you have prepared her?"

"Yes, now I suppose I should have. I just always assumed that Harriette would take care of it when the time came. I never expected to outlive my niece."

"Why did you put restrictions on Harriette herself?" Sniffle asked, not knowing absolutely that he had. Roger had hinted at it, but it was not clear.

"You mean my opposing Mr. Lescouth?" he asked. They nodded. "There were several factors. One is purely selfish; I did not want Vanessa to prefer him, but that would never have been an acceptable reason to oppose Harriette's marrying him. I was far more concerned about his son and Vanessa; I thought if I could keep Harriette and Roger apart, it would keep Vanessa and young Roger apart as well."

"I don't think life works that way," Sniffle said.

"You are aware of their mutual interest?" Nosemitt cautiously asked.

"I am aware of a great deal," he said. They could not tell how much to read into that. "But the son carries a genetic predisposition to serious illness too. I believed their chances for healthy children were slim."

"I am beginning to suspect that Fredricka was not the one most concerned about the gene pool," Sniffle said. "Is anyone free from the hazards of heredity? But also it strikes me that Vanessa and young Roger might have had less interest in each other had they become brother and sister."

"You do find a different angle every time, don't you?" Walter said, shaking his head. "I suppose that I may borrow your phrase and say that I don't think life works that way all the time either. But as to gene pools, yes, Fredricka and I had a few things in common, including an unfortunate selection of mates. I at least did not repeat the error."

"You have indicated that you have 'sources,'" Nosemitt said; "paid informers, you mean?"

"That sounds more sinister than it is," he said. "I have placed young people in positions where they could be of use. It started with my niece long ago– Harriette and I had a close working relationship in all the years she was at the newspaper. I provided her with information to help her do the community a great deal of good, and sometimes I would ask little favors of her."

"Adopting Vanessa is not a little favor," Sniffle said. "Especially if her husband objected. Or was not even asked."

"No, that was not a little favor. I had in mind having her do things comparable to my getting jobs for friends and relatives of hers. Her nephew Fred is on my payroll; Dustin started out working for me but saw much larger opportunities elsewhere; at her request I got young Roger his first job before he went to Blackburn, but he was not interested in serving as a channel for me. She asked me to find work for a young woman who had been fired unfairly from the paper's advertising department, and I did. Those are my little favors for her, but, for example, she would send me likely candidates for my information network; she would pass certain kinds of stories along to me before the paper carried them. She helped make certain arrangements for me. We saw ourselves as a team, as I believe I have made clear. As for Marvin's objections to adopting Vanessa, that marriage was a divorce waiting to happen. I did not feel at all responsible for causing it. She should never have married him in the first place."

"You know," Nosemitt said, feeling that there was no more to be learned about little favors, "Roger senior has been implicated strongly because, as you and Vanessa told us, he was the last person known to have been with Harriette. Yet we cannot believe he did it. Do you really think he is the one?"

Walter studied the backs of his hands for a while and then looked far away. "I don't know," he said at last. "I do believe he loved her, and I know she did love him. If he did it, then I will have to ask myself if I drove him to it. But wouldn't it seem more likely that he would have come after me? So I suppose I do know what I think. I think he did not do it."

"I suppose we think the same," Sniffle said.

Vanessa entered the room to ask if they were ready to come to dinner. "If my plate is poisoned and I keel over," Walter whispered, "you will need to rethink this matter." Nosemitt could never quite adjust to his ability to joke about the matter, even though she was accustomed to Sniffle's weird way of coping, but nothing had a chance to happen– Roger had made his excuses to Vanessa and had left. After a quiet dinner in which the young woman heard and accepted the news of her birth with astonishing calm, Vanessa took Walter back to Aunt Emmaline's.

"At least," Vanessa would say much, much later, "I still can call her Aunt."

Thursday, January 18

When they met with Lesley Duke at ten in the morning to go over some of the new findings, they were surprised to learn that she was down in the basement pistol range. They were sent down there

95

and found her blistering the target with more than bullets. Muttering angrily and swearing vehemently the entire time she was shooting, she did not notice them for a while. When she did, she flushed a very bright red and put the gun back in its holster.

"Shot someone quite thoroughly dead," Sniffle observed.

"He'll never notice," Duke said. She put on her heavy jacket and invited them to ride with her through the park. "Bird patrol," she explained; "another batch of little winged corpses and the chief sends me out to collect them. We can talk out in the open air; it will suit me to cool off."

"How many specimens do you need?" Nosemitt asked. "And what did they find out from the others?"

"Rodex, all right. Now it seems to me that you quickly pointed out what should have been an obvious connection, and is anyone but me grateful? No, instead of regarding it as the strangest but most significant clue we have so far, the chief acts as if it is a ridiculous suggestion and tells me to spend more time tracking down the bird killer and let the men handle the real crime. The men– meaning Art and the chief– aren't handling anything either."

"So it's the chief you riddled," Sniffle said. "Serves him right."

They drove into the park to the playground and got out to hunt for the evidence. A few preschoolers and their mothers were at the swings, and one little girl wandered over to the drinking fountain. She came running back quickly, pointing excitedly to the fountain. "There are this many dead birds!" she called out excitedly, holding up a mittened hand. No one knew how many. Duke went over with a large plastic bag and a pair of work gloves and found three birds at the foot of the fountain. Breadcrumbs were all around.

"It would be nice to solve this without the men," Duke said wistfully.

"We've been wondering if there is quite a bit more to solve than meets the official eye reading the official reports," Nosemitt said.

"Oh? Like what?" Duke asked, definitely interested.

"Well, you say there have been no murders for years," Sniffle said, "but according to the death certificate for Harvester Kettle, he was poisoned. I wonder if you know anything more about that?"

"Before my time. Must have been suicide," Duke said, "or it would surely be in the homicide file."

"Or a cover-up of some sort," Nosemitt suggested. "There's a lot of poison in one family."

"More?" Duke asked.

"Over twenty years ago little Albina Marie Kettle was found poisoned in the woods behind the house. It seems the family is fatally involved with Rodex or one of its variations."

"Twenty years ago! You aren't suggesting that the same person is responsible for all three murders?"

"Why rule it out?" Sniffle asked. "If we consider that the murderer might be in the family... ?"

"Well, why murder a child?" Duke asked. "And what do you think the motive for poisoning Harvester Kettle was?"

"We don't know," Nosemitt said, "but we think there could be a common thread. Once again, the jewelry could be the link. Perhaps at one time Albina was the intended beneficiary; perhaps in later years Harvester tried to get his mother to change her will. There are so many possibilities when family wealth is at stake. There could be motives we've no way of knowing."

"All true," Duke conceded, "and in fact I haven't made much progress tracking Marvin or Dustin. I keep running into a brick wall."

"Perhaps your chief has motives of his own?" Sniffle suggested.

Duke looked at her. "Like what?"

"I don't know. I just keep wondering why he wanted you to go after Vanessa but refuses to allow a connection with the bird murders. Why, if Harvey was poisoned, was there no homicide investigation at the time? Why, since there seems definitely to be a drug dealing scheme involving the car agency, has there been no effort to uncover it and arrest anyone?"

"You're right– the chief keeps us on Vanessa and Walter and says he has others working on the drug case; but we can't figure out who. I do think if Mr. Kettle left any kind of suicide note that here in this community no one would question it. But still, the chief thought I was right to check into Marvin and Dustin but made it clear that I should concentrate on the other two. It makes no sense to keep everything in separate compartments like that."

"Until you start to question everything," Nosemitt said. "Look at the overall picture."

"It is just like Nosemitt," Sniffle said, "to want to see the overall picture of separate compartments."

"We haven't yet seen one," Duke said. "We have a public figure murdered; she is the heiress to valuable jewelry, but she also posed a threat to a suspected drug ring. She was in a position to expose their activities but did not live to do so."

"That is part of the picture," Nosemitt said. "Now consider that her son was probably part of the drug ring; her ex-husband may or may not have had a part behind the scenes. The owner of the paper in which she wanted to expose the drug activity is the former owner of the car agency; does he have an investment there still? Is he involved at all? Why did he refuse to publish the story?"

"Given all this," Sniffle said, "who has more motive– Vanessa and Walter or any of several people connected with the drugs?"

"Add in this new angle," Nosemitt suggested. "What if your chief has been paid all along to look the other way?"

"Then he puts the least experienced officers on the case," Sniffle said.

"But then one of them runs into unexpected help from outside sources," Duke said.

"Which infuriates the chief," Nosemitt went on.

"Who keeps the detective busy gathering dead birds," Sniffle said.

"And then of course," Nosemitt added, "we may be off the scent completely."

"Stick with me," Duke said; "the scent I'm on is strong." She sealed the plastic bags a little more tightly and carried them to the trunk of her car.

"Look, Moonbeam and his friend are back," Sniffle said, pointing to the familiar shiny black car that was pulling out of one of the parking spaces near the empty tennis courts. As the car drove past them, they could hear radio music blaring and could see a skinny girl with close-cropped red hair clinging to the driver. Hanging from the rear-view mirror, where one might expect furry dice, was a brassiere that clearly could not have belonged to the redhead.

"Charming," Sniffle said.

"Another nice touch on the license plate," Nosemitt pointed out. The eloquent plate said E-REDDY. "And I'll bet he is."

"I recognize the girl," Duke said, smiling. "When I went over to Marvin's to ask some questions, she was just leaving. I think she's the babysitter."

"I hope so," Nosemitt said. "At least, maybe I hope so."

"Did you learn anything from Marvin?" Sniffle asked.

"Not especially. He says that he had occasional communication with his ex-wife, more often from her. He says he didn't call her much at all. When I asked what she would call about, he indicated that she would ask about Dustin mainly. She was worried that he had taken on a job that was too demanding."

"Those were Marvin's words?" Nosemitt asked.

"Yes. He said that he always told her that Dustin could handle anything and to quit worrying about him, that he was a grown man who did not need to be looked after as if he were still three."

"Do you have any information linking Marvin with the auto agency?" Nosemitt asked.

"No, do you?"

"Walter suggested that possibility. It's clear that a great many complex relationships exist within this family, that everyone knows a great deal more than they're saying, and that none of them really does know who killed Harriette, except the murderer of course."

"I'd like to be able to draw all the information together," Duke said. "If it turns out that the alleged drug ring is responsible for the murder, though, I wonder how or if Birdman fits in. Maybe he doesn't."

"We still don't know for sure that he is not a she," Sniffle said. "I think you ought to have a chat of your own with Portia."

"You can't think she's out killing birds and people," Nosemitt said. "I thought we had ruled her out."

"No, we just don't think she is physically up to it; she could have been involved. She could have planned at least parts of it all. I'd like to know more about the Blackburns too … and the Waldos. I would not be surprised at this point to learn that everyone is related and all of them had a hand in everything."

"I don't mind talking with Portia Kettle," Duke said; "but I doubt that I'll learn anything more than you already got."

"Do we have any justification for a meeting with this man, Carl Blackburn?" Sniffle asked Nosemitt, who could not think of any.

"I'll tackle that one too," Duke said, getting out her notebook and jotting names down. "I don't have to clear everything with the chief ahead of time. You have me very suspicious of him now; I keep thinking of how many times he said to suspect everyone and then would reject as absurd some of my suggestions on how I wanted to proceed."

"How about the Waldo brothers?" Nosemitt said. Duke wrote their names down.

"Is there anyone we should be seeing?" Sniffle asked. "Emmaline, I think, but who else?"

"I wonder if that babysitter for the Kettles could tell us anything about Marvin's comings and goings," Nosemitt said. "I wonder if she babysat the night of the murder and, if so, where Marvin and his wife were. Want to add her to your list?" Duke nodded and added the name.

"I'm glad to have all your suggestions," Duke said. "Neither Art nor I knew where to start, but I do wish I didn't now think that that is why we were put on this case."

"It's good for us to feel that we aren't simply useless and in the way," Nosemitt said. "I still don't completely understand why Walter hired us in the first place."

"He did say that he needed outside objective agents," Sniffle said. "He didn't trust the police to do the job." Duke could hardly argue.

"I think I have a full afternoon's work ahead of me," she said. "Why don't you meet me here tomorrow at noon and we'll see what has come of it all."

"Fine," Nosemitt agreed. "Maybe we'll go visit Walter and Emmaline, if it's all right with them."

They knocked on the door and waited. At first there was no answer and so Sniffle rang the bell. They were about to leave when they thought they heard a tiny voice asking who was there. The voice seemed to come from above, though, and they looked up. For a moment they could see no one and hear nothing, but then an upstairs window opened and Emmaline's voice came through a little more clearly: "I said, Who is it?" Nosemitt stepped back several feet and came into Emmaline's range of vision. "Oh!" she said; "I'll be down quite soon."

"How long is quite soon?" Sniffle asked Nosemitt softly. "You know her better than I do."

"I would guess within five minutes," Nosemitt said. "She is very slow on the stairs."

Emmaline made it down in four minutes, breathing hard. They apologized for disturbing her. "No bother at all, my pets," she gently wheezed. "Come into the parlor and sit while I fix us some tea."

"No need," Nosemitt insisted, but Emmaline was gone surprisingly quickly. The two somewhat precarious investigators studied the parlor more closely. Within its dark walls and all over its multiple carpets the odds and ends of collected furniture gleamed almost luridly. The regal purple chair that Walter had sat in during their first visit was now covered with a cerise afghan. A stiff and uncomfortable loveseat in the middle of the room had been upholstered originally in a forest green brocade but now boasted chocolate brown corduroy slip covers that had slipped more than they covered. Four throw pillows, apparently made by Emmaline from kits that had lost their directions, graced the corners. They were lumpy and misshapen and their designs had faded in a misguided washing.

"You know," Sniffle said, "I begin to understand why you've been in a hurry to finish our waiting room. This is almost painful."

"There is no almost about it!" Nosemitt said. "And we have to finish that room the minute we get back."

"I do believe we were given yet another false story; I really don't think Walter is Vanessa's father; I'll bet you Emmaline is her mother. Anyway, they are definitely blood relatives."

They heard the squeaky sound of the wayward wheels on the teacart and a few meek exclamations from Emmaline as the cart took a header into a wall. Something fell to the floor and broke, but fortunately it was only a saucer. Cart and driver entered the parlor at a peculiar angle, and Nosemitt hurried over to help.

"I believe Walter is still napping," Emmaline whispered.

"That's perfectly all right," Nosemitt said, carrying three cups and two saucers to one of the many little tables. "We were hoping we could chat with you for a while."

"How nice, how lovely. I would be delighted. I'm afraid I no longer have many topics left in my repertoire. There have been so few opportunities. I am able to discuss needlework with some small expertise and then teas. I do not have a small knowledge of teas. This one, for example, is one of my own blending and is quite the thing for bruises of the feet."

"It is that specialized?" Sniffle asked, incredulous.

"Oh, I think not," Emmaline said with a genuine horror at having misspoken. "I myself am frequently bruising my feet and so can testify from experience that this tea makes a wonderful soak. It is also tasty, however. I use much less salt when I am going to imbibe it."

Sniffle set her cup down firmly, and even Nosemitt was quite determined to be too full for even a sip. "Actually," Nosemitt said, "we did have another topic in mind. Perhaps you know that your brother invited us–"

"Yes, he told me the other day to expect you, that he was looking forward to your visit, but he did not tell me that you were coming today."

"True, but he invited us to come to St. Edwards for a very specific reason. Not just here to see him, but to do some work for him."

"How kind of him, I'm sure," Emmaline said with a smile. "He is always doing good. He must have known you were wanting to do some work?"

"We were, yes, but what I am getting at is that he hired us to learn more about Harriette's death. The circumstances, the facts, the details."

"The murderer," Sniffle said, steeling herself to the word.

"So sad," Emmaline murmured, "but these thing seem to happen more and more these days. I'm sure you will do a splendid job. Tea?"

"Thank you, no," Nosemitt said. "Many details have already come to light. For example, we now know that Vanessa was adopted and that her real father is—"

"Oh, that old story! I never believed it for a minute."

"Which old story do you mean?" Sniffle asked.

"Why, the Vanessa story of course. I ask you, does it make sense to you that Walter would have gone to Chicago to adopt a baby girl for Harriette to raise? Really, does he take me for a nincompoop?"

"So, what do you think?" Nosemitt asked.

"What do I think? It's as plain as the hands on your face," she said. "Oh, excuse me, that's what I say to the clock sometimes. I do speak to things; one does in my situation. Anyway, it's as plain as whatever you want on your face. She's Walter's daughter. There, I hope I haven't shocked you."

"Actually, we knew that already," Nosemitt said gently.

"Well, good for you. I suppose Walter thinks we women are fools, but we see things he thinks are quite secret. Men can be so blind."

"True," Sniffle agreed, looking around the room and wondering what all she herself was missing. They could all be blind.

"So then, you probably don't know any of the details of Vanessa's real mother, I suppose," Nosemitt said.

"Only that the mother had some fatal illness that Vanessa could inherit. I imagine Walter might have made that up, but he has taken great pains to see to it that there was plenty of money for her if she should need prolonged or expensive medical care. I think that part must be true."

"It occurs to me," Sniffle said, "that you might know the Kettle family fairly well."

"I know some of their doings," she said primly. "I know a few things."

"Do you remember an Albina Marie Kettle? A child a bit older than Vanessa? She was Harvester and Portia's daughter."

"Albina Marie? That family was a great one for repeating names. Albina Marie. Oh, Albina Marie! That poor little girl they found in the woods?"

"Yes. Do you know anything about the circumstances?"

"Does anyone? What a terrible thing that was. You know, I think Harvester never stopped grieving for her. I know that he took his own life after years of grieving for his daughter."

"He definitely committed suicide?" Nosemitt asked.

"Who knows from definite?" Emmaline asked, sipping her less salty tea. "Some assumed suicide, said there was a note, never published of course. Portia grieved too, but she took a different path. Harvester had become more and more active in all kinds of hobbies; Portia spent most of her time being ill. And then, after Harvester's death, Portia had to come out of her cocoon to try to run the business. She hated it, you know, and eventually she sold it for a very good price."

"They have a son," Sniffle said. "What is he like?"

"Fred? Oh, he's just your run-of-the-mill spoiled young man. Used to hunt and fish with his father. I don't know what he does for a living. I believe he still lives at home, although I may be mistaken. He never went to college, probably never finished high school. I seem to have it in mind that he had some kind of reading problem or learning problem. I know he dropped out of school several times, but I don't know if Harvester ever got him to finish or not. Harvester would have been the only one who could have made the boy do anything. Portia was always terrified of losing him too; she let him do as he pleased."

As they drove away, Sniffle suddenly suggested that they stop at the newspaper office again. "Don't tell me you haven't forsaken Herbert Molecott," Nosemitt snorted.

"No, he wasn't on my mind at all. I was curious about Harvester's obituary. I wonder what it said about cause of death."

"Probably nothing," Nosemitt said. "Why would they be interested in announcing anything? And if they did publish something specific, wouldn't everyone know?"

"Yes, I suppose. But let's look anyway. Maybe there will be something there."

They found someone at *The Edwardian Times* who was willing

to take a minute to conduct them to the basement where a damp room filled with file cabinets served as newspaper morgue, and an older woman wearing a yellow sweater with the sleeves worn and raveling served as librarian. She was surprised to see them, having met the Nosemitt woman after the memorial service and having been told that she and her friend were just visiting for a while, staying with Vanessa for the first few difficult days. Nosemitt felt awkward but Sniffle filled the gap. "We had quite a bit of time on our hands and thought we would like to catch up on a lot of odds and ends of news from the past several years." It was the truth and all were pleased.

"Where would you like to begin?" the woman asked them. They thought up several time periods, including the few days on either side of Harvester's death. Melba, the librarian, went slowly through several file cabinets and brought them stacks of newspapers. "We've heard rumors of microfilm out there in the bigger world," she sighed; "you'd think we could modernize. I'm sorry you'll get so filthy from these old papers."

"I love them; I prefer them," Nosemitt beamed. "Microfilm is all right, but I prefer the real thing." They went out in the hall where there was a small table and some chairs and began reading. Melba found a couple of pairs of thin latex gloves for them. Nosemitt put one pair on and soon was having a good time rooting through very dated advertisements and social news. Fairly quickly she found the obituary.

KETTLE, HARVESTER FREDRICK beloved husband
of Portia Lockett Kettle; dear father of Fredrick and the late
Albina Marie Kettle; dear son of Fredricka P. and the late
Horatio M. Kettle; our dear brother, brother-in-law, uncle, and
cousin. No flowers. Contributions may be made to the
Humane Society of St. Edwards. Private service. No visitation.

"Nothing newsworthy here," Nosemitt said.

"Here's an article from the next day," Sniffle said, reading it out loud. " *'Friends of animals and people alike are mourning the untimely death of Harvester Kettle. Better known to one and all as Harvey, he was a devoted sportsman and proud advocate of healthier and more sanitary conditions for animals at home or in kennels. Harvey developed the KettleKennel, 'a dandy little haven for your hound'; the KettleKatKastle, 'a palace for your puss'; and the KettleKage, 'a veritable paradise for your bird'. He established and wrote the original charter for the Sensible Hunting Club, an organization devoted to the hunter who knows the value of life and who voluntarily restricts his activities to the legal and selective shooting of small numbers of designated targets. Harvey set up on his own property a wild life preserve in memory of his young daughter who tragically died there many years ago. He is survived by his wife, the former Portia Lockett, his son Fredrick, his mother Fredricka Kettle, and several brothers and sisters, nephews, nieces, and cousins.'"*

"So?" Nosemitt said.

"I guess I find it strange that a man devoted to a wildlife preserve and safe conditions for animals and limitations on hunting would poison himself out of grief that his daughter died years and years earlier."

"I don't think it's entirely unusual," Nosemitt said. "Besides, we don't know what his reason was. Maybe it was to feel united with his daughter. You're going on Emmaline's theory."

"No, I'm questioning it. Also, would a man dedicated to shooting kill himself with poison?"

"I have no idea. Why not?"

"Maybe he would; it just rings funny to me. You know, live by the gun, die by the gun."

"I believe that usually says 'swords,'" Nosemitt pointed out. "Next you'll be thinking that because Emmaline said 'hands on your face' she must be the one who suffocated Harriette."

"Probably not," Sniffle said; "I understand talking to things."

They read several more items in the papers Melba had brought them, thanked her for her help and left, bumping into a perfectly coiffed but confused-looking woman carrying a miniature poodle into the cramped quarters. "Melba, Melba, what shall I do with Céstlavie while I have my hair done? I can't think where she could stay."

Melba sighed heavily. "Really, Mrs. Blackburn, I have asked you to find some other person to help you out. The dog is not happy here. I told you she is always wanting to make a puddle on the files."

"You know that is a friendly gesture on her part," Mrs. Blackburn said. "You are my only hope. By the way, darling Céstlavie is to have next week's shampoo and trim at the same time I have mine, but it simply could not be arranged this time. There, there, my little precious, you will be quite the beauty whenever your appointment is. All the little people in the shop simply adore cutting my baby's hair and shampooing her. They positively fight for the privilege."

Sniffle could hardly contain her disgust, and Nosemitt feared that she herself would do accidental damage to the files if they lingered. They waved goodbye to Melba, who looked jealous of their freedom. As Nosemitt and Sniffle left the building, they saw a highly polished navy car with a uniformed driver waiting at the curb right in front of the doors.

"She has a built-in staff and she descends upon the employees of the paper to watch her dog?" Sniffle fumed. "Perhaps now we know why someone in advertising lost her job unfairly. I thought this kind of thing died out years ago!"

"Apparently not in St. Edwards," Nosemitt said. "Céstlavie Blackburn– I doubt that he lives in a KettleKennel."

"Probably it hasn't died out anywhere," Sniffle said sadly.

Friday, January 19

They met Lesley Duke at the park the next day; and, as it was very pleasant for January, especially after the icy rain that had been falling off and on since their arrival, they brought lunch with them. The three women sat on one of the park benches, its paint faded and peeling, and watched as the usual small assortment of three or four preschoolers arrived with a couple of moms. Duke had already made a quick search and had found no additional feathered corpses. She relaxed over her hot coffee and lukewarm hamburgers picked up at the Burger Quik. "Whom all did you get to see yesterday?" Nosemitt asked her.

"I tried to make contact with that redhead in the car, but the best I could do was get her name from Vanessa's stepmother. Candace Applewhite, high school student. That's it for now. I did ask Mrs. Kettle if she and her husband were out the night of the murder. Do you believe it– she asked what murder? Anyway, she got out her calendar and, yes, they were out that evening. They were at a party given by Frank and Clarissa Waldo. They were there until shortly after midnight and then went out to a nightclub with another couple, the Harrison Dibbles."

"Dibble?" Nosemitt said. "Wasn't that the newest Mrs. Kettle's maiden name?" Sniffle wasn't sure.

"Yes, you're right," Duke said; "she did say he was her brother."

"Very nice set of alibis provided for each other," Sniffle said. "The Waldos are taken care of by hosting the party; Marvin and Harriet are there; afterwards her brother is their witness to being at a nightclub.

Was Dustin there too? For that matter, was Chief Bigguns?"

"In fact, yes to Dustin," Duke said, checking her notes. "I did ask her for all the names of the guests she could remember. The woman is not a mental giant, but she did recall a few and mentioned the Blackburns. I think she said most of the agency staff seemed to be there."

"Then did she mention young Roger Lescouth?" Sniffle asked.

"No, but that doesn't mean he wasn't."

"Considering the time, he probably wasn't," Nosemitt observed. "We can be pretty sure that he and Vanessa were at the Park-Jackson apartment."

"Check," Duke said, making more notes. Sniffle wondered if she were telling them to check further or if she would or if she meant it as an okay. Little ambiguities often bothered her, but she decided to ignore this one.

"Did she indicate the reason for the party, or was it just a holiday kind of thing?" she asked.

"No reason given."

"What kind of reason were you expecting?" Nosemitt asked.

"Well, it's not as though I imagined that the Waldos said, 'Let's throw a party because then we'll all have an alibi when Harriette gets murdered tonight.' I just wondered if there was anything to celebrate– a major transaction or something. Walter thinks Marvin is involved, which now seems more likely; but I wonder about the Dibbles. What is their connection?"

"That I can tell you," Duke said happily. "I did finally do some extra family research of my own. Harrison Dibble's wife was Leonora Waldo. If Mr. Wrothwell is right about Marvin being involved at least financially, then it seems reasonable to think that his wife's family is the connection. Perhaps they invited him to join a family venture."

"Good work!" Nosemitt said, failing to suppress a note of surprise. Duke did not care; she had surprised herself as well and had reached the point not only of liking the two women but also of wanting to be allied with them. As far as she was concerned, St. Edwards was not going to become a hotbed of major crime. She was less ambitious than Art Bradley and had job security as long as she wanted it, despite Chief Bigguns's objections. She had a couple of connections of her own, and they too involved family.

"So now we have a larger picture filling in," Sniffle said. "An interesting canvas, so to speak. We have at least as a strong possibility a drug ring operating out of the Waldos' agency. They have a network of investors, mostly from family or influential associates like Carleton Blackburn. They have a team of salesmen who may or may not know what is going on but who create an appearance of legitimacy. One of their investors may well be Marvin Kettle, with the probable addition of his son Dustin, who may be involved in other ways besides investing. They may or may not have the police chief in their pocket, giving them local protection at least. In comes Harriette– and Walter, we'd have to say– with the threat of exposure. Carleton Blackburn protects them at the first level, but Harriette presses to investigate and publish. Herb Molecott advises her, possibly on behalf of his boss, Blackburn, that what she wants to do is dangerous to her and her family. He may or may not be involved beyond speaking for his boss."

"And," Nosemitt continued, "all of this puts us squarely back to the likelihood that someone involved in this scheme is responsible directly or indirectly for the murder of Harriette Kettle. But we haven't even an inkling as to who actually did the deed. We are overrun with potential motives; and yet, for a small community, St. Edwards is chock-full of suspects."

"I still think we should be looking for someone sadistic enough to kill innocent birds," Sniffle said.

"Innocent birds," Nosemitt repeated. "Innocent birds. Harriette. Perhaps Harvester directly or indirectly. Remotely, Albina Marie. And then of course pigeons and sparrows and all the others."

"Ducks," Duke said grimly, as two little boys came dragging a dead duck from the edge of the pond. She went over to them and asked to see the duck, which they held out to her like a trophy.

"Dead," one said.

"I don't think you should be carrying it," Duke told them. "It may have been poisoned; you need to make sure those gloves and mittens get thoroughly washed. Tell your moms right away."

All three women went to the pond shore and looked for crumbs or other telltale signs of poisoning. They found a small scatter of what looked like cracker crumbs floating and bobbing a few feet out. Duke found a small branch with a few dead leaves clinging to it and raked the crumbs back in. Several stuck to the leaves. She got a plastic bag from the supply in her car to take everything to the lab. As she was leaving, Nosemitt suggested that Duke might want to check with Mrs. Waldo and get a guest list for that fatal night.

"Of course," she sighed. "I should have done that already."

"With all the crumbs so close to the edge," Sniffle said, "wouldn't you think they had to be thrown in recently?" She shuddered but looked with Nosemitt for footprints, finding only some elongated scraped tracks, as if someone had not taken steps but had slid along. There were no tread marks or other distinguishing features in the tracks. Was he or she still hanging around? She shaded her eyes against the winter glare to scan for a figure amid the trees. A figure amid the trees— that presumably was what had been present the day Albina Marie went into the woods. But who would have let her, so little, so young, wander in the woods alone? It did not seem at all likely to Sniffle that the toddler had been off in the woods without anyone. It was that time-distant puzzle that haunted Sniffle most; she was sure there was a link to now. But Portia? They really needed to talk to Portia again, though it would be so painful, so difficult. They really needed to do that, and so they drove there next.

11 Princewood Place
Portia's home

"Why would you want to bring that all up again?" Portia cried. "What possible point could it serve?" Nosemitt and Sniffle together, alternating whispered sentences, outlined why they thought that there just might be a connection. So fearful that Portia might somehow be the one and yet not believing her truly capable of it, they dreaded every word they spoke and every tear she shed. It was the poisoning, they emphasized— the inescapable fact that three people in Portia's family had been killed either by poisoning or suspected poisoning in a community that claimed to know only the most minor of crimes. That of course was not necessarily the case, but it was the claim, they said.

"But Harvester's death was not a homicide," she said quietly. "I know from the letter he left me that he took his own life."

"He indicated the reason?" Nosemitt asked. Portia nodded mutely.

"Can you tell us?" She shook her head sadly. They sat there in silence.

"Could you show us?" Sniffle asked. Portia looked up at the two women, their eyes and voices and total expression so compassionate and so tearful for her, and yet they did persist. She felt that they wanted to help and perhaps they could. Perhaps at long last someone could. She took a deep breath and went to her desk and unlocked it slowly. For a moment they tensed, not knowing whether she would bring back a note or a gun or what. They had not thought until right then that their actions could bring great danger; they had considered only how difficult an emotional situation they were going to encounter. She brought the note.

My dearest Portia,
I am so sorry to leave you this way, but I cannot go on. This week, while on our hunting trip, I learned what I had long suspected but never faced. I used to tell myself No, this act does not mean that act. What act? you will ask. It is so hard to write this.
You know, we have always tried to shield Freddy from his own actions. We have limited his hunting trips to one or two a year with me and kept the guns locked away from him ever since we found him shooting the dog. And we knew, deep down, that he had killed so many of the others. We told ourselves it was bad luck that so many died so early– this one in a trap, that one run over by a neighbor's car, although the dog had just been leashed, another poisoned.
We knew, didn't we? And now I know another terrible and totally unendurable fact that we have refused to consider: I know now certainly that little Freddy, four-year-old Freddy, took Albina into the woods and gave her poisoned candy. How do I know? He told me. Just like that, after all these years. No remorse, no sense that it was wrong. No guilt, no shame. He did it because she was smaller and he could. He wasn't angry. When have we ever known Fred to get angry? He just knew that he could do it. He rolled the candy in the insecticide out in the garage.
I cannot go on. Forgive me.

"Your son?" Sniffle said, barely audibly. Portia was crying uncontrollably and Nosemitt went to embrace her. "And yet you have said… ," but Sniffle could not finish the sentence. The image of poisoned candy in the hands of a little boy just stuck there in her mind.

"I understand why you told us you had no idea who had taken your daughter," Nosemitt said softly. "But I hope it is a release that at last you can say what you have known and kept hidden for so long. I hope it helps." Portia sobbed and sobbed.

When she finally was able to speak again, she could only say over and over, "But you see, it had to be someone smaller than he. He could not have killed Harriette. Harriette was bigger than Fred. She was bigger than Fred. My boy is not big. Harriette was bigger than Fred." She showed them his picture on the chest in the corner, and he was indeed rather slight. He looked a match for no one, and yet there was something far more disturbing than his size. The look in his eyes…

"What kind of car does he drive?" Sniffle asked, although both she and Nosemitt knew the answer.

"Why?" Portia said, wondering what his black Mustang had to do with anything. "And he's so proud of it, always polishing and cleaning and caring for it. He can be such a good boy."

"He really isn't a boy any more," Sniffle said softly. "He must be in his mid-twenties."

"Yes, but Fred is not really like most young men his age. He was always a little slower to develop. He never did well in school, you know, never really even learned to read. He said it was all a jumble to him, made no sense. All those letters squiggling around made him nervous, he said. I tried to tutor him, but he just wanted to play. But I never let him play with the guns, never."

Sniffle placed the call to Lesley Duke to inform her of this terrible connection. She had to wait a long time for the detective to come to the phone; but when Duke finally did pick up the phone, her first words to Sniffle were a real shock. "We have arrested Roger Lescouth Senior. Art went over there with the chief and a search warrant, and they found the blue cushions."

Speechless, Sniffle hung up. "I don't believe it," she said all the way to Vanessa's.

"Neither do I," Nosemitt kept responding. "There must be a mistake."

When they got to the house, they found a note taped to the inside of the front door.

Have gone to police headquarters. Will call.

They sat in silence in the living room, restless and yet in a kind of paralysis. With all the people who had some kind of perverse reason for wanting Harriette out of the way, they could not believe that the one who most wanted her alive and nearby would have killed her. "Maybe there's a perfectly good reason he had the cushions," Nosemitt said, but they could think of none.

"Maybe they were put there after the fact," Sniffle suggested. Which fact?

"I don't suppose he would have borrowed them?" Nosemitt

wondered. Probably not.

"We don't actually know that they were the weapons," Sniffle reminded them both. True.

Slowly time passed. The windows blackened; the room went dark. Nosemitt made her way to a lamp and turned it on. A few cars went past the house but none pulled into the driveway. The phone did not ring.

And then suddenly and startlingly it did. Nosemitt raced to get it, reaching it on the second ring. "Hello!" she panted. Sniffle stood at the kitchen doorway, trying to understand both sides of the conversation. "Yes," Nosemitt said. "Oh? Yes? Oh? Not? Not really? Oh." Sniffle was going mad trying to make anything of this nothingness. At last Nosemitt smiled and said, "See you very soon." It was the smile that helped.

"Well? What? What?" Sniffle demanded.

"It's all right. It really is all right."

"What is?"

"They were not Harriette's blue pillows. They were definitely not even nubby. They were almost not even blue. And they had belonged to Roger for years. Vanessa had to go through quite an ordeal of questioning before they got around to showing her the pillows. They are releasing Roger. She will take him home and then come back here."

"Funny, we didn't even think of that possibility."

Vanessa arrived home exhausted, staying downstairs with them only long enough to say that the chief had insisted on putting her through a polygraph test when she denied that the pillows had ever been Harriette's. "He wanted Roger to be the one," she said tearfully and then went to her room.

A few minutes later the doorbell rang. It was Detective Duke, wanting to make sure that Vanessa had gotten home all right. "She looked pretty shaken when she left, and I was worried about her."

"I think she'll be all right, but it was an ordeal," Nosemitt said. "Can you sit down for a few minutes? We tried to tell you our own findings earlier but there was no chance." Duke came all the way into the living room and sat down.

"We think we have your bird murderer and maybe more," Sniffle said. "Remember the black Mustang?"

"Yes. In fact, before I forget to tell you, I have some information myself. At two this afternoon, after I took the duck to the lab and after

I spent some time with Mrs. Waldo, I went to the high school to see if I could get a chance to talk with Candace Applewhite."

"And did you learn who her boyfriend is" Nosemitt asked.

"Everreddy is all she called him. The license plate is short for that. Anyway, she confirms that she did babysit for the Kettles that night and that they went out all dressed up for a party. She gives you the impression that she wouldn't remember anything, but she can tell you every detail of Mrs. Kettle's dress. The real reason she remembers the date, though, is that her boyfriend was supposed to come by for a while and he didn't. She was pretty angry about it, but they must have made up. All she wants to talk about is dropping out of school and marrying him."

"Her boyfriend is Fredrick Kettle," Nosemitt said.

"The black Mustang is frequently in the park," Sniffle said, "but that is not the most significant thing about Everreddy."

"He has a history of killing small animals," Nosemitt announced. "Dogs especially but probably birds as well."

"And," Sniffle added, "the most unsettling fact is that he does not seem to need a reason. Harvester Kettle's suicide note tells the story. Toddler Freddy gave his little sister poisoned candy just because he felt like doing so."

"How do you do this? You get more information than we do!" Duke asked.

"Are you and Sergeant Bradley really working on this case together, or are you in competition with each other to solve it?" Sniffle asked.

"A little of both," Duke admitted.

"You might want to try more of one and none of the other; see if it works as well for you as it does for us sometimes," Nosemitt said. "Which isn't to say that we don't occasionally get exasperated with each other, but the goal is what counts."

"Yes, you are right, but it would help even more if we could think of the right questions," Duke said. "We have had no training, no real guidance from anyone. Neither of us thinks the right way yet. I can't believe we arrested Roger without knowing if the pillows were the right ones. Art and the chief's thinking was to get him first; ask later."

"Well, we don't want to make the same mistake with Freddy," Sniffle said, "but we also don't want to wait much longer to see him brought in for questioning. My fear is that Portia will want to protect him and that he will leave St. Edwards."

"Then I'd better go right now. I think I will call Art now, though, and have him meet me at the Kettle house."

Twenty minutes later Duke called to tell them that Fred was indeed gone. Portia did not say that she had told him he was suspected of killing anything or anyone, but she did not deny that she had expressed great concern that he might be in some kind of trouble. Did he need a little vacation? she had asked; she insisted that that was all. She said he had been very appreciative, had told her she was a great mom. He had taken a few things and had gone out to the garage, but she did remember that he took time first to turn the hose on. "He just goes a little crazy when the birds soil his car," she said.

"She seems so harmless," Sniffle said; "but now isn't she guilty of obstructing justice? What are you going to do about her suggestion that he needed a vacation?"

"Here in St. Edwards? Portia Kettle?" Duke said. "Probably nothing. She would be universally regarded as a concerned mother who has had too much to put up with and who would of course be entitled to help her son. I can't imagine that we would go after her."

"I think I like that," Sniffle said, "but I'm not so sure it is really okay. What she is doing seems natural, reasonable, defensible. I just hope you find him anyway." Nosemitt felt that Portia could have been worried about her son without urging him to leave town and compound his own problems.

"Besides," she said, "her own husband recognized that they had protected him too long. She doesn't seem to think so."

"Since when do a mother and father have to see things the same way?" Sniffle asked. "He was probably right, but how could she bear to see her son tried as a murderer– assuming that he is the one. I doubt that she thinks he did it, and it may look like willful blindness; but she has been in denial about many things for a long time."

"But in her heart, don't you think she now fears that maybe he might be the one?"

"You know what Art said to me?" Duke said at the end of the conversation. "He said he thought we had solved our first murder, that we had found the Bird Killer. He's going to take me to dinner if it turns out to be true, and I'll let him– but I can't believe that he thinks we solved anything at all. Anyway, I have a small surprise for him. He left before I did and I came away with a little surprise."

"I won't ask what, but now what are we to do about Freddy?" Nosemitt asked. "If he has left town, surely you don't expect him to return? What does Sergeant Bradley wish to do to capture his first murderer?"

"We have taken a few steps," she said. "The chief has sent out Freddy's photo and a car description."

"Including the lovely mirror-hanging?" Sniffle asked.

"I don't think he included that," Duke said, "but the license plate of course and the color and model. We got the picture of him from his mother. Also, we have alerted the airport and bus terminals, just in case he takes either of those ways out of town. Let's see– I have an appointment early Monday morning with the principal of the high school, Oliver McRilfin, who will sit in on an interview with Candace in his office. I think that's it."

"Shouldn't you be following up with Candace sooner? I can't see waiting until Monday. She may know where Freddy has gone," Nosemitt said.

"Well, I tried to arrange a meeting for tomorrow, but Mr. McRilfin will not be available. It was his suggestion that he be present at the interview with the young lady. I don't know whether he thinks he will be protecting her or finding a reason to expel her."

"May I suggest that you contact her again tonight?" Nosemitt said. "You really can't afford to let so much time go by." Duke agreed with that and then got up to leave. "If I succeed in seeing her early, I will inform the principal of the reason."

"Before you go, what did you learn about the guests at the party?" Sniffle asked.

"Ah, that! I have a copy of the guest list with a check mark by the name of every person who attended."

"Attended or said they would?" Nosemitt asked.

"I assumed attended," Duke said, crestfallen again. "I don't know. I guess it's basically worthless unless that point is clear." She crumpled the list but then smoothed it out again. "It's a start," she said. "Besides, I may put it in my scrapbook as a reminder of what all I have had to learn the slow, hard way."

"They say that sometimes that's the most lasting way," Nosemitt said, trying to sound consoling. In fact, it was simply a reflection of experience.

"They're the same ones who say 'Practice makes Perfect,'" Sniffle observed, "and we know how true that is, don't we? Just yesterday I walked into a glass door, and I've been walking for years, even through doorways."

"I did say 'sometimes'," Nosemitt repeated.

"You did," Sniffle agreed.

"Anyway, may we see the list?" Nosemitt asked. Duke handed it over, smoothing it one last time. Many of the names meant nothing, although a few did stand out. Dustin's name was right below Marvin's and Harriet's; a Fred Keckhopper was on the list just below Dustin. They knew nobody with that name, but it stood out at them– perhaps merely because of the asterisk after it. Roger Lescouth Jr.'s name was there, too, similarly marked.

"This probably is the invitation list, not the attendee list," Nosemitt said. "Perhaps the asterisks are by the names of those who did not attend. That should be easy to learn." Duke nodded again, took the list back, and left.

"Any suggestions for how we spend the weekend?" Sniffle asked Nosemitt. "Anybody we can visit or question or eavesdrop on?"

"Eavesdrop? What an idea! No, I think we should just wait and see what evolves. Something will happen."

"We read too many novels," Sniffle said. "There something has to happen."

"Yes," Nosemitt said, "and a good thing, too."

Saturday, January 20
Way too early in the morning

"Sorry to call at this hour, but something very interesting has turned up," Duke said excitedly over the phone. "Come meet me at the county airport." Nosemitt got off the phone looking smug and went to knock on the bathroom door to encourage Sniffle to hurry out of the shower. When she couldn't sleep, she often took a hot shower and then went back to bed.

"I know you wanted to go back to sleep, but you can't," she called in; "we are heading to the airport."

Sniffle emerged from the bathroom, hair wet and slightly spiky, robe serving as towel as well as covering, fatigue still apparent in her eyes. "Why" she asked. "Are we fleeing? Are we meeting someone? Have they found Rodex on the runway? What time is it anyway?"

"Almost 5:30 and you aren't likely to go back to sleep now anyway. Let's just have some toast or something and get going." Five minutes later, Sniffle joined Nosemitt in the kitchen for a hasty cup of instant coffee and a very lightly toasted slice of bread. They grabbed coats and left for the airport, a small airfield about a mile and a half outside the town, not far from the county dump.

"I wonder what all one might find there," Sniffle said, yawning.

"Just head straight for the main entrance to the terminal and let's find Lesley," Nosemitt said.

"Is there more than one entrance?" Sniffle asked, not yet seeing how to get to a parking lot at all. "Are we sure that there is an entrance? Are we sure there is a terminal?" In fact, there was a driveway but it was hidden from immediate view by overgrown shrubbery. After passing it, Sniffle turned around and drove directly to the small gravel parking lot. Lesley Duke was waiting for them, and she was standing right by the shiny black Mustang with the well-known license plate.

"Something interesting indeed!" Nosemitt said as she got out of the car.

"It gets more so," Duke assured her. "I don't know if you will be glad or sorry about this next part, but Art and the chief are on their way out here too. I felt that I had to call them."

"Well!" Nosemitt said; "it must be really something!"

"I have been curious about the chief anyway," Sniffle said.

"Everreddy Freddy must really be quite stupid," Duke said. "Not only did he leave his car here in plain view; he left the trunk unlocked and a credit card in the glove compartment."

"Away from trees," Sniffle said. "So, what have you found?" She was still not fully alert but was more or less coming around.

"See for yourselves," Duke said, leading them to the unlocked trunk, opening it, and pointing straight at a turned-over box of Rodex. There was a small brown bag of crushed crumbs, presumably ready to be scattered. Next to it was a little tangle of blue threads. It looked as if someone had pulled them from a larger piece of fabric and played with them, braiding some strands and knotting some. It looked quite odd lying there in the trunk with the bag of crumbs.

"Is this the way it is supposed to work out in your favorite detective fiction?" Sniffle asked Nosemitt. "Everything just comes together in one place and that is that?"

"You are assuming too much, too soon," Nosemitt said. "Clearly, though, we are really closing in on our prime suspect."

"Closing in? You call this merely 'closing in'? The Rodex that we already were pretty sure would be in his possession, the car of the man who as a child calmly poisoned his own little sister? Blue threads that could have come from a blue cushion? Even the threads look nubby. Closing in?"

"The threads do look significant," Nosemitt said, "but they may not be."

"There is another factor," Duke said.

"See?" Nosemitt said to Sniffle.

"What?" she asked Duke.

"The credit card is in the name of Frederick Keckhopper."

"Damnation!" Nosemitt said. "So now we have to find out who he is and what his credit card is doing in this glove compartment."

"Maybe it's just an alias Fred Kettle uses," Sniffle suggested.

"Or maybe not," Duke said. "I asked Art to look up the legal registration on this car and bring that information when he comes. I am trying to learn how to ask more questions and get more answers."

"Well, that is a good thing," Nosemitt said; "but we are sure that the driver of this car is our very own Freddy Kettle and that he is the one who acknowledged poisoning Albina Marie."

"But do we know who was driving it this morning?" Duke asked.

"Valid point," Nosemitt agreed, smiling approval.

"I suppose it is possible that two cars drove out here this morning, setting this one up to mislead us all," Sniffle mused. "Do we know if anyone named Fred took a plane anywhere?"

"No one is here yet to ask," Duke said, "but usually there is at least one agent in by seven. I don't know of any flights out of here before nine. In fact, we don't have many flights at all. There is a daily commuter flight to Chicago, and there is an evening return flight as well. Beyond those two, it's mostly a charter-your-own deal. It seems to be a paying proposition, however."

"I wonder if the Waldos have a running account," Sniffle said.

"So, either Fred came here yesterday morning and flew out, or he came at any time and flew out on a chartered plane, or he simply parked his car here and may or may not have left St. Edwards at all," Nosemitt said.

"Who might have paid for a charter flight?" Sniffle asked. "We could find the auto agency involved here, protecting him," clearly determined to bring the Waldos to justice.

"I see you are partial to the agency theory, but what about Portia?" Nosemitt suggested.

"Well, here come the chief and Art," Duke said. "I will be eager to know what you think of our boss." The two men got out of the patrol

118

car and strolled over to the Mustang.

"Better have something worth our trip out here," Bigguns said.

"I think we do," Duke said, taking him around to the trunk of the car and showing him the Rodex but not the blue threads just yet. She had put them into a specimen bag to take to the lab.

"Well, look at that," the chief said, staring at the trunk. "Whose car is this?"

"Fred Keckhopper's, sir," Bradley reported, "whoever he is. I never heard of him until I looked up the registration on this car."

"Good thinking to do that," Bigguns said, patting Bradley on the back. Bradley said nothing, and Duke glared at him.

"How did you know to do that?" Sniffle asked him. "How did you know what car was out here?"

"Uh, well, my sidekick here called me and asked me to look it up," he said softly.

"That's what a sidekick is for," Bigguns said. "Glad you are contributing, Duke. Now let's get this exhibit back to the station. I'm not quite sure why you needed to have me come out here," he said. "Or was there more?"

"A bit more, sir," Duke said; "but first I'd like you to meet Ms Nosemitt and Ms Sniffle, both of whom have really made some major contributions to our efforts. They have saved us quite a lot of work." Bigguns grunted something about not liking outsiders to be involved and headed for the patrol car.

"What else did you find?" Bradley asked. The chief turned back, waiting to hear the answer.

"I got this last night," Duke said, pulling a sheet of paper from a file folder attached to her clipboard. She showed the chief the photocopy of Harvey Kettle's suicide note. Even Nosemitt and Sniffle were surprised that she had obtained it, but the chief simply said he didn't see its relevance. After all, that was a past event referring to an even more remote event.

"This car is regularly driven by Fred Kettle, who poisoned his own sister with Rodex over twenty years ago. No matter who Fred Keckhopper turns out to be, Fred Kettle is the usual driver of this car. We think he does work for the Waldos' car agency, and you know that we list the agency or its employees on our suspect list. How could it not be relevant?" Duke was betraying her frustration and anger and now stood there silently to keep from screaming.

"Well, that's quite a chain of evidence you are assuming," Bigguns said. "Write it all up and we'll keep it in the files. Maybe something will come of it after all. Meanwhile, I'm going for breakfast. Want to join me, Art?"

"Why not impound the car?" Nosemitt asked.

"No need," Bigguns said and motioned Art to get in the car.

"I guess they are off to cook up some way that Art can get most of the credit for this information," Duke said bitingly as they pulled away.

"Well, look at it this way," Sniffle suggested: "maybe they won't give it any credit at all."

"That is really cheering," Duke said sadly. "Well, I'm going to wait until the airport opens and see what I can learn about chartered flights or if anyone was seen leaving this car here. I think I'll look around the grounds here and then write up my notes to take back to the station. Thanks for coming out so early."

"Do you keep a camera in the car?" Sniffle asked.

"No, but that is a good idea," Duke said. "I'll go back to the lab to get one and come back here. If I find anything, I'll document it all."

"I'd start with a photo of the trunk," Sniffle suggested.

"Did you make contact with Candace" Nosemitt asked.

"No, her mother said that she was spending the weekend with friends in St. Cleves. I will have to wait until Monday."

"I wonder if Everreddy is one of the friends," Sniffle said.

"Have you had breakfast?" Nosemitt asked.

"Just coffee," the detective said. "I almost always have a thermos in the car. It's okay. I will call later to let you know if anything comes up or to see if you have found the answers. I kind of hope you do." She was more visibly distressed now than she had been when Bigguns left. It took her a few minutes to realize she had not mentioned the blue threads.

Saturday, January 20
noon

Sniffle had headed for a nap the minute they returned to Vanessa's. That plan was thwarted by a loudly barking dog. Instead, she and Nosemitt had an early lunch and settled in the living room to read. Nosemitt returned to Harriette's columns and Sniffle brought out a puzzle book. It had been her love of puzzles that allowed her to think that she could merge that with Nosemitt's love of detective stories and skill at deducing the solutions and maybe actually do some sleuthing together. Never once had she contemplated that they would be involved in anything serious, certainly not a murder case; and although she was finding the details of this mystery intriguing and more complex than she would have ever believed likely, she felt vastly out of her depths. Puzzle books were more to her taste. Still, she had to admit, they really were getting somewhere. They really were helping. Amazing!

"Listen to this," Nosemitt said, letting her glasses slide down her nose.

"Dear Ms. Ettikettle, please advise me on the proper response to the question, 'So, what do YOU do for a living? It is usually asked by someone who has just informed you that he or she works twenty-five hours a day in a Very Indispensable Position and volunteers for a hospice program during lunch break and is chairperson of the community Symphony Benefit every year. And there I stand, trying not to say that I take care of my two small children and isn't that valuable too?'"

"And what did Harriette say?" Sniffle asked.

"She said, *'I can imagine many responses I would enjoy. I'd get some pleasure from thinking that you could happily stand taller, look the person directly in the eyes, and say that you are a lifeguard– after all, you do guard precious treasure full time. I'd also enjoy the thought that you might simply say you are a fulltime caregiver. What could be a More Important Position in this world? Not everyone remembers that, but I hope you always know it is true. Probably what I would enjoy most of all, of course, would be the unlikely possibility that people would stop asking such questions in ways that are unkindly meant and that you and all of us would never feel required to answer them. I am not much help, am I?'"*

"I like that," Sniffle said. "It's a genuine response, whether it is helpful or not. I don't like when people just say, 'Don't worry about it.' Still, I can empathize with the writer there. You know, there are people like you, thank goodness, who think that artists make a significant contribution to the world and others who think artists are simply self-involved overgrown children who do no real work at all, who just play."

"They have no idea," Nosemitt said.

"But the fact seems to me," Sniffle added, "that what all of us do is find ways to fill our allotted time with something that gives us meaning, unless we are in such a restrictive or desperate life that we are not free to do so. Life is experience and the content may be irrelevant. I think collectively we experience everything possible."

"Yet wouldn't you say that the content is relevant to who you are and what goals you have?" Nosemitt suggested.

"But does who we are really matter in any absolute way? Our goals matter to us, but do they matter to anything larger?"

"Well, you know I think they do," Nosemitt said. "I think they matter– and so do we, even if we don't see how or why."

"Well, I don't believe that time really can be wasted in a cosmic sense, even though I believe we waste it all the time personally. The dog has stopped barking; I think I will try for a nap again," Sniffle said, getting up and heading for the stairs. "And right now, napping does not seem like a waste of time. It seems essential."

"Dream about what matters," Nosemitt suggested.

Same day, naptime

It started calmly enough: a circus scene with clowns and elephants and a parade of bright colors, noiseless and in a pale blue light that softened all the possibilities. She was seated off to one side, not near the main ring at all and only with difficulty able to see anything that was going on there. In the ring before her, silently and beautifully, a woman in a silky costume the same color as the light went through incredible contortions and defied all thoughts of what a human form or shape could shift to. Sniffle admired the flexible grace and seamless motion the dark-haired artist displayed.

A man wheeled out into the ring a tank of water some six feet high. The water was of that same soft pale blue of lights and costume. The woman turned cartwheels all the way to the tank and somehow seemed to take wing as she vaulted into it. The man silently applauded, encouraging the audience to do the same. Off to the far left, tigers waiting for their act paced restlessly in their wheeled cage; and somewhere an elephant trumpeted and the clowns stumbled. Dimly Sniffle heard a burst of music from the main ring, and dimly she sensed a shift in the atmosphere in this ring too. The woman had managed to twist into a pretzel shape in the narrow confines of the rectangular tank. How like a coffin, Sniffle thought, a watery coffin.

Somewhere a gunshot went off and a monkey screamed and the crowd shrieked. Somewhere a puff of smoke rose as high as the tightrope wire and a child cried. Somewhere in the farthest ring a stilt walker moved across the path of the circus pony, and the pony startled and neighed and stopped. And in the ring before her eyes, Sniffle watched in horror as the man reached into the tank and held the woman's head harshly down in the water, and the woman drowned. Pale blue silk in pale blue water: very little of the woman was visible any longer.

The voice that tried to scream but failed was Sniffle's, and yet it echoed in her brain as it ended the dream abruptly.

Now she sat with a cup of hot tea in the living room– sorry she had tried to sleep, sorrier that she had succeeded. "All this evil in the world!" she said, but Nosemitt knew that Sniffle was merely at the surface of the dream; and neither of them ever liked staying there too long.

"The world's evil?" she asked over the rims of her glasses.

"Not quite ready to assume my own," Sniffle murmured. "Maybe I could think about the word horror instead, although we are presently immersed in more of that than I care to think through.

"Immersed? Appropriate word. So is your lady in blue."

"And dead," Sniffle said. "The artist is dead. I don't like anything about that."

"The contortionist is dead," Nosemitt pointed out. "Maybe we need to stay much more straightforward and skip the circus act about our identities. The dream doesn't have to be about the artist as such. Right now, we are both recoiling at all the subterfuge."

"We aren't adept at it, I'm glad to say; but I don't think our identities are a source of horror," Sniffle said, holding the cup of warm tea to her aching head.

"No, but they are becoming a source of confusion that we had not foreseen. We are increasingly uncomfortable with all the layers of secrets that we have discovered can lead to serious problems. I don't think our aliases are a serious issue, but maybe they are a symbol for you and for us."

"There is a lot that I at least did not anticipate. Why again did we decide to do this?" It was a rhetorical question, and Nosemitt chose to leave it as such. "I can't say that it isn't fascinating," Sniffle continued; "but will I ever paint again?" That was not a rhetorical question; it was one of several recurring agonies for Sniffle, and Nosemitt knew it was pointless to say anything. She slid her glasses back into place and returned to reading, relieved at least that the question this time wasn't *Will I ever sell another painting?* Nosemitt knew that Sniffle would

123

paint; sales, however, were never safe to predict.

"Why *drowned*?" Sniffle asked out loud, but neither of them pursued it.

Saturday evening, Jan. 20

To give Vanessa and Roger some evening time without questions or guests, Nosemitt and Sniffle decided to eat out. For Sniffle it was always a risk. Not only had her many allergies provided her pseudonym; they had also kept her from enjoying a wide range of foods. People like Olga Berlin were always finding their way into her life and meals; Sniffle viewed it as a private curse laid on her by some gastronomic demon who spent eternity seeking out concoctions that gave one far more than indigestion. Nosemitt did not have this demon; she could eat practically everything. Dining out together was generally a challenge. At home they cooked what both liked or separately, as the mood required. Breakfast was always the easiest meal of the day.

"How about The Gravel Oyster?" Nosemitt asked, poring through the three pages of restaurants in the greater St. Edwards phonebook. "I can't imagine that they serve only one item."

"Should we call and ask?" Sniffle wondered. "I never eat oysters."

"Why don't we start at what is usually the end of these habitual conversations and just say what we would like?" Nosemitt asked. "It will save time, and I'm hungry."

"Not Mexican," Sniffle insisted. Nosemitt already knew that was out. "Not Indian." Curries had never been on the list of tolerated foods. "No pasta. Maybe shrimp or crab? Lobster tails do sound wonderful. If your oyster place has any of those, we could both be happy. Unless they only fry the shrimp and serve the crab whole and bake the lobster. Should we call?"

"Go right ahead," Nosemitt said, settling into the couch with her coat and purse in her lap. Sniffle went to the phone and called The Gravel Oyster. The person who answered could not understand what Sniffle was asking and kept repeating that she did not know. "Ask if they have shrimp on the menu," Nosemitt said. "You haven't been direct enough. Asking if they serve only oysters isn't working."

"I don't think the problem is what I'm asking; it's a hearing problem. Can't you hear the background music from where you are sitting? It is horrible and earsplitting. Let's go somewhere else."

Nosemitt slid down lower into the couch. She handed Sniffle the phonebook and closed her eyes for a while. "There is a steakhouse in the downtown area of St. Edwards. I didn't realize that what we saw on our rambling would be considered a downtown area, but it appears that it isn't far from the library," Sniffle said.

"All right. Do we need a reservation?" Nosemitt's eyes were still resting. Even from across the room, she could tell that it was not going to be their destination. After hanging up, Sniffle reported that reservations were required and that two days in advance was the best time to call, preferably by eleven in the morning.

"Italian?" Sniffle asked. "Here's one called Casa Bologna."

"Why not call and see if they serve more than deli sandwiches," Nosemitt teased. In fact, it was not an Italian restaurant; deli was all that it did serve; and it was about to close.

"Chinese?" Sniffle suggested, fearing they were destined to be deafened at the oyster place.

"Sure," Nosemitt said. "Let's make it an adventure and not even call ahead."

They arrived at The Golden Pagoda behind a couple who seemed in the midst of an argument over where they would be willing to sit. "At least that isn't one of our issues," Sniffle whispered. The woman, henna-haired and shapely, wanted to sit in a quiet booth away from others; the man suggested that they be nearer the buffet. Finally, while their argument progressed, the owner of the restaurant offered to seat Nosemitt and Sniffle, whose only preference was for nonsmoking. As they followed the owner to their table, they heard the man say to his companion, "Okay, okay, Chick! Whatever you say." Sniffle briefly stood up a little straighter to hear if Chick would call her man Mel, but Chick didn't call him anything repeatable at all. Sniffle chose to believe he was Mel and was glad she had not opened the hotel room door. She was, however, sorry not to see their faces.

Over sesame chicken, usually safe for Sniffle, and teriyaki pork with broccoli for Nosemitt, the two women quietly reviewed their notes. They paused whenever anyone passed by, but there were few customers that evening. "Do you think we need to attempt to verify that Vanessa's real mother did have a fatal genetic disease?" Sniffle asked.

"Do you think Walter would tell us her name?" Nosemitt asked in return. "Or do you think her real name is on Vanessa's birth certificate?"

"I have the name written here somewhere, the one on the certificate

I mean." She flipped through her three notebooks.

"I never know why you don't keep just one," Nosemitt sighed.

"I am more likely to lose one than three," Sniffle said.

"True, and you are definitely likely to lose at least one; and it will be the one with the information you are looking for. I guess three makes some sense, but I still think you should get a laptop and keep your notes on it."

"And then lose the laptop?" Sniffle asked, horrified. "Anyway, here it is, if I can read it. It looks like 'Amelia Bedelia'. Surely not."

"Where are your glasses? Better yet, let me look at it." She took the notebook and studied the name Sniffle had written. "Didn't you have your glasses on when you wrote it?"

"I might not have," Sniffle said. "I was in my Let's Act Totally Incompetent mode."

"Well, maybe it was too good an act. Anyway, I think it might be 'Amelia', but the last name looks like Beddloe. It's enough to go on, I think. I hope Walter's story is true. I hated the thought that he might not really have Vanessa's genuine interests at heart. I just wish he had let her know his reasons. As it is, she may in fact be in serious danger without knowing that she could be tested for the disease."

"Yes, she may be. She might not want to know, though; but somehow she should be able to make a decision affecting her own life so strongly. And she especially should know if a child could be afflicted."

"Yet it is understandable that Walter never thought he would have to tell her."

"You know, your mentioning laptops has me wondering if there is a library or business locally where I could make use of a computer. I don't want to drive to the capital again," Sniffle said.

"So, that item is on our to-do list. What else?"

"I am totally in the dark about Chief Bigguns and even Sergeant Bradley. He was so pleasant when we first met him. What do you think is really behind the change? Is it as simple as Lesley makes it seem– that the chief is putting pressure on his sergeant to be the one to solve the crime and to do it without any outside interference? It seems ridiculous."

"I certainly agree that it is ridiculous, but I don't think it accounts for the rudeness. And I don't like the implication that women don't measure up. I don't know," Nosemitt said, savoring the last drops of tea. A waiter appeared with a fresh pot.

"That was quick!" Sniffle said; "do you think we can be heard as well as seen?" Both women looked around warily and thought that perhaps they really ought to leave. "Too soon to return home," Sniffle said. "Ice cream?" They left and went looking for an ice cream shop.

So they sat in the car, cold though it was, one sipping a chocolate milk shake that she had requested be heated and the other enjoying a hot fudge sundae with most of the usual extra toppings. "Not bad," said Sniffle, using the straw to get at some of the syrup in the bottom of the cup. "We haven't talked about Emmaline much. What is your current impression?"

"Kind of a caricature," Nosemitt said, wiping a spot of fudge from her chin. "And yet not really foolish. I kind of like the fact that she talks to the clock. I sympathize. And while she may be unaware of most or even all of the facts of her brother's life, it isn't because she chooses not to understand. She is not given many facts at all."

"She seems to come straight out of a British comedy," Sniffle said smiling.

"*The Lady Killers*?" Nosemitt suggested.

"Now there we go, accusing her again," Sniffle laughed. "Maybe Walter should have put her on his payroll. I think she would have enjoyed it."

"That reminds me– don't we need to find out if Fred Kettle and Fred Keckhopper really are one and the same?"

"Good idea, but I have been mulling over another question: why would the Waldos accept Harriette's nephew working for them? This town is larger than Sunford but still too small for all such relationships not to be known. Are you adding all these things to our list?" Nosemitt got out the one small notebook she kept and added the new topics.

They drove aimlessly about town after the ice cream. They did not wish to intrude on Vanessa and Roger, and they could not think of anyplace they would be likely to learn anything at this time of night. "Do we know which street Harriette was found on?" Nosemitt asked.

"I think so," Sniffle said. "Try the first notebook."

"You finally numbered them?" Nosemitt asked, sounding pleased.

"Just the first one," Sniffle admitted. "I hadn't planned on using a third."

"Is that supposed to sound rational?"

"Not really."

Nosemitt turned on the overhead light in the car and began to skim through the notes. Sometimes Sniffle's handwriting was clear and direct; sometimes it was more like the scrawl on a prescription pad. This time the paragraph that referred to her note on the crime scene was quite clear and the street name very legible: Greenwood Road. Nosemitt got the town map out of the glove compartment, and they made their way to Greenwood.

"It doesn't fit its name," Sniffle said, looking at the small rundown houses on the heavily potholed street. Here and there, houses still had Christmas lights up and a few were lit. Quite a mound of trash sat in front of one house, and another seemed as if it were about to collapse. A couple of teenage boys, in jackets too thin for the frosty night, stood huddled beneath a dim lamppost, smoking and staring at the two women. Nosemitt checked to make sure the doors were locked, and Sniffle drove on down the street a little less slowly.

"It makes everything all the sadder," Nosemitt said. "What a grimy, shabby place."

"Maybe the snow made it a bit less so," Sniffle said, remembering that the snow had helped narrow the timeframe that awful night. "Maybe the light was a pale blue because of the Christmas lights, and perhaps Harriette tried to escape. Maybe she vaulted into her midnight walk, feeling safe and secure in the presence of someone she trusted. I have her mixed into my nightmare, now, and she becomes the contortionist, suddenly twisting to get away. It's all a dark circus, and the tigers are always pacing."

In the rearview mirror Sniffle saw the two boys leave the lamppost and walk in the direction she and Nosemitt had driven. She pressed on the gas pedal and they left Greenwood Road. "No need to come back here," Nosemitt said, shivering. Sniffle reached over and turned the heater up a notch, even though the temperature in the car had nothing to do with the shivering. She was pleased that the heater had decided to work again.

It was still not very late and they needed another destination. "Want to see if there is any sign of life at the airport?" Sniffle asked. Nosemitt had no objections. They drove out there, passing the entrance yet again and turning back. There were three cars there now but no black Mustang. "What do we make of that?" Sniffle asked.

"I guess that someone removed it," Nosemitt said with only a slight tinge of sarcasm. "In fact, quite definitely someone has removed it."

"I see," Sniffle said, grinning. "What else do we make of it?"

"Hmm. What are the possibilities? Freddy came back and got it.

Someone else came back and got it. Someone had it towed away. I suppose the most important first question is, Where is it now?"

"But still, by whose hands or orders?" Sniffle added. "Think that the chief impounded it after all?"

"And, once again, who is Fred Keckhopper?"

"He stays firmly on our list," Sniffle said. "If he is a native St. Edwardian, we ought to be able to find him in a yearbook, if he ever graduated, or in the newspaper files. And I still want to find public computer access. At a machine, I don't have to pretend to be any more or less competent than I am."

"It has always surprised me that as an artist you are comfortable with modern machinery," Nosemitt said. "You are a humanities person."

"I don't see any conflict between the two," Sniffle said. "All inventions of every kind are the results of human imagination and creative effort. I can't admire inventors of bombs and I would not ever want to use that kind of invention, but for me Creation is what life is."

"But the great irony is always that Creation paves the way for ultimate Destruction," Nosemitt said.

"And then the human experiment may end and a new experiment begin. All things come to an end."

"You are sounding more complacent about that possibility than I think you really mean," Nosemitt declared. "Since when have you been comfortable with the thought of annihilation?"

"Not comfortable in a personal sense. Only in a detached and off in the future sort of way. In the 'Après moi, le deluge' sort of way. Individual, personal destruction is a whole different thing. Like time-wasting."

"What is that?" Nosemitt asked, pointing to a distant light that came and went.

"Looks like a flashlight being turned on and off," Sniffle said. "I think it is coming this way. Should we leave?" She started to pull away from where she had parked, but a voice called out and the light flashed on and off repeatedly. The voice was muffled because the car windows were closed, so Nosemitt lowered hers by about a quarter of an inch. Then she could hear a man's voice calling to them to stop and explain why he should not call the police. In a moment, he was at the side of the car, pointing the flashlight at them and at the whole interior of the car.

"What is going on?" he demanded. "You are trespassing. What

are you doing here?"

"How can we be trespassing at a public airport?" Nosemitt asked. "It is a public airport, isn't it?"

"It isn't public after seven p.m.," he informed them. "That is when it closes. There are no incoming or outgoing flights, and there is no reason for anyone to be here."

"We are visitors to your community and did not know any of that," Nosemitt argued.

"Well, now you do. State your business in coming here, please."

"We were in need of entertainment and decided to take a drive," Sniffle said. "We thought we would see where the airport was in case we ever come back."

"And now you know," he said. "So get going."

"I fail to see any need for your harshness," Nosemitt said. As she spoke, she saw headlights go on near what she thought she remembered was a hangar. They went out almost immediately. It was fortunate, perhaps, that this unpleasant man was standing with his back to the hangar area. The man stepped back and motioned them out; Nosemitt closed the window; and Sniffle hastily exited the parking lot.

"I assume you saw the headlights, too," Sniffle said, eager to get away.

"Don't you wish we were brave enough to search for a back entrance to that area?"

"I do and I don't," Sniffle admitted.

"Want to bet that the airport is tied in with the Waldos?"

"I think I would lose," Sniffle said. "I wonder if there is a black Mustang back there. I wonder if that was a chartered flight coming in or leaving."

"It's almost ten," Nosemitt said, busily writing in her notebook in the dark. "I think we can go back to Vanessa's now."

Monday morning, Jan. 22

Nosemitt was in the bathtub, humming the irritating tune that continued to pester her mind; and Sniffle, working the daily crossword puzzle while the bacon sizzled on the griddle next to the French toast, was trying to remember any mythological character whose name contained six letters and started with 'L' or possibly 'V'. "Not Vulcan," she muttered, erasing four of the letters. She heard a disturbing noise and looked up and around and down on the floor. She checked to see if the radio had been turned on low and was now making itself heard. A loud crackle drew her attention to the griddle, where the bacon was snapping and hissing and the toast was just beginning to burn at the edges. Quickly she removed all to a plate and went on with the puzzle.

"It almost smells really tasty in here," Nosemitt said, coming into the kitchen just as the clock struck seven-thirty. "I hope you didn't burn the bacon."

"No," Sniffle assured her, "and I think the toast only needs a tiny bit of scraping." In fact, once the edge of the bread was trimmed off, breakfast was quite delicious. Nosemitt poured a second cup of coffee and picked up a couple of sections of the newspaper. "Anything worth reading?" Sniffle asked.

"I'm not seeing anything of immediate interest, unless you are inquisitive about the winter sales at the mall. Good prices on tents, just in case you want to camp out in the wooded area around the airport."

"Not I, thank you very much."

"And a very deep discount on walkie-talkies," Nosemitt added, yawning.

"Now those might be useful if we really are ever going to do anything like this again," Sniffle said, interested.

"They appear to have range of a thousand feet. I don't think they would be useful for anything other than communicating a sighting of Olga Berlin if one of us is out walking and has not gone far."

"Seriously," Sniffle said. "We ought to look into a decent set. They could be very handy just in our own house, whether we use them here or not."

"You know you'd lose at least one, and then we are back to the usual shouting."

"Well, let's add them to our list and just put a question mark next to them." Sniffle really could have pointed out that Nosemitt was equally likely to misplace one, but she seldom saw a need to do so. "Are we almost ready to get going?"

"Let's finish clearing up here first," Nosemitt said, beginning to wash their few dishes. Sniffle dried them and put them away, and they got their coats and headed for the door. In reaching for her gloves in the coat pockets, Sniffle discovered a note. It was from Roger Jr., thanking both of them for the previous evening. Nosemitt had a similar note from Vanessa. The notes warmed the day immediately, and now the two women really did leave.

"First stop?" Sniffle asked.

"Walkie-talkies," Nosemitt said. Sniffle was pleased and showed her appreciation by being very efficient when buying them. Nosemitt only had to wait in the parking lot seven minutes.

"Do you want to drive? Sniffle asked.

"You just want to play with those things, don't you? We can't use them in the car."

"No, but I can read the instructions. I've always wanted a real pair of these things and now I need to know how to work them." Nosemitt started the car but wasn't sure where they were heading next. When she asked, she got no response. Sniffle's mind was fully engaged in deciphering the manual, which had to have been written by someone with little knowledge of English and only an occasional interest in a translating dictionary.

"It says, 'Concoct wire A to thing at beside of little button on right.'"

"You have to assemble these?" Nosemitt asked unhappily. "Concoct?"

"That's what it says," Sniffle said, "and please note that I am wearing my glasses. I am willing to 'concoct' wires, but I don't see which button they mean because there are two rows of them, and obviously each row has a button on the right. Also a little thing beside."

"So both rows have a 'thing' on the left?"

"Yes. Identical things. However one row's button on the right is red, and the other's is blue. The directions make no mention of color."

"Is one button smaller than the other? It did say the little button on right."

"Well, you might be onto something, but I would need a much stronger pair of glasses and a scientific measuring device to know for sure. Otherwise, no, they look the same. I think I have to make an assumption here. Let's say that that we concoct wire A to the thing at left of little button on the first row, which I am now naming Row A."

"Sounds reasonable," Nosemitt agreed. "What next, and where am I driving to now?"

"Take your pick from our list and surprise me," Sniffle said, studying the directions again. "Hmm, 'Repress button on right for purposes of testing. See if noise emits.'"

"Do you think it means 'depress' button or are you really going to attempt to repress it?"

Sniffle connected a wire to the thing to the left of the button on the right of Row A and pressed the button. The only sound emitted was that of Nosemitt, gleefully cackling in a most unrepressed manner. "I guess you passed the test," Sniffle said, adding in extreme disappointment that they probably needed to return them.

"Maybe you should play incompetent again and see if either of the Rogers can put them together," Nosemitt suggested. Such compromise was not an easy decision, but Sniffle agreed to ask. "Now, should we go our separate ways again this morning?" Nosemitt asked, still grinning.

"I guess that works out best. You can take me to the library, please. Wait long enough for me to find out if they have an available computer. I'll wave to you from the door if I'm staying. Where will you be going?"

"I have a hunch that Portia may be needing a 'consoling' visit, although it can't stay consoling for long. I'll see if she will allow me to come in." She drove to the library and waited only a few minutes before Sniffle came back to the library door and waved her on. Then she drove out to Portia's, wondering at her own willingness to get so involved in other people's lives. Over and over, she and Sniffle marveled at what all they had not contemplated that this adventure they had chosen would entail. She wanted to do as professional a job as they could manage, but they had both been such private citizens for so long. This departure from all that they had been had sounded like fun– more fun than wearing purple hats and spitting as they aged, more fun than traveling with tour groups, more fun than confounding their adult children's assumptions in minor ways. And if they could stick with it, they might have the enormous satisfaction of feeling that they had contributed something worthwhile in their later years.

Nosemitt had always denigrated her many civic contributions, feeling that they amounted to little more than attending endless meetings, chairing too many of them, repeating worn-out pleas for new volunteers, and too often ultimately accomplishing less than she had dreamed. She had envied Sniffle's creative life, whereas Sniffle was forever unhappily subject to the accusation that she didn't really do anything and was out of touch with reality. Sniffle admired Nosemitt's dedication to causes and her respect for all of the arts; Nosemitt respected her friend's great productivity and knew that, whatever the outer appearance, Sniffle was thoroughly in touch. And yet they were alike in many ways; and they were able to co-exist in a real harmony, despite surface bantering and occasional cacophony. Not only did they have mutual respect and true caring for each other; they shared the same political views, and that alone kept quite a bit of peace in the house they shared.

She arrived now at Portia's home and went half-tentatively and half-assertively up the walk to the front door, noticing this time that the wind chimes were in the shape of birds. She wondered if they had been there before or if they were new. Were they possibly a gift from her son? Seeing them brought her back to the business at hand. Slowly Portia came to the door, and clearly she was not entirely happy to see this visitor; but at least it was only one and not two. She invited Nosemitt in and offered tea.

In the library, Sniffle had to settle for using a computer quite different from her own. After a few minutes of experimenting, she came to a semblance of terms with it and began to do some online searches. Not expecting to find anything, she went ahead and typed Fredrick Keckhopper's name into the search field and was surprised to find six references. Two links led to the same paragraph on a family website celebrating a great-great-great grandfather of a woman in Maine. Grandpa Fred was apparently a family character, known locally as a practical joker. His most beloved prank, one he seemed to have inflicted regularly, was to get people to walk half the distance to a wall. He would ask them to go halfway again. And again. He would keep encouraging them to go "just" halfway and would tell them that by doing so they would never get to the wall. When they naturally bumped into the wall and, rubbing their heads ruefully, let him know his theory was wrong, he would laugh and laugh. Clearly this was not the Fred they were seeking.

Two other references were to the websites of two different insurance salesmen. She checked to see if this was just one salesman with two different offices, perhaps in different cities, but it wasn't clear. Both had the same middle initial, but there was no photograph on either page. If they were two individuals, neither was in St. Edwards. She read a little more than she wanted to know about one's personal philosophy of maximum insurance, and she followed a few links on both pages, rapidly getting bored.

The last of the six links was to a quotation in Bartlett's Revisited: "I have had my fill of Keckhoppers," author unknown. A footnote indicated that no evidence had been found to support the theory that it was written by a very young Shakespeare. In fact, probably it had been written by a victim of great-great-great Grandpa. Sniffle took the quote as a divine sign and moved on to the next topic, the death certificate of Amelia Beddloe. Since she already knew where Vanessa's birth had taken place, she assumed that the woman's death was probably also in the Chicago area; and it was. She was not able to locate any online information about the cause of death, but she did find the phone number to call to request such data. That number went into her notebook. "Now for marriage data," she said.

Portia looked very weary. Sunken cheeks and dark circles under her eyes seemed to suggest worry and sleeplessness. Nosemitt had no doubt that there was ample reason for Portia's condition. How to approach the topic of her son's whereabouts was now the problem.

"You are without your friend," Portia commented. "Is she well?"

"Yes, we are both fine," Nosemitt said. "And you?"

"I am not at my best," Portia said. "I am not sleeping well at all. I hope you aren't here with more questions, although of course you must be."

"I have been worried about you since we were here last," Nosemitt said gently. "We both have been. All of the questions raise such terrible memories, and we are not insensitive to that. I am really very sorry that any questions are necessary at all."

"Thank you for that. I suppose I should be grateful that you have come here rather than Ms. Duke again. She tried to be diplomatic, but she does have to be rather impersonal, you know. At least she was more courteous than Sergeant Bradley."

"I'm afraid the direct impersonal way may sometimes be the only way to proceed in such matters. Otherwise, crimes could never be solved. Somehow the facts need to emerge."

"Yes, I even allowed her to make a copy of Harvester's last note. I suppose I finally accepted the fact that hiding it just kept it more real and more constant in my mind than acknowledging it. But I would not have let the sergeant take it. I tried to cooperate with Ms. Duke."

"I can understand that," Nosemitt said, struggling to find things to say to avoid the point of her visit, though she could not postpone it indefinitely. Finally she felt she could delay no longer. "Have you seen Fred recently?"

"No." She sighed heavily and looked far away, through the frosty window and out toward the woods. "No, I haven't." Nosemitt knew it was not true, sensed the evasiveness in Portia's mind, but wasn't quite

135

ready to challenge it– almost but not quite.

"Do you know where he is?"

"No. I did think he was looking a bit peaked the last time that he was here. I hope he is off someplace relaxing."

"How long ago was that? Did he seem just tired, or did he seem to be under stress?"

"No, I don't think Fred was stressed. But he works hard, and I imagine he plays rather wildly too. He just looked tired. That is all. Nothing suspicious, if that's what you are expecting."

"Have you seen his car? Might he have left it here?"

"No, I doubt it. I haven't looked in the garage, but he never leaves it here. Why is his car of interest? You brought it up once before."

"So, when you suggested that he take a vaca–"

"What makes you think I suggested that?" Portia asked, her voice tight and strained. "I never said that."

"Apparently you did say that to Lesley Duke."

"Did I? I don't recall saying that. Why would I have said it?"

"Perhaps it is true and then you forgot that you said it?" Really, Nosemitt did not want to suggest anything, but she felt very sorry for Portia. The woman was only wanting to protect her son. Nosemitt was experiencing a similar ambivalence. She understood the desire to protect but wanted to make this woman see that aiding him only added to his problems.

"Fred is just a boy. He doesn't know what he is doing sometimes. He doesn't mean harm, and if he did poison a dog or maybe two dogs, well, I know he didn't think it meant anything. I doubt that he knew what death was. I am sure he thought that they would be up and playing again soon. He loved cartoons, and you know none of those silly creatures really ever dies."

"And doesn't that make him a dangerous person?" Nosemitt tried to say as softly as possible. "He does need to be protected," she said, hoping that approach was better. "He needs to be protected from his own impulses and his own nature."

"But not in jail," Portia said adamantly. "Not in prison. If they want to put him in a hospital and help him, that is one thing; but no one has ever said Fred needed treatment. And I still say he did not murder Harriette. Treat a boy who hurts little helpless animals, but don't turn him into Harriette's murderer. He is just a boy," she said, receding back into her tired, faded voice, "a little boy who never grew up."

Nosemitt thanked her for the tea and went to retrieve her coat. "I am sorry that we had to have this talk," she said. "I hope you are right. I hope that Fred is not the one; but I also hope, very much, that you will see that it is never too late to find help for him, whether he thinks he needs it or not. You are still treating him as a boy, and really you have to regard him as an adult. By the way, does Fred have a job? I think I was told that he has sometimes worked for Mr. Wrothwell."

"I really am finished with the conversation," Portia said. She walked Nosemitt to the hall, asked her not to come back, and closed the door firmly. Then she slowly made her way to her bedroom and to the assortment of whiskey bottles she kept there. She filled a very tall glass and drained it. She got in bed, pulled up the covers, and screamed into the pillows until at last she was totally exhausted and fell asleep. She dreamed of being lost somewhere in a black night and so did not know she was dreaming at all.

Sniffle had found no state or county or local record of Harriette's marriage to Roger. She realized that they probably had married out of state, but she wasn't sure where to start a more extensive search. She figured that Roger would be willing to show them any proof if they really felt a need for it, but it occurred to her that she probably ought to be talking to the librarian. "Later," she murmured to herself. She looked over her notes, not sure what exactly she wanted to hunt for next but decided to look at the shelves of local reference works and pulled out several issues of the *Yerebooke*, hoping to find the unknown Fred, holder of the title to the Mustang. She found him in one and was about to put the others away but was curious about the quip below his picture: "Same time, same place, next year." She checked the following year's book and found him there, too. In both photos he appeared to be of a stocky build, with a broad face and yet small features. His quip the second time around was "Free at last." Sniffle looked over his list of activities, a very short list that merely mentioned that he had spent only his senior years in St. Edwards, having gone to school in Minnesota before then. Sniffled jotted a few things down and put the yearbooks away.

Suddenly she had an entertaining idea. Chuckling to herself, she entered a phrase into the search engine and happily proceeded in her investigations. This kind of search was much more to her liking. She got nowhere for a while, but then inspiration struck.

Nosemitt left Portia's, looked at her watch, and decided it was too early to get Sniffle. On a sudden whim, she stopped at a public phone booth, looked up the Waldo agency, called, and asked to speak with Fred Keckhopper. She was told that he was out of town and would not return until the following week. "I think that is the person I need to speak to," she said. "Is he the tall one?" She had no idea of what Fred looked like, but it was worth a question or two.

"Not at all," the receptionist said. "Perhaps you mean Roger?"

"No," Nosemitt said. "I am fairly sure I was told to contact Fred, the tall one."

"We have only one Fred, and he is short and rather heavy," the woman said. "May I ask what you need? Perhaps I might be able to help direct your call."

"Thank you very much, but I think I ought to get more detailed information from the person who recommended Fred. I will call back another time." She hung up the phone, pleased to have learned that there was a Fred Keckhopper and that he was not the slightly built Everreddy. For good measure, though she had not thought otherwise, he also was not Roger under an alias. One more secret pseudonym just might have made her throw her hands in the air and give up.

Next she called Gladiolus Press. She had a favor to ask and this time Roger Sr. was there. She explained her goal and asked if he knew of a source of help. He told her not to worry, that he could take care of it. He would bring the item over after dinner that night. Nosemitt was pleased and checked off a highly coded item in her notebook: L2S. Pseudonyms might be wearing thin, but codes still held an allure.

By the time Sniffle was ready to speak with the librarian, she had compiled a motley list of questions, one of which was to ask where the nearest store might be that carried the item she wanted. She was delighted to learn that there was such a place within walking distance, but she discovered at the door that it had begun to rain. It was cold enough to turn icy, and she knew better than to walk over there in such weather. Falls were no fun. She found the public phone and called the shop, learning at first to her disappointment that they had nothing like what she wanted in stock and then to her happiness that their computer indicated that it was available from one of their affiliates and that they could have it for her within a few days. Although she had had very mixed responses when she had found it, she knew that she wanted to have this item for Nosemitt. She was very satisfied with herself and with the upside of benevolent machines.

She returned to the library computer and attacked the list of answers and suggestions that the librarian had given. Two hours later, Nosemitt arrived and came into the library to hunt for Sniffle. It was not a difficult task; the library was small and Sniffle had stayed near the only window with a decent view. They sat and reviewed most of what they had each learned, saving some surprises for another time. They left, stopping at the grocery store to pick up more tea bags and a few other items and went to Vanessa's. "A productive day?" Nosemitt asked.

"Ah, yes," Sniffle sighed, thinking mainly of the item she had ordered.

"Same here," Nosemitt said, thinking chiefly of Roger's promise.

Later that evening

They had a quiet dinner on their own. Roger Jr. was still out of town and Vanessa had been invited to dinner and a movie with the Park-Jacksons. The vpi's chose uncharacteristically to find TV trays and eat while watching the evening news. They both felt completely detached from the world, a situation they ordinarily did not mind at all. Now, though, Wrothwells and Kettles were too much with them. "And I too have 'had my fill of Keckhoppers,'" Sniffle said, puzzling her friend. They declared a moratorium on conversation about the case and chose to be appalled instead by the horrors of the world scene. Finally they both had enough of that, and Nosemitt switched channels and found an opera playing on the public television channel. She settled herself comfortably to watch it and to revel in the music, while Sniffle imagined how she would have designed the set and costumes. Midway through an incredible aria, the doorbell rang. Sniffle went to the door and, of course, asked who was there.

"Special delivery from Roger," the familiar soft voice said. Sniffle opened the door just slightly and was happy to see the elder Lescouth.

"What do you have there?" she asked, curious not only about the large box but also the handwritten label on it: Harriette's.

"It's for you," he said, "at least for as long as you are here. But maybe you will want to keep it." Nosemitt came to the door, her eyes twinkling.

"For me?" Sniffle asked, baffled. Roger set the box down and took out his penknife to slit all the tape.

"A laptop!" Sniffle almost shouted. "How wonderful! But I can't keep it. I will be happy to use it, but it is yours. You keep it."

"I have several at work and one at home," he said. "This was Harriette's and Vanessa hates computers. You are more than welcome to it. Please take it and enjoy it. Just don't go to any obscene web sites."

"You mean it is already configured for access?" Sniffle asked, overjoyed.

"Yes, I just need to set it up by a phone line. You show me where you'd like to work. I already changed the name on the account. I hope you don't mind that your identity is just SNIFF. Would you believe that 'Sniffle' was already in use?"

"I don't mind at all." Sniffle beamed at Nosemitt, knowing whose idea this had to have been and only sorry that her own special purchase was not the equal of this. Nosemitt continued to look quite pleased with herself.

They thought about setting it up in the kitchen, but Sniffle didn't know who would bother whom more. She didn't know which rooms had phone jacks, but Roger did. He suggested the study where Harriette had always worked, and at first Sniffle hesitated. It was, after all, where the nubby blue cushions used to reside; and she didn't know if that association would distract her too much. And was Roger really sure he didn't mind? He was quietly emphatic that he did not.

While he was making sure the connection worked, Nosemitt fixed a pot of tea and Sniffle debated about getting the walkie-talkies. Maybe she should just return them and not bother this kind man; but then he asked if there was anything else he could do. He was restless and lonely and needed to have something to occupy his mind and his time. "Do you think you could fix our new gadget?" she asked. He could, and he was nice enough to agree that the directions would be a challenge for anyone. It was, in the end, a simple job; and Sniffle went happily and gratefully about the whole house with one of the gizmos, testing the range and trying out different volume levels while Nosemitt whistled or hummed or sang back to her. The exchange went on for several minutes, and Nosemitt tired of it. "What is your estimated time of arrival back in the living room?" she asked. "It would be nice to see you again."

"Coming in from the landing any moment," Sniffle said, more quickly descending the stairs than she normally could. She put the walkie-talkies on the coffee table and sat down to tea. "Do we have any cookies?" she asked and off she went again to see.

"Do I want to know what you two have been learning?" Roger asked.

"We are still learning possible leads," Nosemitt said. "Perhaps, though, you can tell us about two Freds– Kettle and Keckhopper, to be exact."

"Fred Keckhopper?" he asked. Nosemitt nodded. "Fred works at the car agency but is one of Walter's people really. There are quite a few on his secret payroll, and I only know about it because of Harriette. She probably was the only person who knew most of Walter's business, and she did not share all of it with me but some. How does he come to show up on your list?"

"Do he and your son do the same thing? Sell corporate cars?" she asked.

"My son is not working for Walter. He really does sell fleets of cars to large and small corporations. I hope he finds out soon how he would really like to make money and spend his life. Fred may be doing the same thing, but I believe he could also well be documenting evidence for Walter. You do realize that I'm not supposed to know that, don't you?"

"So, how does Freddy Kettle fit into the picture?" Nosemitt asked, nodding. "Walter says that Freddy is on his payroll too."

"Still? I am surprised. Fred Kettle is not at all competent at anything. He wouldn't be capable of understanding what might be important and what is totally irrelevant, let alone documenting it. I wonder what Walter has him doing. I can't imagine he is at the car agency."

"Well, I am quite sure that he did not hire him to decimate the bird population," Sniffle said. "That seems to be more of a hobby of Freddy's."

"And that is not a surprise," Roger said, "although I didn't know it. I would think or guess he is a messenger boy or something along those lines. Maybe I should say a delivery boy; I wouldn't trust him with a message."

"Why is that?" Nosemitt prodded.

"The boy may have a recordable IQ, although he gives little evidence of it."

"Well, he passed a driver's license exam," Sniffle observed. "He had to have been able to read the questions."

"I wouldn't be sure that he did," Roger said.

"Couldn't read or didn't pass?" Sniffle asked.

"Either," he said.

"Does he have any connection with the other Fred?" Nosemitt asked, still wondering about that car registration.

"It's possible. When I first got to know the family and specifically met Freddy one afternoon, I remember asking about him and that Harriette did say something about his having a high school friend who felt sorry for him and looked after him. A sort of guardian angel kind of guy who kept Freddy from being beaten up regularly. I wouldn't be at all surprised to learn that it was Keckhopper."

"So, he is a decent sort?" Nosemitt asked.

"My son thinks so, and he is a pretty good judge of character."

"Demonstrated by his choice of a wife," Nosemitt said, smiling.

"Then what does Roger think of the Waldos?" Sniffle asked. "Is he aware of whatever mysterious doings they are suspected of engaging in?"

"He takes the position that being suspected does not equal being guilty. If it ever is established that they really are involved in shady dealings, let alone outright criminal activity, he will be out of there immediately."

"So you feel sure that he cannot point to anything that would support the accusation."

"As sure as I can be," he said.

"And what is your own opinion?" Nosemitt asked.

"I am of the opinion that there is plenty going on there, but of course I have heard things through Harriette that my son hasn't. Do I want him out of there? Yes, I do. Does he need that job? Yes, he does for now. I have stayed out of the whole matter, as far as Roger is concerned."

"I think we ought to find out if Mr. Freddy really does have a driver's license," Sniffle said.

"One more question," Nosemitt said. "Do you think Walter is a bad man? Or are you angry with him only on personal grounds? Not that you don't have cause, but is there more?"

"Aside from dictating things he has no business dictating, Walter is a very good man. If he hadn't interfered with our personal lives, there isn't a man I would trust more to do the right thing for the common good. He just overstepped decent bounds when it came to controlling Harriette."

"And do you know why he felt free to do so?" Sniffle asked.

"No. Harriette never went into the details, and that was the only source of difficulty between us. Maybe, when all of this investigating is over, if you can enlighten me about Walter's behavior, that will be the greatest good that you could do for me. And then, my friend, you definitely may have the laptop. I will insist. And dinner too."

"So many carrots, so little time," Sniffle said, thinking that perhaps they might be well onto Freddy but would they ever understand Walter?

"Did I already ask you what makes you think that Freddy is of interest?" Roger asked. "I did finally ask Vanessa what the lab results were. It was not a poisoning case. Even if Fred is poisoning the local wildlife, I don't see any reason to make a connection to him."

"All of the descriptions of him include his amoral nature– ," Nosemitt began.

"Or his amoural nature," Sniffle added, remembering the first time they encountered him.

"Yes," Nosemitt groaned, remembering the same scene, "and his stupidity. We are going on the premise that these two qualities make him a very dangerous person. Otherwise, we are prepared to learn that we are only slightly maligning this young man and that we are wrong about the extent of his crimes. So far, though, he is the only one leaving visible tracks."

"And the fact is that he disappeared right after Portia alerted him in some way to the trouble he might be in."

"Well," Roger sighed, "I hope you are wrong. He was grateful that she got him work. Besides, he isn't at all strong enough physically to have overcome Harriette."

"That is what Portia says too," Nosemitt said soberly.

"I just can't see any possible reason," he said, shaking his head slowly.

Tuesday, January 23
breakfast time

"You know, this lack of a motive really is a fact we are deliberately avoiding," Nosemitt said. "I am thinking that we have pinned way too much of our theory on his undoubtedly being Bird Killer. We need to be looking at others and thinking more broadly."

"Yes," Sniffle sighed. "But at least we did help Lesley get him on her radar. I hope she can track him down."

"So, which direction do we want to pursue now?" Nosemitt asked, holding her coffee cup with both hands to keep them warm.

"I was so hoping we were about to go home," Sniffle said, sighing.

"It is time for this to be over."

"I do not understand why there is not more activity going on to investigate the automobile agency," Nosemitt said, frowning. "If there is even a slight chance that they knew of Harriette's work and that they felt threatened, why wouldn't they be the most constant subject of scrutiny?"

"How does one go about finding out if they did know?"

"Maybe that's our next conversation. We need to know what, if anything, happened with Lesley's questioning of Candy Apple."

"Ah," Sniffle said; "I detect a note of scorn."

"Clever of you."

forty-five minutes later

"Yes, I really did get some worthwhile information from her," Duke said. "You had suggested that I find out about Freddy's job. She confirmed that he does work for Mr. Wrothwell. She said she doesn't know what all he does; but, according to her, Mr. Wrothwell couldn't get along without him."

"Did you ask about the birds?" Nosemitt asked.

"Yes, she said he hates birds because he is fanatical about keeping his car polished."

"So, did she say he is the one who is killing them?" Sniffle asked.

"She said she has never seen him do it."

"Does she know where he is?" Nosemitt asked.

"No, she was upset that he hadn't called her for a couple of days. She expects to hear from him soon, but I'm not sure why she expects that. I did ask her if he traveled often, and she said no. Then she said that every once in a while he does disappear for a short time. Maybe that's why she assumes she will hear from him shortly."

"Did you ask if she knew who Fred Keckhopper is?"

"Yes, I did, I'm happy to report. And yes, she does. She said he is Freddy's best friend. She thinks maybe the two of them go on fishing or hunting trips, that that explains his occasional disappearances. She did say that Mr. Keckhopper does travel a lot."

"Does she know where he lives?" Sniffle asked. "I couldn't find him in the phone book."

"I didn't ask that. I suppose if he travels a lot, he might have an unlisted number; or he might even live somewhere else. I will be stopping at the Waldo agency today and will try to get a little more information about him from the receptionist."

"Good," Nosemitt said.

"Speaking of the Waldos," Sniffle said, "we were wondering just this morning why they aren't being pursued more diligently. Or are they?"

"Yes, because of the interstate trade they conduct– whether just cars or more. I'm told federal agents are working on that. I don't know what all Art knows about what is developing there, but I am not in the loop at all. I'm just supposed to track other leads. No one is telling me anything specific."

"Well, I am glad that they are not just being ignored," Nosemitt said. "It did seem odd."

"Did we ever tell you about our experience at the airport?" Sniffle asked. "And the light that went on back where we think the hangar area is? And that we were chased off the parking lot?"

"No," Duke said. "What about all that? What are you thinking?"

"Wondering if the Mustang might be back there," Sniffle said. "Wondering if someone moved it back there to hide it."

"I take it Freddy hasn't shown up?" Nosemitt asked.

"Not that I know of," Duke said. "I think I can justify a visit out there, looking for the car of the bird killer. Thanks."

"If you could just happen to find out anything about the Waldos making use of the chartered flights, that would be a plus," Nosemitt added.

"Or a minus, if the chief thinks I'm overstepping my assignment," Duke said sadly. "But I'll keep it in mind." Again she made some cryptic notes.

"I haven't seen Uncle Walter for a while," Sniffle said. "Shall we drop in?" They drove to Emmaline's and parked across the street from her home. Usually there were no cars on the street but on this day a large section of pavement was blocked off. "I hope he can tell us more about what some of his agents do," she said.

"On the trail of Fred Keckhopper now?" Nosemitt asked.

"I am curious about why he is the owner of the car Freddy drives, not to mention knowing more specifically what Freddy himself does. I haven't given up on him entirely." They got out of the car and walked slowly to the door, pausing to watch three city workers high up in the trees, getting ready to cut some limbs down. Nosemitt, not liking heights, shuddered. Sniffle, once an avid tree climber, envied the young men's agility and fearlessness. After a couple of minutes, they went and rang the doorbell.

Once again Emmaline slowly made her way to the front hall and peered out through the tiny opening she allowed. Then she even more slowly unlocked the door and, unable to avoid a small sigh, politely invited them in. She led them into the parlor and said she would see if Walter was awake.

While they waited, both women looked around the room more carefully than they ever had before. There were no books in view, no magazines on any tables, no ashtrays anywhere, no unscarred table surfaces. On a positive note, there were countless tiny china cups and souvenir dishes, many small figurines, a few very old photographs in dented or cracked frames with cracked or spotted glass, and hundreds of pencils. "Pencils!" Sniffle said.

"I bet she works puzzles," Nosemitt suggested.

Some of the plants in the room had recently been watered; others seemed to be gasping for liquid refreshment of any kind. The dark draperies exhaled dust as one passed near them; and, oddly for a room with no ashtrays, there was on one table a rather large carved pipe holder with eight pipes in it.

"I wonder if she used to smoke," Sniffle said, smiling.

"Perhaps it was provided as a service for guests," Nosemitt conjectured. "It's such an odd mix of a room, looking in some ways like the Edwardian Arms and in other ways like a set for a horror film." In fact, Nosemitt was exactly right. Emmaline had a great love for the gothic and in her twenties had been the decorator of the Edwardian Arms lobby. Few people remembered that now; few remembered her at all. Hers had been a secluded life, but it had not always been so.

They were looking intently at the ancient andirons in the small fireplace and had not noticed Walter's arrival. He had quietly sat down and enjoyed observing them, and then he coughed ever so slightly. The women both were startled and apologized profusely. "No need," he said; and then he told them those few facts about his sister. They found themselves enchanted once again and chastened somewhat by the reminder that we all are more than we seem, except when we are less.

"I am happy to see you," he said, motioning them to sit near. "What news have you for me?"

"More questions, we fear," Nosemitt said. "There are so many threads and you probably know best how to weave many of them together."

"Ask away! I am feeling stronger than I did the last time you were here."

"What exactly did you hire Freddy Kettle to do?" Sniffle asked. "Everyone who mentions him indicates that he is not very competent at all."

"Fred is retarded, yes," Walter said. "But he needs work and I give him errands to do. He drives; that alone makes him useful. Would I trust him to understand anything complicated? No. I don't give him any complicated tasks, just simple things. Sending him to get the mail from my office, back when I still maintained an office. Giving him sealed packets to deliver to others who share my concerns. Occasionally I have sent him to water plants for a friend who is often out of town. Things of that sort."

"And there is another Fred, who might be working for you. Fred Keckhopper. His name came up in connection with Freddy's. He apparently owns the car Freddy drives."

"That Fred used to work for me. He was one of my young agents on the lookout for any kind of proof of criminal activity at the auto agency. At first he was eager and even rather stimulated at the thought of checking up on others. Perhaps that should have warned me off. He got a little too eager, and I began to suspect that he was making some things up, and then I began to wonder if was working both sides of the fence. I told him that I appreciated his services and that I thought he had made very helpful contributions. I gave him a month's extra pay and said I no longer would need further information for the present."

"How did he take that?" Sniffle asked.

"I would say that he was fine with it. He said that he doubted that he would learn any more than he already had, that he was being sent out of town more and more and no longer had access to any company files. He said that if he learned anything on his travels, he would gladly contact me and we could work out some kind of free-lance payment, so to speak. I have been very comfortable with that."

"And has he contacted you?" Nosemitt asked.

"I believe just once," Walter said. "He suggested that I have someone take a look at airport records, if there were any to be looked at. And I have contacted him a few times, not often."

"We have asked the police to check airport files too," Nosemitt said, pleased. Walter beamed at them, clearly happy with his choice of whatever kind of investigators they were. They were more than meeting his expectations.

"Very good! Tell me what led you to do so" he said.

"Being ordered off the airport parking lot," Sniffle said. "We always are suspicious of unpleasant people who angrily decide they need to wave flashlights in our faces. It's a rule with us."

Walter laughed and said, "Of course." Then he asked why they were looking into the backgrounds of the two young men named Fred.

"In a roundabout way, Freddy came into view," Sniffle said.

Nosemitt snorted. "Sniffle means that we first discovered him when he was mooning some children."

Walter snorted too. "Well, sad to say, that does indeed sound like something he would do."

"I'm quite sure you are aware of the decline of the native wildlife population here in St. Edwards," Sniffle continued. "Birds especially?"

"I am aware of it, but I haven't gotten involved in any of the details," he said, looking interested. "Tell me more."

"We have been working with Lesley Duke, who was assigned to the Bird Man mystery," and we thought we had found her man– or boy," Nosemitt said.

"And all the evidence does support it," Sniffle added, "including the discovery in the trunk of his car of the poison that was being used."

"I see," Walter said grimly. "I see all too well, I'm afraid."

"And then, of course, we learned at some point why his father committed suicide," Nosemitt said.

"Really? You have even gone into that territory? How amazing and how thorough. What did you learn there?" There was a sudden racket outside as the tree trimmers began sawing. Three chain saws all going at once were two or three too many.

"We assume that you do know that secret," Sniffle shouted.

"Ah, you are being discreet and testing me first," he said loudly. "That is good. Yes, I was visiting Portia when she found the tragic note. She allowed me to read it, and we agreed that we could not go to anyone with the news that a mere toddler had poisoned his own younger sister. I am fully aware of that terrible history."

"Then you understand why we put Freddy at the top of our list of suspects," Sniffle said, her voice not used to the strain of speaking above a conversational level. "Even though Harriette was not poisoned, she was found with poisoned crumbs scattered upon her. The same poison even. Rodex."

"But each person we have asked says that Freddy is too slight and

148

too weak to have overpowered his aunt and suffocated her," Nosemitt loudly joined in.

"They are right," he called out, cleaning his glasses. "The set of circumstances looks very bad, but I would have a difficult time believing that Freddy could have done it. Nor do I see any reason."

"That is also what everyone says, but did he have a reason to poison his sister?" The sawing sound died out abruptly.

"No, so I do understand your reasoning," Walter said, lowering his voice and obviously relieved to do so. "I just have to sit here a bit and contemplate your theory. It is very troubling in all sorts of ways. Not least, it brings into question the decision Portia and I came to about what to do with the facts we had there in Harvey's note. Yet, I have to remember, yours is a theory, not at this point a fact. Oh, I hope it is not true. I hope it cannot be."

They could see his face go gradually paler and paler, the strain and fatigue returning. They apologized for having disturbed him, although he insisted he was glad they had come, and got up to leave as Emmaline was trying to lug the rolling cart across a thicker than usual wrinkle in the carpeting. She saw them already standing and wearily turned the cart around to drag it back to the kitchen. "It's all right," she said to them in her weak voice, "the cookies were a bit stale anyway, and I only had half a pot of squash tea brewed." For a change, Walter walked them to the door, thanked them again for their very good work, and watched from the door until they were safely in their car.

"A narrow escape," Sniffle said, pulling away quickly.

Nosemitt wrinkled her nose and wondered if she herself would have liked squash tea. "I like squash," she mused, "but tea?"

"You have no idea if she meant it was made from squash or if it is just named that in honor of some unlikely food she squashed."

"You are becoming quite the pessimist," Nosemitt observed.

"Hardly. At least I credited her with crushing some edible item. I could have been far more pessimistic. Cynical, even. Now, if Harriette had succumbed to poisoned tea, we would have only two suspects– three if we include Olga."

that evening

When Sniffle had begun using the laptop, she had wondered if Roger knew that there were still files on it that he might want to look over or delete before she went any further. He glanced at the file names and assured her that she was welcome to look at anything. For more reasons than one, he really did not want to destroy any of Harriette's documents. "I would not want to be accused of even the possibility of having destroyed anything that might provide clues," he had said.; "and then, too, you might find something that would be helpful. You are most welcome to look at anything on there."

Mostly what Sniffle had found seemed to be research notes on Native American women, notes and a few images of tribeswomen, and many more images of their handwork. There was nothing about letters to Ms. Ettikettle or personal letters, although there was correspondence with some Midwestern museums and several historians at various universities around the country. Everything was in a single folder called N.A. Project. It was work far removed from her daily assignment at the newspaper, and clearly Harriette had been deeply engaged by it.

This evening, as she was preparing to summarize the notes she and Nosemitt had compiled so far, Sniffle ran into a problem with her program crashing repeatedly. She decided just to get rid of the preferences for that program and let it start fresh; but when she went to do so, she noticed a folder that had a mysterious title. The folder was not at the main level of the computer, and she would not have found it had the software program not acted up; but it had and she had... and so she called Nosemitt to come look.

"What?" Nosemitt said, carrying her glasses and book.

"Look at this with me," Sniffle said. The folder was named *Just for Me*, and Sniffle felt a little qualm about opening it. "Should we?"

"I think it is okay under the circumstances," Nosemitt said.

Sniffle opened the folder and then opened the first document in it.

"I am a little disturbed by how often F has been coming around. Sometimes he has a real topic to discuss, but mostly he just sits down and looks around. I can't tell anyone about this yet. I need to know what he really wants. He never stays long."

"Which 'F' do you think she means?" Sniffle asked.

"I haven't any more idea than you do," Nosemitt said. "It might not be either of the two we are thinking of."

"Do we have anyone else with that initial on our list?" Sniffle asked.

"Don't I remember hearing that one of the Waldos is named Frank?" Nosemitt asked back.

"Could be," Sniffle answered, not remembering at the moment.

"What else does she write?" Sniffle scrolled down the page.

"F showed up very briefly at the newspaper office today. When I asked what he needed, he said he was just bored and wondered what the newspaper office looked like these days. I asked him how he had time to come by, but he didn't answer. I asked him to leave, telling him that we normally don't allow drop-in visitors to the newsroom or the offices. Not strictly true, but I was getting more and more disturbed."

"So, it still could be anybody with 'F' as an initial," Nosemitt said.

"And apparently someone who had been there before," Sniffle pointed out. "Let's see what else."

"Maybe I am getting paranoid with all the concerns Uncle Walter is expressing. It seems to me that everyone is potentially a threat. If I tell R, he will want us to move immediately; and I can't yet do that. Maybe soon, though. Meanwhile, I am becoming more nervous about being alone.

I think R may finally get to move in. Will talk to him about that, but he may then suspect that I am under more pressure than I've let him know."

"Oh, my," Nosemitt said. "This is really upsetting. Is there a date on that file?"

"She hasn't dated it, but the computer indicates that it was last modified just before Christmas." They spent another hour reading through more of the Just for Me files, getting nowhere in being sure just who 'F' really was. One minute it seemed as though it had to be Freddy; the next minute that seemed an impossibility. The visitor sounded like someone of importance in some entries and just a nuisance in others. Their frustration grew, but they decided that the next morning they would look over Lesley's list and see if there were other individuals with the frightful initial.

early next morning

"Yes, I still have the party list," Duke said. "I'll bring it over. No

151

need for you to come here. The chief has been angry with both of us all week. He doesn't think Art is getting anywhere, which is true, and he doesn't want me to succeed. That's more and more obvious. I'm okay for the critters but not for the people crimes."

When Nosemitt hung up the phone, she asked Sniffle if they were going to show Lesley the files.

"I don't know yet," Sniffle said. "What do you think?"

"I think we should first look at the list."

"Won't we be withholding evidence?"

"I think we are just checking things out, and then we will proceed with caution."

Lesley arrived a short time later and sat down at the kitchen table with the vpi's. "Breakfast?" Nosemitt offered. Lesley smiled and accepted toast and coffee.

"What are you searching for?" she asked.

"You were right, Nose, it is Frank Waldo," Sniffle said. "Oh, we are looking for everyone with either a first or last initial 'F'– probably more likely the first initial. And here is a fellow named Farley. Do you know who this is?" she asked Lesley.

The detective paused to swallow a sip of coffee and then looked at the name. Farley Petersen. "I don't have anything written down about him," she said. "Wait, yes, I do. I have 'FP, stepson of Marvin Kettle by second marriage. Mechanic at the airport."

"Hmm!" Nosemitt said. "And have you learned anything out there?"

"Yes, that's why he wasn't in my set of notes about party guests. I met him when I went out to the hangar. The name Buddy was on his shirt, and that's what they call him. I had forgotten his real name."

"So, what did you find out when you were there?" Sniffle asked.

"No car hidden inside the hangar. No car in the parking lot. No car in their shed near the hangar. I asked him if he had ever seen Fred Kettle's car in the vicinity. I said that it had been reported missing, and we were looking for it. He denied ever seeing Fred at the airport, although he acknowledged that he doesn't see any of the travelers on regular flights, only a few of those who charter planes."

"And did you ask him who were some of the people who chartered flights?" Nosemitt asked.

"You will be happy to know that I did, but he wasn't willing to answer. He said he never paid much attention, just saw silhouettes coming and going outside on the small runway right next to the hangar."

"So he isn't a pilot or anything?"

"No, he is strictly a mechanic. He was working on a small plane while we talked."

"Well, he could share in the family business, couldn't he?" Sniffle said to Nosemitt. "It's pretty handy to have someone at the airport as part of your team."

"Could be," Nosemitt agreed, "but are there others on that list?"

"I'm finding few," Sniffle fretted. "I don't suppose we can throw in a 'Phil' or a 'Phineas' either."

"Is there a Phineas?" Nosemitt asked with interest. They both laughed at some private joke, leaving Duke puzzled.

"So now what?" Sniffle said, leaning back in her chair and slowly stretching. "Where do we go next with any of this?"

"I probably should mention his name to the chief and let him hand it over to the F.B.I. agent," Duke said. "Just as one more name. Probably he has already been questioned."

"I don't see how we can pursue anything directly," Nosemitt said. "Maybe if we think of questions, you could go back and try for answers."

"Sure," Duke agreed.

"Maybe you could ask him if he knows if his stepfather ever mentions using the chartered flight service, not just if he has seen Freddy," Sniffle suggested.

"Or how you can obtain a list of clients who have repeatedly used it," Nosemitt said. "No need to mention Freddy again at all."

"I am sure I should be able to get a warrant to get that information without bothering Buddy again," Lesley said, "provided I keep it related in the chief's mind to getting our bird killer. Otherwise I think he will say yet again that I should not be trespassing on federal investigations."

"Whatever," Sniffle said.

"We might want to bother Buddy again," Nosemitt suggested. "He remains a candidate."

"For what?" Duke asked, not knowing about Harriette's secret files.

"We have been reading documents," Sniffle said, not sure of how much to reveal yet.

"And?"

"And we are trying to make sense of them," Nosemitt said. "We just discovered them last night and aren't meaning to keep them to ourselves. We just don't understand them yet."

"I think you need to tell me more," Duke said, sounding stern but also disappointed that they hadn't shared the information immediately.

"Harriette writes shortly before her death that someone she has identified only by the letter 'F' has been scaring her. Of course my mind went straight back to Freddy immediately, but Nosemitt's sense prevailed. We are looking for any male with that initial."

"I see," Duke said, still a little irritated at being treated again as an appendage. "Well, you are leaving out Willard Ferguson."

"Who's he?" they both asked.

"The airport manager, not that he's a likely suspect. He's probably the one who chased you out of the parking lot, though. And you have not included Barney Forshaw, whom I interviewed last week when I was at the newspaper office. He is the custodian there and knows quite a bit. Unfortunately, none of it was particularly helpful."

"Please, we did not mean to hurt your feelings," Nosemitt said. "We just did not have time to go through the material and know what to do with it yet. We see ourselves as agents for you every bit as much as for Walter."

"We really do," Sniffle agreed. "We are even newer at all of this than you are."

"You have other things going for you," Duke said.

"Age, you mean," Sniffle said. "It isn't all it's cracked up to be."

"I meant experience and an ability to take a bigger perspective," the young woman said. "I look at a thing and try to understand what it means. You look at it and try to understand its context, how it fits with other things. Oh, you joke and make wild connections for the fun of it; but really you are looking for what makes sense."

"Actually, we aren't," Sniffle said. "There isn't a whole lot of sense to be found. We are looking for what seems human and therefore what is essentially absurd."

"Never trust the strictly logical," Nosemitt added.

"It's good for some things," Sniffle acknowledged, "but it is useless in understanding people and their behavior."

"And because of that search for absurdity, I now propose that we add Reverend Fibble, friend of Marvin and epitome of foolishness– not to mention possessor of the initial 'F'– to our list of suspects." Duke laughed. Her hurt feelings were soothed, all irritation gone.

"And don't I remember that a Funston or Fenwick or Fungus was one of Marvin's adopted brothers?" Sniffle asked.

"Fenton," Nosemitt said, surprising herself that she remembered. She added the minister and the brother to her notes, although she did not believe for a moment that Reverend Fibble was a serious contender.

"Have we run out of names?" Sniffle asked. Is there no 'Felipe' or 'Ferdinand' or 'François' we can go hunting for?"

"There is someone here on the party list with that first initial," Duke said. "An 'F. Scotch Whiskey.'"

"You are joking of course," Nosemitt said.

"No, that is really here on page two. Oh, how dumb of me. I think she gave me more than the guest list; I seem to have the shopping list as well. Right below that is 'G. Bourbon, and below that is C. Soda. I suppose the initials tell her what label to look for."

"I think that's a bit of a relief," Sniffle said. "As names, those would be a bit disgraceful to impose on anyone." Then, remembering something she had found for Nosemitt, she added, "Of course, as things in this case go, it would be a lesser disgrace." Her eyes twinkled, but no one noticed. Nosemitt did not even hum, and Sniffle was pleased.

Later that day

"Rog will be back from his trip tonight," Vanessa said when the vpi's arrived home that afternoon.

"Then we will have dinner out," Nosemitt said.

"No need. I am already fixing dinner for all of us and Roger. And, just for the two of you, I did not invite any neighbors." It was nice to see her able to joke and be more comfortable than they had previously ever seen her. They admired the outfit she had assembled: sedate gray slacks whose hems she had trimmed with yellow braid, a yellow sweater with a large green appliqué of a tree frog, red socks that actually went with the red of the frog's eyes, but purple and white sneakers.

"The frog is nice," Nosemitt said.

"I like him very much," Vanessa said cheerfully.

"The socks surprise me," Sniffle said, delighted that there really was some color balance. Balance was not something she expected of Vanessa.

"Yes," the young woman said, putting assorted chicken parts into a roasting pan and attacking them with whatever seasonings appealed to her, "I thought I would surprise you."

"Good job," Sniffle said, slightly intimidated by what might be lurking in the bottles of seasonings. Not one of them retained their original label, but so far she had been able to eat Vanessa's cooking. Still, Sniffle was becoming increasingly uncomfortable the longer she was away from her painting. Seeing a few of them no longer was a sufficient bond. She wanted the case solved; she wanted to pack up; she wanted to go home. "I keep seeing new threads opening up," she said to Nosemitt, who agreed. "Will they ever stitch into something that is substantial?" Nosemitt hoped so, even though she too felt that they could not really have access to what would most help anyone make a breakthrough. Until Freddy showed up, for example, how would they or Duke or Bradley make any headway? Until the car agency's doings could be known, how would they know if that was where the answers really lay or if that was a separate matter, a blind trail in pursuing Harriette's case? Perhaps something might be learned tonight at dinner, but they were not optimistic.

Half an hour later, as the aroma of dinner was beginning to be tantalizing, Rog arrived home. He and Vanessa disappeared, and dinner went on hold. Nosemitt and Sniffle found carrots and celery to munch on. Roger arrived, and that helped. He had brought a bottle of wine, and they decided that the three of them would make it feel welcome and appreciated.

"So, how are you getting along?" he asked. "What's the current status?"

"Two depressed, aging women, wondering why they are here," Sniffle said quietly. "Tell us, how many men in St. Edwards do you know who have the initial 'F'?"

"First name or last?" he asked. "Or epithet?"

"Take your choice," Nosemitt said.

He named all the men he could think of whose names began with 'F' but not as many as they had already listed. He did, however, add a couple of new ones: Farley-Buddy, Marvin's stepson, had a twin named Skip (whose real name sounded something like Furrell or Furl); and Harriette's own source at the Waldo agency was Dave Fillmore. Nosemitt had fetched her notebook and now added these names. But then, of course, Roger wanted to know why they were looking for 'F' names. Sniffle went for the laptop.

"I wish she had told me," he said. "I loved her independence, but now I could wish she had been a little more dependent. At least she could have shared her fears with me."

"She says she was sure you would want her to give up the job and move away."

"Yes, I would have. And when I see that she was about to say that finally we could have lived together, it makes me miserable all over again to know that we were so close to having a real marriage, not one legally only but the reality of it, but were prevented yet again." The two women looked at him with tears of respect and sorrow.

Dinner was quiet and the vpi's felt nothing but sadness.

Thursday morning, Jan. 25

Sniffle awoke in a decisive frame of mind. They would turn Farley-Buddy firmly over to Lesley; they would consider meeting Dave at the auto agency if Roger Junior thought it would not appear out of the ordinary; they would see if the receptionist at the newspaper kept a record of visitors and would see if she listed anyone with the foul initial coming to visit Harriette; and they would claim the lesser fee and go home. Unfortunately, Nosemitt was of a different decisive frame of mind. She was willing to let Lesley have Buddy; she was willing to check with Roger Junior about talking with Dave but not about going to see him at the agency; she was very approving of checking the receptionist's possible logs; and they would stay on in St. Edwards.

The decision being made á la Nosemitt, Sniffle reluctantly agreed to pursue the Keckhopper connection a little further, although she didn't know where to go next. Nosemitt herself would meet with Lesley for the purpose of refining a list of the questions to be asked of the unknown Dave, the missing Freddy if he ever showed up again, and the girlfriend with the cropped red hair. "I need something else to work on in case I get nowhere with Fred Keckhopper," Sniffle said.

"What about seeing what kind of trade-in the Waldo agency might offer you for your car?" Nosemitt suggested. "We might get some other perspective on the sales staff that way."

"Back to the pretenses, I see," Sniffle groaned. "Back to the incompetent act. Well, in this context, I won't have to pretend."

Sniffle dropped her partner off at the police station and proceeded to the car agency. It had occurred to her to ask Vanessa to let Roger Junior know that she would be at the dealership for a while and that he was not to acknowledge her. Once there, she wandered through the large showroom and walked a bit faster outside in the chilly display lot. No one approached her, and she went back inside. She was considering sitting behind the wheel of a very luxurious, leather-laden, sleek-styled, ridiculously priced car when a salesman did approach. He admired her taste; she smiled weakly and descended into her routine. "I am just looking," she said. He let her know that women with her sophistication and appreciation of such elegant styling had all the right instincts to own such a machine. She smiled as if she believed him.

"I am sure price is not an object," he said. She wondered why since she was dressed well only in contrast to her usual standards of paint-spotted jeans. This time she was wearing plain black slacks. She did not own any expensive clothing, and so she was even more suspicious of him than she would have been of a salesman at a more ordinary showroom. She seemed not to need to go too incompetent, because the salesman clearly wasn't too great at his role himself.

She asked his name, and he said it was Dave. How would she find out if it was the Dave who presumably was a friend to Harriette? Or was Dave Fillmore really a friend to her? Was he the 'F' who had frightened her?

"Come on into my office and let's discuss this," he suggested. "You're under no obligation." It seemed one way to have a brief conversation, but about what? She followed him into his cubicle and sat down opposite him. He got a stack of papers out of his top drawer and began to shuffle through them. With a broad smile on his face and with the speed of much practice with the paperwork, he began talking in a very low voice– as if by seeming to confide in her, he could offer her a deal too good for her to resist and something he would have great difficulty getting his manager to approve. She had trouble hearing him and said so.

He leaned forward and said, "I know why you are here." She was alarmed and started to get up.

"I don't understand," she said, quite honestly.

"No need to leave," he said, motioning her to sit down. "I am a friend." She did not trust him at all.

"A friend of whose?" she asked, showing genuine puzzlement.

"Well, let's say a friend of Roger's and go from there," he said, not once failing to look as if he were busy with the paperwork and with the attempt to sell her a car.

"Roger?" she asked, determined to be more discreet than past performance would guarantee.

158

"Indeed," he said, frowning for a moment at a particularly tricky bit of wording on one of the documents but then quickly filling in whatever it was he was choosing to fill in. "I received a call from my friend asking me to make sure that I looked for you."

"And did this friend of yours tell you what kind of car I was interested in?" she asked.

"Not specifically. He did say that you were not a person to be rushed and that I should take the time to answer as many questions as you had."

"I am quite puzzled," she said, feeling that his answers were a bit too generic and did not tell her what she most wanted to know. She began to doubt Roger Junior. "Is this 'Roger' someone I know?"

It was his turn to look perplexed. "Roger Lescouth," he said. "You do know him?"

"I have met him," she said warily. "In fact, I've met two men with that name."

"Oh," he said. "If you know both of them, no wonder you're puzzled. You might be thinking I mean my colleague here, but I am a friend of his father's too. It was his father who called me. He asked me to work with you, but he didn't get any more specific than that."

"I remain puzzled," she said. She was thinking that Vanessa must have misunderstood which Roger she had asked her to alert. "Is there a phone I could use?" He immediately offered his own and tactfully left the cubicle, closing the door.

Once she felt he was far enough away, hoping that she could communicate without any direct references to the situation, she called Vanessa and asked how things had gone that morning. "I am at the car agency now," she said. "Were you able to reach your husband?"

"No," Vanessa said; "he had to rush off while I was in the shower, and he left me a note that he would be unavailable all day. I think he had meetings in St. Cleves all day. I called Dad instead." While it was nice to notice that Vanessa had begun calling Roger Senior 'Dad', this was not the time to dwell on that fact.

"Just wondering why," Sniffle said, trying to be brief.

"I knew he would come up with something," Vanessa said.

"Okay. Thanks. By the way, do you know Dave over here?"

"Fillmore?" she asked.

"The very one."

"Mom respected him a lot. That is all I know."

"Good. See you later." She hung up the phone and went out to

159

find Dave to let him know that she had finished with her phone call. He came back in and sat at his desk again.

"So, did Roger confirm that he called me?" he asked, sounding as if he were teasing.

"Oh, it wasn't Roger I called," Sniffle said, leaving it at that. Dave just looked blank. Sniffle had no idea where to go in any conversation with this young man. She and Nosemitt had thought perhaps they could glean a few insights, but now she saw no way to do so. "How long have you been a salesman here?" she asked in a conversational way.

"My third anniversary with the company is coming up," he said.

"Does sales work suit you?" she asked. She was pretty much relying on basic conversational devices, with no specific aim; and she hoped he thought so too.

"Well, it works for now. Sales is not my life ambition, though."

"What would you do if you could do anything at all?"

"Roger did say you would probably want to know a little about me. I guess if I could do anything, I would travel the world as a photographer," he said, looking off into the distance out the small window in his cubicle.

"Then it is good to know Roger Senior, isn't it?" she asked. "He is a very nice contact to have."

"I suppose so. I don't think I've ever seriously considered that I would end up really being a photographer. I assume it will stay a hobby."

"Have you ever tried selling any of your work?" she asked innocently. Dave's face flushed and he stammered a bit as he said just a few photos now and then. Sniffle's antennae went up. She tried to will herself to remember to search through Harriette's laptop for other files, possibly photos. Perhaps there would be something about the Waldo agency lurking among those yet-to-be discovered documents. She could not make notes here at the agency, but she did as soon as she left. Dave assured her that he looked forward to her return. "I know we can put you in the driver's seat," he said, smiling. She wished she knew how figuratively she could take that.

As she was getting into her car, Duke arrived in her own vehicle, not the squad car. When she saw Sniffle, she discreetly signaled to meet her around the corner. A couple of minutes later they were having coffee at a little deli on Albert Street. "Where is Nosemitt?" Sniffle asked; "and where is your car?"

"In the shop," Duke said. "It probably is just as well not to have a police car on the lot here. I dropped Nosemitt off at Vanessa's so that she could continue working on questions for Freddy and Candace. I have my list of questions for Mr. Fillmore."

"I just spent some time with him. He turned out to be a salesman here, and there isn't one thing he said that tells me whose side he is on."

"Would you expect him to?" Duke asked, surprised.

"Not ordinarily, but I would not expect everything to be ambiguous either."

"Like what?"

"Like saying he's a friend of Roger's, who it turned out was Senior, and telling me he's on my side. But he seemed to think I was really there to buy a car. So, was he telling me, as salesmen do, that he would advocate for the best price for me, or was he subtly telling me that he was a friend of Harriette's?"

"Oh," Duke said. "How did you treat it?"

"As if he is a car salesman, which I think he is. But maybe more? I don't know. I was reluctant to make any additional assumptions."

"Probably smart. Why not ask Roger himself?"

"Yes, I'll do that. Thanks, Lesley. What questions did you and Nosemitt come up with to ask him?"

"We're sticking with two threads with Mr. Fillmore: we're starting with the questions about Freddy, just to see if he also knows that young man and where he might be. The idea is to give him a safe topic in case his bosses ask what I was doing there."

"That seems like a good idea. And the other thread?"

"If I can bring him outside, I will be more able to ask him other questions. So I want him to meet with me at the park where Freddy was last seen. I hope he can get there during his lunch break. That's where I will be questioning him about his relationship with Harriette Wrothwell."

"Why the need to be outside?"

"Just in case there is any spy or spy hardware in the vicinity inside. We do not want the Waldos to have any reason to get rid of Mr. Fillmore. They already know that they are being investigated by federal agents; we don't want them to think that we are locally involved in any way with their doings or that he is, either."

"Sounds good. I haven't figured out how to learn anything new about Fred Keckhopper. Any suggestions?"

"No, but do you want me to ask Mr. Fillmore anything about him?"

"Maybe a character assessment? Maybe what he knows about his role at the agency? I'm not feeling terribly creative."

"Sorry. I know you hate that, but I'm sure you will come up with something soon."

"Mmm," Sniffle said, doubtful. Nosemitt knew this pattern of temporary despondency that Sniffle endured when everything seemed blocked and solutions looked bleak. She was not fun to have around during these moods; they usually led to the use of such words as *marketing* and *salability* and *why?* and *bah!* They just had to wear off. "Just out of curiosity," she said dully, "what's the chief's first name?"

"Fred," Duke said.

"What? You are kidding, right?" Sniffle said, stirring to life and grabbing for a pen.

"Gotcha!" Duke said. "His name is Patrick." Sniffle subsided into gloom again.

Back at Vanessa's, Nosemitt was finding her own interest in writing questions waning too. She was still more absorbed in the case than Sniffle was, but her stamina for the details was wearing thin. As a mystery fan, she knew that two weeks or so was a very short time in which to gather all the data, analyze it, double-check and triple-check everything, and proceed to a conclusion. She knew it was not like a game of Clue, where you made your guess and either won the game or lost. Even so, she was yearning for closure for Harriette's sake, the family's sake, and their own. When would it come?

She sat at the kitchen table with her short lists of questions and no new ideas. Maybe if she did something else for a while, she might get inspired. She found the morning newspaper and worked the crossword puzzle. She fixed a pot of tea and drank all of it with some scones she had picked up the day before. She rinsed the pot and the cup and wiped the crumbs from the table. The crumbs. Something should come to her from the crumbs, she thought. She tried to get into a meditative state but kept being distracted by some annoying little sound outside the kitchen window. It sounded like a half-squawk. From the window she could not see anything to account for the noise, so she got her coat and went out. There in the grass was a dying grackle. Bread crumbs lay in a small circle nearby and a thin trail of them wound out toward the front yard and to the street curb. Nosemitt instinctively pulled back, thinking first of the possibility that the murderer had been right there and not too long ago, then of the possibility that he–she?–might still be nearby. Her mind leaped a little brook and rushed to Olga Berlin and her odious cooking, and yet she could not see that impossible woman as a deliberate killer. Just on the off chance, though, when she went back inside, she looked the Berlins up in the phone book. There were two listings but only one on this street, and the name was Floyd Berlin. Nosemitt plopped down at the kitchen table, feeling slightly ill. Sniffle arrived home and came looking for her.

"What's the matter?" Sniffle asked. Nosemitt pointed to the open phonebook, but Sniffle had no idea what to look at or for.

"Look at Olga's husband's name," Nosemitt said.

"Floyd?" Sniffle said. "It is an 'F' name, but so?" Nosemitt told her what she had found outside and her new theory. She laid out the scenario of a man hungry for a real meal and constantly being fed foul food. Finally, fed up, he went insane and took the latest batch of inedible foodstuffs, filled them with fatal amounts of Rodex or whatever, started to eat it himself, could not quite get that far, and took it outside away from his own home, and flung it far and wide. Well, in a narrow range of far and wide. Better the birds than his wife, he must have thought. He could get life in prison for doing Olga in, but– if he killed off some of the wildlife– only a too-brief stay in some mental facility where he would be fed real food. It was all too clear, too sad, and way too understandable.

"And so you think he did Harriette in, too?" Sniffle asked, highly entertained and only slightly worried about the possibility that Nosemitt might be taking her own theory a bit too seriously.

"Maybe he had done this poisoning bit several times," Nosemitt said. "Maybe he used to come and talk with Harriette as an antidote to the wife he lived with. Maybe he came in one evening with the bag of crumbs still in his hand and he sat down to talk with Harriette; and maybe he set the bag down and left the room for a minute and Harriette thought those were croutons in the bag and decided to sample them. Or maybe Floyd said something like, 'This is what she gives me to eat! Here, you taste it! Isn't it awful?' He had forgotten, you see, that he had put poison in them, until Harriette fell over. Then he had to get her out of there and far from this street. It all makes sense now. Such a needless accident, such a terrible thing." Tears rolled down her cheeks.

"Hogwash!" Sniffle said, "but delightfully far-fetched." Nosemitt was incensed and said so. Sniffle became more and more amused. "I especially enjoy the thought that Harriette confused bread crumbs with croutons that she could not resist tasting. Wonderful!" She could not stop laughing. Tears ran down her cheeks too.

"It accounts for the intimidating person who was dropping in to see her," Nosemitt said coldly.

"You think Floyd in his misery brought Olga's cooking to the newspaper office?" Sniffle asked, going again into a coughing fit of laughter.

"It's possible," Nosemitt said archly. "I fail to see the humor. It seems entirely plausible. Everything fits."

"Except the fact that Harriette was not poisoned."

"Oh," Nosemitt said, turning quite red.

"It was quite brilliant apart from that little detail."

"Very funny. We'll see who is laughing when this is all over."

"I think I still will be. But maybe Floyd fuffocated her," Sniffle said and went into another fit of hysterical laughter.

After dinner, the two women seemed to be back on their regular terms, even though Sniffle occasionally had to cough lengthily and Nosemitt had to sigh heavily every time. "Get over it already," she said.

"What questions did you come up with for Ms Candy-Apple?" Sniffle asked.

"I am not in the mood to discuss it," Nosemitt said and turned on the television to watch the evening news. Things had not returned entirely to normal, but at least Sniffle's mood was much improved.

Friday morning, January 26

Breakfast was companionable. Nosemitt had only the slightest of edges and Sniffle was able to refrain from any reference to the Berlins. She told Nosemitt about her meeting with Dave at the car agency and her concerns when his conversation could be taken either of two ways. "I want to ask Roger about it," she ended.

"What's your theory?" Nosemitt asked; but Sniffle quickly sensed a possible trap and insisted she had none. "Oh, you must have some thought in mind," Nosemitt coaxed.

"Not really," Sniffle repeated. "I just don't know if he was really telling me that he was Harriette's friend or not. I don't know if he was sending a signal or just being affable."

"What about Fred Keckhopper? Did you get any farther?"

"No, I didn't even know where to go next. What we need is for both Freds to be in town and for Lesley to interrogate them. What about Candace?"

"I do have a few questions that need to be asked, but I don't know who should do the asking," Nosemitt said.

"You know, I think I do have a fear. It isn't a theory."

"Are we back to Dave?" Nosemitt asked.

"Yes. At first I kept thinking he was talking about Roger Junior. I still don't know exactly what is bothering me, but do you think Roger Junior could be more involved in the car business than his father thinks? Or, possibly, maybe his father knows and is protecting him. We have let our sympathy put us firmly on his side, but are we right to do so?"

"I assume you don't think either Roger is involved in Harriette's death?"

"I do not. It's the car agency doings that I am wondering about. Something feels wrong."

"Because Roger Senior called Mr. Fillmore to alert him to your visit?"

"Not exactly. Well, maybe. I don't know."

"Because you think the man should have come right out and said he was a friend of Harriette's?"

"Not exactly, no."

"Well? I don't see that anything about the automobile agency is in our job description. We are supposed to be finding out who killed Harriette."

"Yes. And then again, I don't know. We have not been able to have any information about that whole car matter, and yet it could so easily be where all the answers are."

"Then we have to hope the federal agents are doing their job. That leaves us to rule others out. And it seems there are enough others to engage us for a while longer."

"We haven't ruled out anyone," Sniffle pointed out. "We have been on the including side. We keep adding more and more suspects." She did not name Floyd.

"That's part of the process," Nosemitt said. "You don't start out with all the answers and put them into a magic sieve to see which ones shake out of the list and which one stays firmly in place. It takes more time than that, and you don't like lengthy processes."

"True."

"I'm thinking that Portia told me never to come back, but she didn't tell you not to do so; and she can't tell Lesley that. Why don't the two of you go back there and see if Portia knows where her son is. See if she can tell you anything about our other Fred. After all, if he and Freddy have been friends for years, surely she knows him."

"Then maybe we can clear our list of two people," Sniffle said, approving the plan. She thought about suggesting that Nosemitt go chat with Olga, but she did have a strong sense of self-preservation. "Maybe it's time for another check-in with Uncle Walter," she said instead.

"All right. Drop me off there and do not forget to pick me up."

"Ah, still a little bit of an edge," Sniffle murmured to herself.

an hour later

"So, you want me to ask the questions about her son, and you are going to ask about Fred Keckhopper?" Duke confirmed when they met in front of Portia's.

"Yes," Sniffle said. "We think she will just throw me out too if I ask her about Freddy. Let me start with asking about Keckhopper, and then you take over. And you know, with birds dying again, maybe you ought to check out the garage. We still are sure he's the one doing in the wildlife."

They knocked on the door and waited. After a few minutes, they rang the bell and waited. They could hear some faint sounds within but no one was coming to the door. Finally Sniffle suggested that they go around to the back. Maybe there was a window in the garage and they could at least see if the black Mustang was there. Just as they were about to reach the driveway, they heard Portia calling to them from the front door, and they went back to it and entered the house.

"I apologize for the delay," Portia said; "I was downstairs sorting laundry."

Sniffle looked around the house, immaculately kept and looking as if no one ever lived there, and doubted that Portia did any laundry. She had observed servants on the first occasion, not just one but three at least. Right now she could hear some shuffling or scuffling sounds coming from the basement, so perhaps laundry really was being sorted by someone. How many did it take?

Portia accompanied them to the living room and offered coffee or tea. Both visitors declined. Then the elderly woman asked what they were here for this time.

"We are interested in knowing a bit about Fred Keckhopper," Sniffle said quietly. Portia briefly looked relieved.

"What would you want to know?"

"Oh, anything really. We understand that he has been a friend of Freddy's and thought you would know him too." Portia looked a bit more wary.

"Do you think that he…," and her voice trailed off, unwilling to say any words that put anything in stone. The entire matter of Harriette's death and of Freddy's problems were topics she did not wish to consider ever again. She wished that the detective were allowed a drink while on the job so that she could have one also.

"We don't know what to think," Sniffle said. "That is our whole problem in a thimble. We need to know about more people in order to know anything at all. I am not here to ask you about Freddy." Portia relaxed again. "What can you tell us about the other Fred?"

"A good young man," she said. "The only person ever really to befriend my son, unless you count the girlfriend. Fred kept my son from many a fight, and I want to stress that Freddy never started a single fight in his life. He was bullied and picked on by all the hooligans in St. Edwards. It is disgraceful what people will do."

"What kinds of things did they do?" Duke asked softly.

"Anything. Everything. Call him names. Hit him. Tease him until he cried. Make fun of the way he walked or talked or ate or didn't walk or talk. No matter how many ways he really was normal, they made him feel rejected and confused. I hate them all."

Sniffle and Duke looked at each other and wondered what to say next. "That is very hard on a mother," Sniffle finally said, "sometimes even harder I think than on the child."

"Yes," Portia said, tears of anger starting to fall. "But Fred was kind to Freddy, played checkers with him when there was no football, gave him his old car to use when Fred began working for the Waldos and Freddy was starting to get some paying jobs. The boys worked on the car together, kept it looking shiny and new. He taught Freddy how to do the kinds of things my son liked– also taught him how to read a little. Freddy never mastered it, though. Mainly, though, he taught him how to drive, which Harvester did not think was a good idea."

"But a good friend to Freddy," Duke said.

"A very good friend."

"And what does Fred do for the Waldos? Do you know?" Sniffle asked.

"Oh, no, he has never talked much about his job to me. I just know that he travels quite a bit for them."

"So, it isn't that Freddy just uses the car when his friend is out of town, I guess," Sniffle said. "It is Freddy's?"

"Oh, I'm sure it was a gift. Freddy was very excited and very specific that it was his."

"Did you think it was an unusual gift?" Sniffle asked, "between friends, I mean."

"I was very surprised, but then I knew Fred was always generous. It wasn't a new car, of course. Fred was given a company car to use and simply had no present use for the Mustang, nor any place to keep it." Duke saw an opening.

"Could we look in the garage, please?" she asked. "Sometimes things get set in a garage, and maybe there might be some notebook or any old thing that would help us in some unpredictable way."

"I'd rather you didn't," Portia said. "I'm sure there is nothing of Fred's still in it."

"In fact, the last time we saw the car, there still was something of Fred's in the glove compartment. We are trying to find him, not just his history. We want to ask him some important questions. Maybe there is a tiny clue about where he is now."

"Ms. Duke," Portia countered, "I am sure that anything now in or recently removed from the car has only to do with Freddy. I don't see how inspecting my garage will be of any use."

"I need to be the one who decides that, Mrs. Kettle. I really do need to make some kind of inspection of the garage." Portia sighed and got up. She pointed to a door that led from the kitchen to the garage but refused to go out with Duke or Sniffle. As they walked toward the door, Portia turned and quietly made her way to a small room at the far end of the house where she could make a phone call in private.

Duke opened the door and just stood there, much to the frustration of the vpi, who tapped on the detective's shoulder. Lesley Duke was considerably taller; she had to step to one side so that Sniffle could see too. There was the shiny black Mustang, complete with its interior hangings. The car was spotless, gleaming. Now, where was Freddy? The two women went back into the house, only to be unable to find Portia. They called out for her, but she did not answer. "Do you mind looking around down here?" Duke asked. Sniffle was not happy.

"What if she has done herself harm?" she asked apprehensively. "I'm not sure I am up to that."

"Then just stay in the living room and wait. I'll check the whole house."

"I don't mean to be uncooperative. If you will give me a few moments, I might be able to be more help then. I just need a tiny bit of time."

"It's all right," Duke insisted. "I wouldn't ordinarily ask anyone else to do this kind of thing. What if you call Art and see if he can get over here immediately? Ask him to bring the camera." Sniffle agreed to do so. Lesley headed upstairs; she even had her gun out, although she had no intention of using it. Was Portia desperate?

"So, still documenting that the Kettle kid is the bird murderer?" Bradley asked.

"Yes," Sniffle said. "You all need to find him. I think there are a lot of other questions he can answer as well."

"I'll come over," he said; "but I need to stop at the station if Duke wants the camera. I'm about five minutes from there."

"All right."

Duke, meanwhile, was not finding anyone. Portia was not to be found upstairs; neither was the housekeeper. Duke returned to the first floor and walked quietly to the back wing of the house. There she found a door open to the winter air and a second garage. Its door was open, there was a scent of gasoline and a tinge of heat in the space there. It appeared that Portia, with or without the housekeeper, had left. Duke looked around the garage. At first glance, it looked as pristine as the house; however, there was one dark corner in the back that the detective now approached. She found only a dented trash can, which she opened. She heard the doorbell ring and assumed it was Art, so she went back inside and made her way to the living room.

"Did you really need me?" he asked. "I've already acknowledged that you found the Bird Man."

"We haven't found him; we've only found evidence that he's the one," Sniffle said.

"I think now, though, we are finding more," Duke announced, more assertively and confidently than anyone had ever heard her before. Sniffle and Bradley looked at her, waiting to hear what. "First, though, call in for someone to go looking for Portia Kettle. Find out what kind of car she owns. She got away."

"Got away?" Bradley said, smiling. "What did she need to get away from?"

"You make the call; then I'll show you," Duke said.

With some irritation he made the call. "Okay, now what?" he asked. Sniffle was eager too. Duke led them to the garage no one could see from the front of the house or from the driveway. There was a second drive, and it led out through the woods and onto an entirely different road. "Interesting," he said.

"Have the camera?" Duke asked. "I want you to take a photo of the trash can."

"Exciting stuff," he said.

"I think so," she answered. Sniffle just listened and watched.

Duke held the trash can lid up and Bradley brought the camera over. "Holy Smoke!" he said; "blue cushions."

"Nubby," added Duke.

Art went to his car and brought back plastic bags. Then all three of them went to the other garage. Sniffle was surprised that Freddy used the one that could be seen from the front, while Portia used the more secret one. She could not understand the rationale, forgetting that Portia rarely drove. It did not yet occur to her that this arrangement was probably more convenient for Freddy and that mattered most.

Art seemed intent now on opening the trunk of the Mustang, even though he and the chief had taken Rodex from it before and had documented the find. Without even attempting to open the trunk, he went looking for a crowbar; but Duke simply tried opening it and was amazed again to find the trunk unlocked. All three heads peered in as she raised the trunk door. There was another box of Rodex, another large bag of crumbs, and this time a dead cat. Sniffle looked away quickly. Lesley got another plastic bag. Art took several photos. Sniffle went back into the house to call Nosemitt and let her know what was going on.

"I am feeling very left out," Nosemitt said.

"You need to remember that it was your idea that we return. We wouldn't have made any headway if you hadn't suggested this, and Portia might have kept silent if you were here too. Besides, this case isn't over. We don't know who did what."

"Or why," Nosemitt added. "I wonder how the chief will turn Sergeant Bradley into the hero who made these discoveries. And why do you suppose Portia used the more hidden garage?"

"I've been puzzled about that myself," Sniffle said. "One more fine little fishiness of Kettles."

"Well, I have been working too," Nosemitt said. "I called Roger Senior for you and asked about his call to Mr. Fillmore. He was surprised that the young man thought of him as a friend. He said that he had called knowing that Harriette trusted him. I told Roger the basic concern you had about how ambiguous Dave's comments were."

"Good. What did he say?"

"He agreed that it sounded very odd. Roger says he just told him that you are an out-of-town friend on an extended visit to St. Edwards interested in pricing a car, not necessarily in buying one, and that he would appreciate Dave's being the one to talk with you because you do not like being given any hype."

"Well, he's right about that. So why would Dave say in a rather mysterious tone that he knew why I was there?"

"Probably he meant he knew you were not there to buy, just to look and ask questions. Maybe he didn't think he sounded mysterious."

"Well, I'm glad I didn't really ask him anything at all."

"Good instincts."

"About time, too. I haven't done so well in that department."

"Bottom line is that we have no idea of his involvement, if any."

"Were you able to pursue anything along those lines?"

"Not yet, but I did figure out how to use your laptop without any crashes."

"Brava! And did you explore?"

"I did. I found a folder of scanned images, but they mean nothing to me. Roger is coming over after dinner tonight so that the three of us can look at them together. Maybe he can identify people. Or maybe Vanessa can, but I don't know if she will be here or not."

"Okay. What was the name of the folder?"

"Ims. Short for Images, I assume."

"No help there. Where was it?"

"Like a little mystery of its own– hidden inside several other folders with very meaningless names."

"All the more enticing," Sniffle said, enthused about the job again.

that evening, after dinner

Roger and the vpi's gathered around the laptop as Nosemitt found the folder of pictures and, one by one, opened each. "Do you know what the 'Ims' stands for?" he asked. Nosemitt said she had assumed

'Images', but Roger doubted it. "Harriette used the abbreviation 'Im' to remind herself to investigate more. We may not find anything pertaining to her recent investigations," he said. "Most of the images have long-ago dates."

"But not all of them," Nosemitt said. "Should we give new names to the ones that seem relevant? That would make more sense to us so that we can find them more easily?"

"Don't change anything about them at all," Sniffle cautioned. "Just duplicate them and give the duplicates the meaningful names." Roger agreed. They kept two or three images on the screen at one time, hoping that they could make connections. Roger was able to identify one photo of Frank Waldo taken some twenty years earlier, but he did not know the other person in the image. Nosemitt duplicated the file and renamed it FW -20yrs.

"Does the photo suggest that she has been investigating him that long or that she simply had a picture from that time?" Nosemitt asked. Roger wasn't sure. He thought it just meant it was a photo she had, maybe for reference purposes. He didn't think that Harriette had been investigating anyone twenty years ago, although you never could tell what Uncle Walter had been looking into back then and how much he had his niece doing.

"Speaking of Uncle Walter," Sniffle said, "is this a picture of him with Vanessa?"

Roger adjusted his glasses and peered at the image. "I don't think so," he said.

"Could it be Albina Marie?" Nosemitt asked. Roger shrugged.

"Go ahead and make a duplicate," Sniffle said, realizing a bit late that she had no idea if Roger knew that Walter was Vanessa's father. He did not seem to have been concerned, or maybe he just had no reaction.

"Hold on," Roger said, looking at another trio of images; "this one definitely is Vanessa. Why would her photo be in this folder if it really is about investigations in the works?"

"Maybe it got put in the wrong folder," Sniffle suggested, believing otherwise.

"Maybe 'Ims' stands for something else," Nosemitt offered a bit tentatively, knowing that it probably did not.

"Strange," Roger said. "I'll be pondering that for a while."

"Any idea who these three people are?" Sniffle asked, clearly attempting a diversionary tactic. She knew she did not want to relay what was bound to be upsetting news to Roger in these circumstances. Let it play out as it will, she thought.

He was definitely thrown off by the photo of Vanessa and took a minute to focus again. "I think the first one might be one of her relatives. I really can't be sure."

"Is it possible that it is a young Portia?" Nosemitt asked, studying the image closely. "It does resemble her, although with that peculiar hairstyle it is hard to know."

"Must be a relative of– well, as you said, Roger, it must be a relative," Sniffle said, wanting to kick herself for almost suggesting that a relative of Vanessa's might not be a relative of Harriette's.

"You think that she was investigating the death of Portia's little daughter?" he asked. "That is certainly a possibility. I could see that she might have a photo of Vanessa here too, then, because it would have made her all the more intent on trying to get to the bottom of that crime for Portia's sake." He seemed to relax at this thought. The vpi's relaxed too, even though they knew all too well that having rational bases for anything was never required of humans.

After looking at more than thirty images, all of them were feeling overdosed and agreed that they would look again another time. "Well, the good news," Nosemitt said, "is that you've managed to identify more than a dozen. The bad news is that there are way, way too many more."

"What is it you're hoping to find here?" he asked.

"As many people as possible who, if they knew they were being investigated, would have been a danger to Harriette," Nosemitt said. She was not ready to say that the blue cushions had been found in Portia's garage. For all they knew, someone might have planted them there just because Freddy might be a convenient fall guy. The more troublesome questions were, to what extent was Portia involved in more than protecting her son? Where had she gone? Who drove? Had she known about the cushions? Would she have known whose they were and how they got there?

The younger Lescouths arrived home shortly after Roger Senior left. Rog said it had been a long time since he had caught up on where Nosemitt and Sniffle were in their work and wondered what new things they had learned.

"I met Dave Fillmore quite by accident," Sniffle said.

"How's that?" Rog asked, although he did not act surprised.

"I went to the dealership to inquire about car prices, and he was the one who came out to talk with me."

"He's a good man," Rog said.

"A good salesman? A good person? How do you mean?" Nosemitt asked with a smile.

"In every way. We both are there for the short term, although Dave could stay on a lot longer than I will. He has other sources of income." It was somewhat awkward that no one said anything. "I'm sure it is all legal, if that's what you're wondering," he said.

"No, I wasn't wondering," Sniffle said. "Just had nothing to say, aside from having met him. I was pleased that he didn't make too great an effort to sell me something I really wasn't ready to buy."

"No, that wouldn't be his style. In fact, very few of us go for the hard sell. I guess it's because our efforts go toward corporate sales mostly. The walk-in customer is a bonus."

"Do you enjoy sales?" Nosemitt asked. "Car sales and corporate sales especially," she added.

"Not much. I went there for the learning experience and because I needed a job. I didn't want Dad finding one for me– or anyone else either. I wanted to do it on my own."

"We both admire that," Sniffle said. Nosemitt nodded, deciding that it was best to forget that Walter claimed to have gotten Roger his first job as a favor to Harriette.

"Do you get experience on the management side as well as the labor side?" Nosemitt asked.

"I had hoped to, but no. I am sales-only. I am not even allowed to attend any meetings unless they are strictly for the sales staff."

"Seems odd," Sniffle said. "Why do you think they have such a policy?"

Rog shrugged and thought that maybe it had something to do with not letting promotional materials get out to the competition in time for the agency to lose out.

"So, you think they don't entirely trust the salesmen?" Nosemitt asked.

"Probably not. Our crew has a tendency to high turnover." He paused for a few moments and then added, "Plus I have heard that maybe not everything is entirely legit. I'd guess that might account for some of the turnover. But I won't leave just on the basis of rumor. I'd need some proof– or a better job offer. Right now I have neither."

"Have you been looking elsewhere?" Nosemitt said.

"Yes," he answered, "but so far nothing has seemed right."

"Well," Sniffle said, "we keep running into strong suggestions that things are not all on the up and up at the car dealership, but we aren't suggesting that you leave on hearsay."

"Did your mother ever say anything about such things, Vanessa?" Nosemitt asked.

"No, but maybe she protected me. I was her assistant only for the etiquette column, not for any of her other work."

"Did you at least know what her other work was?" Sniffle asked.

"Only that it was work that Uncle Walter paid her to do," she said. "I think the real reason that he found ways to prevent Mother from marrying Roger was that he knew Roger wanted to move west and re-establish his publishing business out where the scenery and the lifestyle were more to his liking."

"Well, at last a reason that makes sense!" Sniffle said, apparently feeling the need for at least something reasonable. "We couldn't imagine why there would be any barrier at all."

"Not that we are sympathetic to such interference," Nosemitt insisted.

"Not at all," Sniffle emphatically concurred, "although from our own perspective it is hard for us to understand why your mother would be governed by her uncle."

"Ours is a very complex family," Vanessa said wearily. "Mother and Uncle Walter had been working together long before Roger came into the picture. It would not be totally out of character for my uncle to have created very compelling reasons for others to do as he needed. Such a generous man– the needs were always for the good of the whole community– but demanding."

"Yes," her husband agreed, "there really was no objective reason for Vanessa to go with him to meet the two of you, but he managed to make it seem essential. Insisted he was too old to travel alone anymore and that she needed a change of scenery. You can't argue with his reasons, but they override other people's reasons for doing differently."

"I do hope the answers are found soon," Vanessa said. "I am enjoying knowing both of you, but I wish this were all over."

"We understand completely!" Nosemitt assured her, standing up to signal to Sniffle that they were wearing out their hostess. Sniffle got up to go to Harriette's study just as the phone rang. Vanessa went to answer it, and she immediately called the two women to the phone. It was Lesley. Both women kept their ears to the receiver.

"We found Portia," she said. "She had driven the car only a short way– far enough into the wooded area to feel alone, I suppose."

"What did she say?" Nosemitt asked.

"She didn't say anything," Lesley said sadly. "She had taken the Rodex with her and is dead." Nosemitt dropped the phone, horrified. Sniffle, eyes larger and rounder than they ever had been, picked up the receiver and tried to say hello. Nosemitt took the phone and managed to say, "Any note?"

"Just a brief one. It says, '*Tell my Fred I'm sorry.*' Please ask Vanessa who would be next of kin besides Freddy. I'm not sure whom to call. Mr. Wrothwell? Marvin Kettle?"

Vanessa had waited by the kitchen door and came to the phone when Nosemitt waved her over. Roger came to the kitchen too. "Here's Vanessa," Nosemitt said into the phone. As she listened, tears began to form in Vanessa's eyes, and Roger was there instantly with his handkerchief. Sniffle began pacing in a small circle. Nosemitt sat down.

"I don't know," Vanessa was saying, reaching for Roger's hand. "She is my father's sister-in-law and she is not related to Uncle Walter, except by friendship. I guess you ought to call my father."

"Does anyone have to go anywhere to do anything?" Roger asked. Vanessa relayed the question, but Duke thought not at that moment anyway. She said she would call back if she learned otherwise.

The four of them sat at the kitchen table, alternately silent and then filled with questions. "Are we to blame?" Sniffle asked Nosemitt. The thought haunted her. Her hands could not hold even a pencil, shaking as they were.

"No, we are not," Nosemitt said firmly.

"Why would she do this?" Vanessa asked. Together Nosemitt and Sniffle pieced together the facts for the young couple that led to the conclusion that Freddy had been the bird killer in the community and that the use of Rodex-poisoned bread crumbs had led them to the initial conclusion that he was the strongest suspect in Harriette's case as well. Vanessa shuddered, and Roger held her hand very tightly.

"But you said 'initial conclusion.'" he said. "Doesn't that mean that he isn't the one?"

"We don't know," Sniffle said. "He is generally perceived as someone too small and weak to have overpowered Harriette. Perhaps it was simply his car that was used, or perhaps he had a helper, or perhaps Rodex is a commonly purchased item in St. Edwards. We don't have any real answer yet. We do know that Portia protected him from as many consequences for his actions in general as she could. Now, I believe, she ran out of excuses for him."

"Or simply felt she could do no more, take no more," Nosemitt said.

"But if he is not guilty, isn't her death a terrible irony?" Vanessa asked. "She must have thought he was the one."

"I'd have to agree that he isn't strong enough to overpower any adult," Roger said emphatically.

"I think even the fact that he was the notorious local wildlife poisoner was enough to make her feel that she had failed him. What else did she have to live for? –in her mind, at least."

"I think our family is cursed," Vanessa said somberly. "Such a dismal, dysfunctional one."

"Honey, all families are," Roger assured her, although he did think hers was fuller of strange personalities than most. Even so, he knew that it was her own unique style that had attracted him to her and that he first loved.

Saturday morning, January 27

Only a handful of people attended the private service for Portia. Walter looked deeply disturbed and exhausted. He seemed at least ten years older since the last time the vpi's had visited with him, and he needed someone to hold onto when he walked. He was not particularly happy to have Dustin fill that role, but he would not have welcomed Marvin's arm either.

Vanessa was in a variation of her mourning outfit: long black skirt with magenta fringe and a dark gray blouse with a tiny pattern of gray elephants. "I guess she doesn't want to forget Portia," Sniffle whispered to Nosemitt.

They heard a stifled commotion in a corner of the room where the service had just ended and looked over to see Walter angrily poking Marvin in the arm. He seemed to be demanding to know why Freddy was not present. "I'm not Freddy's guardian," Marvin said. "Leave me alone!" Vanessa went over and helped her uncle away, inviting him back to her house to spend the rest of the day. Walter looked slightly confused but agreed to go with her. He smiled weakly, almost grimly, when he approached his vpi's but then asked to stop and rest on a nearby bench. His pocket handkerchief had seen a lot of use that morning; and it was disheveled now, marring his usual elegant appearance.

"I am not up to hearing any reports today," he said apologetically.

"That is perfectly understandable," Nosemitt said.

Back at Vanessa's, the two women retreated to Harriette's study and left the small family to themselves in the living room. "I keep wondering if Portia made any attempt to contact her son before she drove off," Sniffle said.

"I imagine we could find out, if you think we might at least learn where he could be. Anyway, let's assume Portia did call her son. If we then can locate him, that's a good thing. We let Lesley take over from there. Then again, what if she didn't? Wouldn't it be reasonable to think that somewhere in her home is an address book where she would keep important numbers? Shouldn't there be a search?"

"I'm sure there should be a search! And checking with the phone company seems worth a try," Sniffle said. "What does one have to do?"

"Let's call Lesley and have her take care of both," Nosemitt said. "I don't know if we have to have some official status or not for the phone company." She went to the study and called Duke to make the requests.

"I'll get on that right now," the policewoman said. "And I want you to know I take very thorough notes of all your suggestions. Who knows when they will come in handy again?"

"Please let us know what you find out from the phone company," Nosemitt said.

"And the search," Sniffle added.

Nosemitt hung up and turned to her friend. "Can you believe that we are mentoring a policewoman? The two of us?"

"Absurd, isn't it?"

About an hour later, Lesley dropped by. "There was an outgoing call from Portia's right about the time we were in the garage," she said; "but it wasn't to her son."

"Worth trying, though," Sniffle said.

"Whom did she call?" Nosemitt asked.

"It was definitely worth trying, and it may be the break we needed. She called Fred Keckhopper!"

"What? Why do you think she called him?" Nosemitt asked, not expecting that answer at all.

"Now perhaps we can find out," Lesley said.

"I'll guess that she wanted to assure that he would go on taking care of Freddy," Sniffle mused. "Was it a local number?"

"No, and that is a problem."

"Where is he?" Nosemitt asked.

"In St. Louis."

"What's next? Can you make him return here to answer some questions?"

"Much as I hate to do it, I may have to let Art handle that part of it. He can sound more authoritative than I ever do. People think they have to answer him; they treat me more as a clerk."

"Well, let the chief know what has been found and that this is your work, not Art's," Sniffle said.

"Not really mine but yours."

"No need to go into that," Nosemitt assured her.

"What about the search?" Sniffle asked.

"Want to go there with me now?" They called the house to see if anyone was still there. The housekeeper answered and agreed to let them in. When they arrived, they had to wait as usual. This time, though, they heard the brisk sounds of heels on the hard floor, very unlike Portia's soft, slow tread. Mrs. Huskins was not in the black dress they had seen her in before; she was wearing jeans and tennis shoes. Her face was streaked, and it was clear that she had been doing major cleaning. They wondered if Marvin had asked her to stay. Duke asked.

"No, doing this on my own. Nobody wanted to have anything to do with the practical needs," she complained. "I'm sorting out the clothes and trying to figure out what should go to charity and what should just be pitched. Tomorrow I'll tackle the summer things. I don't know what young Freddy will want done with anything."

Sniffle asked if she had heard from him, but she shook her head. "Only one who's called has been Mr. Keckhopper. At least he gave some thought to what Mrs. Kettle might have liked to have done and was considerate too. Suggested I just take care of the inside and let him deal with the grounds and the garage and the car. Nice man. I won't be surprised if he does offer to pay me." The three other women looked at each other, all with the same question in their minds but not one they would be asking directly.

"So, was Mr. Keckhopper always a big help to her?" Nosemitt asked.

"I'd say so! Even if he did nothing but be a friend to young Fred, that would have been more than most people have ever done for her."

"It sounds as if he did more," Nosemitt suggested.

"Oh, yes. He's kind of an amateur inventor, I guess you'd say. Always coming up with some device or other that he would ask her to try out for him. Like, you know, that special collar he invented for the dogs. It not only kept fleas away; it had a little tiny speaker in it. Mrs. Kettle could talk into a little gadget in the house and call the dogs back to the house if they were out in the woods. Worked just dandy." Sniffle was intrigued.

"And then, too, he would send her all kinds of gifts– foods from around the world when he traveled, that cane she used, samples he used to get from other salesmen he knew."

"He sounds more like a son than her own son does," Nosemitt said.

"Well, there are some who think he really is her son, not that I believe it. Folks will talk, especially if they think there is any sin involved."

"Wasn't he known here in St. Edwards?" Nosemitt asked. "Why wouldn't people know if he was in this family?"

"Well, with all due respect, there was some kind of hushed up scandal back around the time he and his dad moved here. His mother had died, so the story was told, and his father brought him here for the small town environment. And Mrs. Kettle, they say, had spent a year abroad. So, put one and one together and get three, as my husband likes to say. I say, Where's the proof? Anyone can claim anything. Poor Mrs. Kettle had a difficult enough life without all the stories going around."

"When was the last time you saw Mr. Keckhopper?" Duke asked.

"Why, yesterday!" she said, as if they should have known. "He stopped by– said he was in a hurry and had to get back to St. Louis but he had driven here to pay his respects to Mrs. Kettle privately and repeated that I should leave the heavy work for him. He did say that I should get rid of all the empty whiskey bottles that had piled up in the closet. She must have still had a few dozen, and I cleared them out just a month ago."

"And Freddy?" Sniffle asked. "When did you last see him?"

"Probably caught a glimpse of him about two weeks ago, maybe. I'm not sure. I heard Mrs. Kettle say he needed a vacation; she wanted to send him off somewhere, maybe Mexico. He always liked spicy food." She turned around and headed for the back bedroom, telling them to feel free to look for whatever they needed. Duke followed her to ask about address books.

"Very spiced," Sniffle whispered to Nosemitt.

"We should have started all our investigating right here!" Nosemitt whispered back. "Now who is our prime suspect– Fred or Freddy?"

"A few things are cleared up if we believe that Portia may have two sons named Fred. For one thing, it might explain the degree of friendship and the gift or loan of the Mustang. Then again, two sons with the same name?"

"It might explain quite a number of things," Nosemitt agreed; "and as many things about it that might implicate one of them, well, that might be how many that clear them. At least one of them, anyway. Is one really the protector of the irresponsible brother? Or does the apparent protector have a convenient scapegoat?"

"Or are they both innocent? And what about Portia herself? Could she have urged one or both of them to harm Harriette out of jealousy? Not for the jewelry but for the daughter?" Sniffle had that sinking feeling that over and over again there was more here than they were prepared to handle.

"But we're doing it anyway," Nosemitt said, reading the expression on her friend's face. "And do you think Portia would have waited all these years if she were jealous of Harriette and Vanessa?"

"Not ordinarily," Sniffle said. "But this was a woman who had never stopped grieving and who was drinking heavily. No wonder it took her so long to answer the door all the time. Probably the cane was for balance. Who knows what she had built up in her own mind?"

Duke returned with an address book that Portia had kept in a drawer of her bedside table. The number listed for Fred Keckhopper was not the same as the one she had called before she drove into the woods, but it was his local number. The women wondered if he ever really lived here. Or perhaps the St. Louis number was a recent thing and she had not ever entered it in this book. For 'Freddy' she had three numbers, including one with 'Applewhite' in parentheses; there was nothing to provide information about either of the other two numbers. Dialing the unknown two resulted only in endless ringing, not even a silly answering machine message.

"You know what?" Duke said; "I am not turning this over to Art. I am going to call Mr. Keckhopper myself. There is plenty to ask!"

"Go for it," Nosemitt said, applauding. Duke got out her cell phone and placed the call to St. Louis, not expecting to reach Mr. Keckhopper but planning to leave a message. She was surprised that he answered. After identifying herself, she asked if he would be able to return to St. Edwards to help the police sort out the random details they had gathered concerning Mrs. Kettle. She did not indicate which Mrs. Kettle, assuming that he would take the reference to mean Portia. At first he was resistant, saying that he had just returned and could not easily spare the time. Then he asked how he would know she really was who she claimed to be. She assured him that if he returned and met with her, he would know that she was a detective on the St. Edwards police force. She was beginning to think he would not cooperate, but he sighed and said he would come back for the day and leave the same night. He thought he could be in St. Edwards by midnight. She asked him to meet her at the police station the next morning at eight, if that was not too early for him. She hung up with a smile.

"All right," Nosemitt said. "We need questions!"

"I think we need random details too," Sniffle said.

"Surely one of them is the question of whether or not he is related to Portia," Nosemitt said.

"And his Mustang," Sniffle added.

"I can't leave out some way of bringing Harriette into our list of questions," Lesley said, writing rapidly in her notebook.

"I'm sorry we won't be able to witness this interview," Nosemitt said.

"Possibly you can," Lesley said. "After all, the three of us were the last to see Portia alive. I think as a group we might get farther. Come on over at eight and we'll see."

Sunday, January 28

It was starting to sleet when the vpi's left Vanessa's, so they arrived on time instead of early. It was not surprising that Fred was also late. "This works out well," Lesley said, bringing coffee, "because neither the chief nor Art comes here Saturday mornings unless they have new paperwork to do."

"Not sure we should be here?" Sniffle asked.

"More that I know the chief wouldn't want you to be here."

They heard a scraping sound that told them that Fred had arrived. He was trying to get the icy mud off his shoes at the main door to the station. Duke went out to meet him and brought him back to her office.

182

He was surprised to see the two women there and asked why they were present.

"These women, Nosemitt on your right and Sniffle on your left, have been helping us in a couple of our investigations. They were with me at Mrs. Kettle's shortly before the incident. I have invited them to join us because I think they have valuable experience and insights that may help us all to understand what has happened."

"I think we know what happened," he said. "Mrs. Kettle killed herself. "

"Yes, but could you help us understand why?"

"I guess life was too hard," he said.

"Mrs. Huskins let us know that you were like a son to her. We hoped you could fill in some of the facts about her that would explain her actions."

"I *am* a son to her," he said bluntly. "By her first husband. They divorced before I was even born. I lived with my father. When I was in high school, I got into some minor trouble and we moved here."

"But aren't you and your half-brother the same age?"

"No, I started school when I was seven and later had to repeat my senior year; Freddy and I shouldn't have been in the same class, not that he graduated. What does this have to do with my mother's death?"

"I'm just trying to get a picture of the family. How come you have the same name as your half-brother?"

"Just the odds of having two fathers who both wanted their sons to have family names. Fredrick in the Kettle family and Alfred in the Keckhopper line."

Duke was feeling pleased with how the questioning was going and the straightforward answers Fred was giving her.

"Many people have said that you are Freddy's best friend," she told him.

"Maybe even his only one," he agreed, "not counting Candy."

"Do you keep in close contact with him these days?"

"Again, I don't see the point of your questions."

"I said earlier that Nosemitt and Sniffle are helping us with a couple of investigations. It was through them that we have been able to find quite a lot of supporting evidence that Freddy is the one who has been poisoning the wildlife in our community. It has reached serious proportions. I am hoping you will be able to help us find him."

"I can't say that the news surprises me. Freddy didn't have normal emotions. He never liked animals, and he saw nothing wrong with destroying them."

"Apparently he saw nothing wrong with destroying more than small animals," Duke said quietly.

"Now I don't know what you mean."

"Portia finally revealed to us her long-kept secret that Freddy had poisoned his little sister."

"She never told me that," he said, a little shaken. "I need a minute to take that in!" He sat quietly staring at his feet for several moments, shaking his head. When he looked up again, they saw one quick tear, but he hurriedly wiped it away. "What else?" he asked. "How did she learn that?"

"Freddy apparently acknowledged that he had done it. He told his father, who kept it a secret himself for years until he couldn't live with it anymore."

"And I imagine that my mother finally felt that way herself," he said slowly. "But what is it you want from me? I don't see how I can be of any help."

"But you can," Nosemitt suddenly said. "I don't think Detective Duke brought you here to contribute information about the cause of your mother's suicide. It is more to understand the picture of how she and Freddy related and, now that we have learned of your own relationship to both of them, how the three of you related to each other. The answers have profound implications for other work being done."

"I'm lost," he said. "How we related? I was her son and he was my brother. What else can I say?"

"Do you think that you and your mother overprotected Freddy?" Sniffle asked.

"I'm sure we did. I hope that is not a crime."

"No," Duke said; "but unfortunately it may have led to crime. You are not here as a suspect, Mr. Keckhopper. We really do need information."

"Is it true," Sniffle asked, "that you have worked for Walter Wrothwell?"

Fred went pale. "Why would you ask me about him?"

"That topic came up," Sniffle answered. "Also mentioned was the probability or possibility that Freddy also worked for him. Can you confirm that?"

"I have done some confidential work for Mr. Wrothwell. I think you need to get your answers from him. I can't discuss anything about my work with him. And I sure can't give you any facts about Freddy in that respect."

"So then the next question," Duke said, "is Where is Freddy? We need to find him."

"Because of the dead animals?" he asked.

"Because of them and because of some other issues too," Nosemitt said.

"If you know where he is or, better, could get him to come back to St. Edwards, it is in everyone's best interests," Duke said.

"Not in his, I guess," Fred said.

"Probably even in his," Nosemitt suggested. "It sounds like he needs to be in a protective environment."

Again he sat silent for a while. Finally he seemed to have made an inner decision; he looked at them and said, "Freddy is here. I am not sure where he is at this moment, but he probably has been staying in Candy's basement or someplace like that. I haven't heard from him in the past few days."

"Does he know about Portia?" Nosemitt asked.

"Yes. It doesn't really mean anything to him."

"How well did you know Harriette Kettle?" Sniffle asked.

Again he looked shaken and uncomfortable. Unconsciously he began to drum on the desk and he tapped his right foot on the floor constantly. "I knew Mrs. Kettle," he said. "They said she was poisoned. Are you thinking Freddy did it?"

"That's the larger issue we are pursuing," Duke said, ignoring the assumption of poisoning. "We want to know."

"Were you ever in Harriette's home?" Sniffle asked.

And again that look of discomfort. "A few times," he admitted.

"Any special reason?" Nosemitt asked.

"Someone was worried about her and asked me to look into taking care of some security installations."

"Mr. Wrothwell?" Duke asked.

"He was not the only one interested in her well-being."

"So, what did you do?" Nosemitt asked.

"I acted as if I was just stopping by for a visit, but I was taking mental measurements of the first-floor rooms for the guys who would be installing security. She was not aware that someone was going to do that for her. It wasn't easy. I could tell that she felt ill at ease with my being there. I never stayed too long, but that meant I had to go back a few times. The layout of the house and rooms determines what kind of system you install."

"Why were you the one to go there?" Duke asked.

"I have a handy skill. I can look at a room and immediately know its dimensions to a sixteenth of an inch. Don't ask me how I know; I just do."

"Did you ever visit her at the newspaper office?" Nosemitt asked.

"I think just once," he said, "but that wasn't about the security matter."

"What was it about?" Duke asked.

"Nothing really," he said. "I was there to drop off our latest advertising copy and dropped in to say hello. I had worked briefly for the paper when I finally got into college but I hadn't been back. I really meant to see Herb Molecott again but he was out." His answers were so clear and reasonable that they wished he would tell them more about his work for Walter, but he volunteered nothing.

"I have to ask you," Duke said, "how far are you willing to go to continue protecting Freddy if it becomes a fact that he is involved in Harriette's murder?"

Fred squirmed and breathed more anxiously. "I don't know," he said. "I haven't given that a thought until now."

"What each of you does for Mr. Wrothwell may turn out to be the most important information you can provide," Nosemitt said.

"You certainly don't think he hired anyone to murder her, do you?" he asked. "He is a demanding person, but anyone who has ever worked for him knows that Mrs. Kettle was one of the two most important people in his life."

"And the other?" Duke asked.

"Miss Kettle, of course," he said firmly. "He probably had a bunch of us looking out for them. I am sure I was not the only one he had asked to make sure they were safe."

"No, we don't think he was responsible for his niece's death," Duke said.

"It has occurred to us, though, that perhaps one of his employees might also have been working for someone else."

Again the sudden paleness and now a trickle of sweat on his forehead. "You look very upset, Mr. Keckhopper," Nosemitt said.

"I am," he said.

"Why would that be?" Duke asked him.

Silence. The chair creaked as he shifted about in it. He was a heavy-set man and he was not used to being questioned like this. He was entirely willing to cooperate with them, but he was miserable with the direction everything was going. All sorts of memories were crowding into his head; little facts he had never put together before were shifting into patterns. He was not a quick man, but he had worked hard to become more capable than anyone would have given him credit for. He had never been much of a student, but he had earned a good education and could hold his own now in a conversation. Time was when Freddy had been his only companion, until football came into his life and he had been part of a team. He liked being on a team. He liked having friends, and he never turned away from his brother. Now, what had seemed a good deed at the time was coming back to threaten his life and perhaps his sanity. How could he tell them what he knew. The silence was becoming unbearable.

"Please," Sniffle said. "We need your help."

It was the best and the worst thing to say to him. He took great pride in being able to help. He hated to turn anyone down. Why else had he loaned Freddy his beloved Mustang when he began driving a company car? Why else had he spent so much time taking care of the mother who had given him over to his father? Why else had he agreed to work for Mr. Wrothwell's causes? Always the answer was that it had been a way to help someone else.

"I am sitting here," he said at last, "terrified at the possibilities."

"How so?" Nosemitt asked gently.

He got out a handkerchief and began wiping his forehead. His eyes did not quite have tears in them, but his face was alternately pale and blotchy red. "I believe that Freddy did odd jobs for Mr. Wrothwell, nothing more. Everyone knew that Freddy was more than slow and that he couldn't handle anything complicated. But I did occasionally receive letters of directions from Mr. Wrothwell at times when I was unavailable, and I would send them to Candy and have her read them to Freddy. Then he would carry out the instructions."

"Didn't you read them first?" Nosemitt asked.

"Most of the time, not always. It depended on what was in the first few sentences. Usually the instructions were maybe one paragraph."

"So then most of the time you would know if there was anything that could be misunderstood," Duke said.

"Yes, and there was never any such thing. But that doesn't mean that Freddy would necessarily understand the contents. I had to rely on Candy. And except for the very last letter, there was nothing that could possibly be misconstrued. I am nervous about that last long complex letter. It was unlike any I had ever received, a little rambling and out of character, maybe even, well, kind of bizarre. I skimmed through it and thought it was weird. But until now I gave that no more thought. Maybe he was ill. Basically he wanted me to deliver a message, which he rarely did anymore."

"What did it say?" Sniffle asked.

"I can't quote it. It was three typed pages. You'd have to get it from Candy, if she kept it. I just know that right now I feel very frightened, and that letter is the reason. You need to find the letter."

"Did Mr. Wrothwell know that you occasionally used Freddy to do some of the work?"

"No."

"Mr. Keckhopper, thank you. You may have just been the biggest help you ever have been," Duke said. "Is it at all possible that you can stay in St. Edwards longer? We will certainly need you if there is any incriminating letter. Let us hope that we are on the right track."

"I will stay. I don't know how I'd concentrate on anything if I were anywhere else."

"Would you be willing to call Candy now and see if she still has that letter? I wouldn't want her to destroy it out of fear that Freddy could get in trouble."

"No, that would not be good at all. She may not have kept it, but I will ask." Duke handed him the phone. "You might as well let me call from my cell phone," he said. "She has Caller ID."

"Thank you for thinking of that," Duke said.

He moved away from the desk a bit, as if he needed breathing room to do this task. He dialed and waited. After five rings, the answering machine picked up. *"This is Candy's very own phone. Leave me messages."*

"Hey, Candy. Keck here. Give me a call as soon as you get this."

"Not there," Nosemitt said, disappointed.

"Not necessarily," he said. "It's pretty early for her." Two minutes later his phone rang. It was a very sleepy-sounding Candace. "Hey," he said to her. "Did I wake you? Oh, sorry. Say, I need that letter from Walter that I sent you. Still have it? Good. Can I come by and pick it up? Great. If you want to go back to sleep, just put it in an envelope and put it under that flowerpot on your front porch. Terrific. Thanks. Say, is Freddy there? I see. Well, thanks again. 'Bye."

"She has it?" Duke affirmed. "I'll follow you over and park at the corner."

"No need," he said. "I'll bring it right here."

"I'd feel better if you handed it to me right there," Duke said. The vpi's silently applauded her again.

"I understand," he said quietly. "No, I am not going to get it and destroy it." Duke looked a bit embarrassed but held her ground.

"Just a minute," Nosemitt said. "What did she say about Freddy?"

"She said he hasn't been there for two days. I'd suggest looking for the car. He used to like to drive to Lakeview Park when he was upset."

"We have the car impounded," Duke said.

"Hmm. Well, did you take my mother's car, too?'

"No."

"Then I'd look for it."

"Upset about what?" Sniffle asked. "You said he didn't often show any emotions."

"He may have realized that his mother is not going to be giving him anything any longer. Her death may not have meant much to him, but her absence probably will." Fred looked completely drained, and they asked him no more questions. "Follow me," he said to Duke, even though she did know the way to Candy's. She followed in her own car.

"I'll come by Vanessa's later," Lesley said to Nosemitt and Sniffle.

noon, same day

Nosemitt and Sniffle were at the kitchen table, anxious to see Lesley and not at all interested in the sandwiches they had fixed. Sniffle was absentmindedly kicking the leg of the table, and Nosemitt glared at her over her reading glasses. "You're making it worse," she said.

"Sorry."

"Did you have any sense of Fred's being almost too helpful?" she asked.

Sniffle thought about the question and looked off into the distance through the window. "I hadn't thought about that," she said. "What do you think?"

"I think he was either incredibly direct and helpful or else he decided that he could implicate Freddy easily."

"If that were true, wouldn't it suggest that he is the guilty one?"

"It could. He certainly acknowledged without knowing it that he is the one Harriette feared, the dreaded person with the 'F' name."

"Yes, and quite a benign cast he put upon it, too."

"I was interested in who the other parties are who were looking out for Harriette."

"You know, I rather assumed Roger."

"I wonder if Herbert Molecott could be one. Fred did say he used to work with Herb."

"Very interesting connections here," Sniffle said, munching on a carrot stick. "I do wish that we wouldn't keep finding more and more alternate suspects. It just drags things out far too long."

"Are you back to wanting to get home?"

"I've never stopped feeling that way."

"I know that you do value the truth, though."

"Of course, but don't you think we really know the answer?"

"Yes, but we could be wrong."

"This could go on forever," Sniffle sighed.

"I wish Lesley would get here," Nosemitt said, reaching for the teapot to pour another cup. "Did you just hear a car pull up?" Both women went to the front door in time to prevent Lesley from ringing the doorbell. "Well, hurry in," Nosemitt said. "Tea?"

"No, thanks," she said. "It was quite a morning, wasn't it?"

"Indeed," Sniffle said. "How did it continue?"

"I have the letter."

"Yes? And?" Nosemitt said anxiously.

"There is a big problem. We really need to go see Mr. Wrothwell immediately, but I have other news as well." Nosemitt and Sniffle waited. "I am officially on the case without Art."

"What? How is that?" Nosemitt asked.

"It seems that the chief gave notice to the police board a month ago that he was retiring for medical reasons. That's why he has been so little involved in any case, and he has been grooming Art to replace him."

"Doesn't excuse Art's patronizing behavior," Sniffle muttered.

"No, but it explains his swagger," Nosemitt said.

"And you learned it today?" Sniffle asked.

"I learned it kind of incidentally. The chief's secretary was in her office when I reported back after getting the letter, and she asked me if I knew. She said there was going to be a retirement party but no date had yet been selected. Anyway, I am now the sole member of our homicide department, unless the two of you would like to apply."

"Ha!" Sniffle said.

"I believe that is a No," Nosemitt translated. "Congratulations."

"Thanks. It means I move up the ladder a little bit, too."

"I'm very glad, but what is the problem with the letter?" Sniffle asked.

"We'll know more when we talk with Mr. Wrothwell. Let's go over there now."

Emmaline opened the door more timidly than usual. "I have had such a scare," she explained. "There is a bird in the chimney, and it sounds very frightened. I do hope it will be able to get out all right."

"At least it is alive now," Duke said, sounding relieved that it was making sounds at all.

"Yes, it is. Very kind of you to observe that. Well, go along into the parlor while I inform Walter of your presence. He is moving very slowly these days, so don't be thinking I've forgotten to get him."

The three women sat down in the parlor. There was a newly patched area of carpet that Sniffle was sure Vanessa must have come over and helped with– pink yarn woven into the old burgundy floral motif. She hated looking at it but could not get her eyes to focus elsewhere. Nosemitt decided to set her purse on top of it, and that helped.

At length they heard the shuffling sounds of feet approaching slowly. Emmaline tenderly escorted her brother to the sofa and assured them she would return with cookies, apologizing in advance for their probable staleness. Walter asked her to wait a while before returning. "Please tell me that you have made progress," he said exhaustedly.

"Yes," Duke said. "We still have one major area to clear up, but we have made great progress."

"Tell me. Tell me immediately. I cannot take any more strain. This has been a most terrible month of shocks and pain. What have you learned?"

"It isn't entirely clear yet," Duke said. "We have to ask you some questions."

"Then do it right now. I cannot believe I have survived all that has happened. Don't delay another moment." Nosemitt and Sniffle shared his intense frustration. What had the letter said?

Duke pulled a photocopy of the letter from her clipboard and handed it to the old man. "Do you recognize this letter?" she asked. He took it, his hands trembling. He adjusted his glasses and reviewed the first page.

"Yes, yes," he said. "It is a letter I sent to Fred Keckhopper. What about it?"

"Please read the whole letter," Duke said.

Walter began reading, muttering, "Yes, yes, here is where I thank him for looking into security systems and recommending a company. And here I ask him to keep the matter confidential. Harriette would have rebelled against the idea, but she didn't accept how increasingly dangerous the Waldos could become. And I expressed appreciation for his visual skills that enabled him to be very helpful in providing the security company with accurate information. Then I go on to give him another assignment." Nosemitt and Sniffle could hear nothing in any of this that provided any clues at all. They were beginning to feel that the case was nowhere near resolution.

"Wait!" Walter suddenly said as he came to the end of the second page. "Where is the third page?"

"That is the question," Duke said. "Where is the third page?"

"I have a copy of the letter in my briefcase upstairs. This is only part of my directive to Fred. Why, anyone can see that it is incomplete. The last line ends in the middle of a sentence and there is no final signature. Call Emmaline. We need my briefcase." He was becoming increasingly agitated and his breathing was being affected. He pressed one hand to his chest, then pressed it to his forehead. "Emmaline!" he tried to shout. Duke hurried out of the parlor to get his sister. She asked where she would find Walter's briefcase and raced upstairs to get it and bring it to him. With difficulty he fumbled in his vest pocket for a small key that he always kept by him. He managed to open the briefcase and with now palsied hands went through the papers he stored there. "Here it is, here it is," he said. "Someone, please read it out loud!"

Sniffle took the letter. She did not read the first page or even most of the second. She went directly to the last paragraph on the second page and read:

"'Finally, while I am pleased with the information and help that you have provided thus far, I must say that I have learned of several matters which you have never communicated to me. Perhaps you did not know them yourself, but foremost among them is the possible marriage of Mrs. Kettle and Mr. Lescouth that I have just learned of through other channels. I need you to contact Harriette discreetly, indirectly, and make every effort you can come up with to get her'

and there page two ends," Sniffle said.

"Get her?" Nosemitt repeated in horror. "Get her?"

"Read on!" he said urgently. "Read on!"

Sniffle turned to the third page and read out loud again, beginning right before the point where she had left off:

"*... other channels. I need you to contact Harriette discreetly, indirectly, and make every effort you can come up with to get her to understand through one more anonymous letter that the car agency scandal is not a mistake but that federal authorities may be looking into it. Tell her that she cannot relax yet; but in fact, it is time that I released my little birds into the world. I have restrained them far too long. Still, they must be vigilant.*"

"So, what have you solved?" Walter said. "Who is the murderer? There is nothing here to answer that question."

"All true," Nosemitt said. "Except for that 'get her' at the end of page two when there is no page three."

"Ask Fred; he should know there were three pages," Walter cried

"Fred did say there were three, but we don't know if he ever read the entire letter," Sniffle said. "He said that whenever one of your requests came in when he was not available, he sent it to Freddy Kettle."

"What? Fred Kettle? Fred Kettle! The boy is illiterate. How could he do anything about my requests? He could no more understand the letter than he could fly. This is intolerable. This is maddening." Again, he clutched his head and his breathing became frightening to hear. Duke immediately called for the paramedics. Nosemitt asked how she might make him more comfortable, but he was beside himself. Sniffle went for a glass of water, but he wanted nothing. He just cried like an inconsolable child.

"Do we have any information from Candy?" Nosemitt asked Duke.

"Yes, I called her before I came to Vanessa's and asked if she remembered how long the letter was."

"What did she say?"

"She said it was two pages and that it scared her. Then she said kind of proudly, "But my Freddy wasn't frightened at all. He just told me not to worry about it and that everything would be okay."

The paramedics arrived and took Walter to the hospital. Emmaline was surprisingly calm and efficient. She had spent three minutes upstairs assembling pajamas and a robe and toiletries for Walter and had a small suitcase ready before the ambulance driver had Walter settled. He was still clutching his head and sobbing.

Nosemitt called Vanessa to let her know about her uncle and to ask what the dinner plans were. She expressed the wish that Roger Senior join them, but she did not say why. "Now what?" she asked Duke. She and Sniffle were both overwhelmed by what had transpired. With all the stress, Nosemitt was starved and Sniffle was yearning for a nap.

"'Now what?' would be the question, wouldn't it?" Sniffle said.

"So many shocks."

"So many ironies."

"So much paperwork to do," Lesley said, injecting the practical note.

"To learn that one is responsible for the death of the person one was trying to protect!" Nosemitt said.

"To release a little bird to a man who killed birds," Sniffle mused.

"To write so much to someone who bounced it all to a man who couldn't read," Lesley said, trying to participate in what was essentially three monologues.

They heard a squeal and a shuffling and looked toward the hallway where Emmaline was back to her role as hostess, bringing a tray of cookies and cake, equally stale, and a pot of bristleberry-cumquat tea. "We women need to keep up our strength," she piped; and for the first time she sat down with the three of them without being asked and shared a little refreshment and also a lengthy anecdote from her days as an interior decorator.

That afternoon, Nosemitt and Sniffle stopped to buy groceries for dinner and arrived back at Vanessa's to find an empty house. One went to the kitchen for a snack; the other took a brief nap. Then the two of them began to prepare dinner. Sniffle started her favorite indoor barbecue recipe and Nosemitt worked on a potato casserole. There was not a single untoward ingredient. Vanessa and Roger Junior arrived home close to five, and Roger Senior was there a few minutes later.

"We have very important news to go over," Nosemitt began.

"We went to see Uncle Walter," Vanessa said. "I think we know much of the news." Roger Junior went to the sideboard and quickly poured out wine for everyone. He was sure his father would need it.

"I don't know anything," Roger Senior said. "What is going on?"

"The case is solved," Sniffle said.

"Who?" he stood up abruptly and asked intensely. He brushed away the wine glass offered.

"It was Freddy," Vanessa said.

"What? Why?" Roger hardly knew what to say or ask. He had thought that knowing the identity would mark some positive turning point, but instead he found that all his anger and hatred were surging to the surface and he wanted to strike back. He wanted to kill. He had not ever really thought Freddy capable.

"It was a colossal series of tragedies," Nosemitt said. Then, as carefully as they could, the two vpi's recounted the interview with Fred Keckhopper and this long day's events. They related the story of Portia's true relationship to Fred and the basis of his concern for Freddy. They reviewed the working arrangement between Fred and Uncle Walter, and finally they described the letter and the horrendous consequences of the missing page.

"But do you know for a fact that Freddy acted on the letter as he understood it?" Roger Junior asked.

"We found the blue cushions and the Rodex and the bread crumbs in his possession," Nosemitt said.

"But you haven't found him?" Roger Senior asked.

"No, but according to Fred and to Freddy's girlfriend, he is still here. They are looking for him, and so are the police. I think they will find him."

"I'll go help them," he said.

"No, Dad," Roger Jr. said. "Let the police find him. You've been through enough."

"I want to find him," Roger said, eyes red and jaw set.

"Please don't," Vanessa pleaded. "We can't lose you, too." That undid him and he kind of sagged into the couch, distraught and in a world of his own pain. There was silence for quite a while. Sniffle got up to check on the cooking and came back. Vanessa left the room briefly and returned with two envelopes. Slowly Roger Senior regained his composure, at least on the surface. He reached for the glass of wine on the coffee table and held it. "I don't think I can eat," he said. "I am very sorry, but I just cannot eat." Then he got up and walked in slow circles throughout the house, looking at everything that was and everything that might have been. The others stayed in the living room, quietly talking. Unlike her father-in-law, Vanessa seemed more relieved that the mystery was over. She had cried enough before.

"How was Walter when you saw him?" Nosemitt asked softly, looking at her.

"Miserable," she said. "But he did feel up to talking, and I now know many things that have always been kept from me. I do not know how I will ever absorb it all. I didn't know how deeply true it was when I said this was a dysfunctional family. That is quite an understatement."

"Which things did your uncle tell you?" Nosemitt continued. Sniffle stayed silent, knowing that her friend would always sound more compassionate than she would, no matter how identical their feelings might be.

"I don't have an uncle Walter, do I?" she asked. Roger Senior returned just at that point. "Dad, did you know the truth?" Roger looked blank. "Did you know that Marvin is not my father and Walter is not my uncle?"

"I knew that Marvin wasn't your father," he said.

"No, Walter is," she said. "It certainly explains some odd facts, but that means that my mother was not my mother. How can I deal with that?"

"Of course she was your mother. She raised you," her husband reminded her.

"You know what I mean," she said.

"And you know that she really was," he insisted.

"But biologically she wasn't," Vanessa said; "and in our case that makes a huge difference. It explains why he didn't want me to marry yet. He told me the whole story of my biological mother." Neither the vpi's nor Roger Sr. knew all of those details, but now they learned.

"What a long list of disasters and heartbreak resulted from his determination to keep those facts to himself," Roger Senior said. "And what was the great basis for his opposition to me?"

Nosemitt answered that one: "He told us that he had hoped you and your son would move west and that there would be no way Vanessa and Roger could have been thrown together. He was always worried about the genetic problems, given that the two biological mothers had died of major hereditary diseases."

"How kind!" Roger said bitterly. "And yet, in his own way, I have to admit grudgingly, his motives were well intentioned; but we all know where that leads, don't we?"

"We have all been victims of good intentions," Vanessa said.

"And I don't doubt that he loved you and Harriette," he said. "I hope I can learn to forgive him for his inability to let others live their own lives. Right at the moment, I cannot."

"Uncle Wal– I mean my father. How strange to say that. Walter

I will call him. Walter asked me to give you these envelopes, and he expressed the wish that you would come see him before you return home." The vpi's took the envelopes.

"Please go ahead and open them," Vanessa said. "I know they do not contain just your fees."

Each of the women opened an envelope and found a very generous check inside that far exceeded their expenses and their expectations. In addition there was a note, stating that they had more than fulfilled all his requests of them and asking them to accept, in addition, dinner with his daughter and son-in-law and Roger at his expense. *"I will be an absent host,"* he wrote, *"but a most sincerely appreciative one.*

"I must tell you that I do not expect ever to recover from these tragic events, nor should I. I have been punished in the most horrific way, but I see it is all my own failure. Do not ever think that I will regret having hired two Vigilant Pursuers Inscrutable, although I am sure that I have not yet hit upon the words you privately intend. I asked you to find the killer, no matter whom the data indicted. Never once did I suspect myself, but I do not ask for mercy on that account. You may also be assured that I will not continue the family pattern of killing myself. I have caused enough pain already."

Nosemitt and Sniffle agreed to stay on one more day so that they could all go out to dinner and perhaps not waste the one that was waiting for them here at home. "Is anyone hungry right now?" Nosemitt asked. "I could eat the kitchen."

"I didn't think I would want to eat anything," Roger said, "but in fact, I think I do want something; and I don't want to go home yet."

"Stay here tonight, Dad," his son said. "Please stay with us."

"I think I will," he said simply.

Monday night, January 29
5:00 p.m.

Nosemitt and Sniffle had brought their suitcases and paintings down and prepared to load the car for their night trip home after dinner. "Are you that eager to leave?" Vanessa had asked. They all knew the answer. "You aren't going all the way home tonight?" Who knew?

"Don't forget the laptop," Roger Senior had reminded Sniffle. That is for you to keep. She smiled happily, thanked him profusely,

and went back upstairs to get it, inadvertently forgetting the walkie talkies. Vanessa and her two Rogers headed off for the restaurant, promising that they would not start without the vpi's. Sniffle went upstairs a second time to retrieve a beige tote bag with a monogrammed **N**, appalled that she had almost left it behind and again forgetting the walkie talkies. "What's that?" Nosemitt asked.

"For later," Sniffle said.

"When can I see what is in it?" she asked.

"Oh, well, now, I guess," Sniffle said. "I can't stand to delay good surprises. Open the larger package inside it first."

"There is more than one thing?" Nosemitt asked happily. She reached for the tote and pulled out the larger package. It was a battery-operated tape player complete with freshly installed batteries. "Why?" she asked.

"Now the smaller package," Sniffle said, pleased with herself.

"Fun!" Nosemitt said. She unwrapped what proved to be a cassette tape, the label pasted over by a sticker to block the view of its name. "May I play it?" she asked.

"I hope you will!"

Nosemitt put the cassette into the player and out came that tune she had been unable to recall fully: *Duh duh da duh duh da duh duh duh...* and the rest of it. Not exactly a political piece but as satirical as she had thought, the link was suddenly clear.

"Of course!" she said. "How did you find this– and when?"

"I took a break when I was working at the library and did a little extra research. I just kept playing with keywords until this title popped up on a list of popular satirical music back in our youth and before."

Nosemitt began singing with the cassette but discovered that there were countless verses she had never heard. One line stood out all too meaningfully in most of the several versions of "The Song of the Temperance Union": *Can you imagine a greater disgrace/than to lie in the gutter with crumbs on your face?*

"So you were tuned right in, as you so often are," Sniffle said.

"Apparently so, but we don't need to try to imagine a greater disgrace, do we?" Nosemitt said. "We have witnessed one first hand."

Monday night, January 29
same time/different place

Drinks and dinner for two that night were at Ye Olde Pub, police

chief-elect Bradley hosting. Not only did he toast Duke's successful work on the bird murder case; he even congratulated her on all of her part in the Harriette Kettle case. He told her it had been very awkward for him because he did like Nosemitt and Sniffle, but he had been directed to keep them out of the way as much as possible.

"You didn't succeed, did you?" Lesley said. "I couldn't have done it without them."

"You have to admit that they have no professional qualifications or skills," he said.

"They have something better," she said. "Sense and imagination. Both go a long way."

"I think it must be that vague thing called women's intuition," he argued. "By the way, you do get all the credit for actually finding Freddy Kettle living in one of the doghouses and putting him behind bars."

"It is such a sad story," she said. "You hate to jail someone that confused and incapable of understanding the meaning of his actions, but he can only be considered more of a threat because of his limitations. Freddy admitted to finding Harriette asleep and suffocating her easily, but he said he had someone who helped carry her out of the house. He claims not to know anything about him. We do still have to find his accomplice, but Nosemitt gave me some ideas. We need to question Fred Keckhopper again."

"Myself, I don't think Freddy should ever be free– not until we can do conscience transplants. I doubt we'll ever have a donation program for such things. Do you?"

"Funny you mention conscience. Freddy said he found the jacket and put it on Harriet so she wouldn't be too cold. So strange. Speaking of donations, though, I do have a little memento to give you." She reached down next to her purse and brought up a small package for him.

"What is it?" he asked.

"Try the direct approach," she suggested. "Open it."

Inside the black wrapping with the silver ribbon was a book. "Where did you find anything like this?" he asked, both amazed and amused. It was a very old book named *The Gentle Art of Sparricide*, written in verse.

"Your friend at the art gallery found it for me," she said gleefully; "and I got two more– one for Nosemitt and one for Sniffle."

Dinner for five was at The Roquefort, an expensive restaurant with all the allowable stars beside its name in *Dining Guide*. Now that all were present, the five were seated immediately, despite a small cluster of patrons waiting for tables. The service was impeccable, the appetizers outstanding even by the standards of one of the Very Persnickety Individuals; and the conversation was subdued but warm.

A slight commotion was developing in the foyer, and it soon became intrusive. An unpleasant, gruff voice that sounded afflicted by excessive cigar smoking and coughing began to demand to be seated immediately. "You got empty tables," he said loudly. Presumably the discreet maître d' was informing him that those tables were reserved, though he could not be heard. The guest was soon joined by his companion, a woman dressed in a crimson strapless dress, with a blonde hairdo clearly not her own. It tipped slightly and so did she.

"I need a quarter," she said in a stage whisper. "I want to find a gumball machine."

"Not now, Chick," the man said. "I'm trying to get us a table."

Sniffle looked up sharply at the name Chick, thinking that Mystery Mel's face was about to be revealed. Just then another voice rang out, a woman's voice just in back of Mel. "Quick! Menus on high!" she whispered to her companions.

"What's the matter?" Nosemitt whispered back, having no interest in the scene in the foyer.

"Olga is here! Hide your faces!" All four responded immediately, delicately raising their menus to study their choices more carefully and to make their decisions most prudently.

"Would ten bucks get us a reserved table?" Mel asked in his same tone of voice. Presumably it did not, although two couples did just then rise from their own table and leave. Their places were cleared immediately, and the two couples there as a result of a winning raffle ticket at the Gourmet Cooking Club's annual banquet were escorted to their seats. Menus stayed high but did not succeed.

"Why, Floyd, look who is here!" Olga said gaily. Floyd nodded briefly in the direction of the five menus, and Olga assured them that the food here was said to be quite tasty, though she was sure she would find it lacking in creative effort and just plain old imagination. "You can't buy that, you know," she said with a wink. Four menus slowly returned to the table, but Sniffle's stayed adamantly in place. Behind the mask, she was intently studying the faces and figures of Mel and Chick in the farfetched but nevertheless perversely possible chance of seeing them elsewhere.

Finally the Berlins continued to their table; and Sniffle dropped her menu, whispering to Nosemitt, "Olé!" The sedate atmosphere slowly reclaimed them all, and attention turned back to the meal. Reluctantly they surrendered their shrimp cocktail plates but then eagerly looked forward to the next course.

"While we are waiting," Nosemitt said, "I would like to offer a toast." She stayed seated but raised her wine glass toward them all. "To your future happiness together," she said softly. "To the longlastingness of your love for each other and of the support you offer each other. May it never waiver." The Lescouth family thanked her.

"And from me," Sniffle said, "to our ongoing friendship. And to Walter, our host and patron, who will never heal but who can be understood." Roger Senior squirmed a bit but finally whispered Yes.

Vanessa raised her almost empty glass and added, "To both of you for coming here, for all that you have done for us, and my apologies for doubting you in the first place." Nosemitt and Sniffle smiled happily, and Roger Junior grinned hugely and tacked on a toast to their return to solve all future St. Edwards crimes. Hoping there would be none, Vanessa said, "or puzzles. Or visit. Maybe as godmothers." Eyebrows went up like question marks. "No, not yet!" Vanessa assured them.

Last came Roger, who asked the waiter to refill the glasses, then turned to his son and asked for his help in keeping him standing. He apologized for his emotional nature and was hushed by the women. He stood quietly for a full minute or more and then, one or two slowly trickling tears starting, he raised the glass another time and simply said, "To Harriette."

WHITE CANOE PRODUCTIONS

Sing to Me While I Can Hear
Finding April Hollow
A Heart and Mind Divided
Laura's Child & The Meandering Road
A Garden of Penguin Proverbs (and fishy observations)
In the Midnight Hours

Copies of our books may be ordered through our website:
www.whitecanoeproductions.com

e-mail for information:
admin@whitecanoeproductions.com